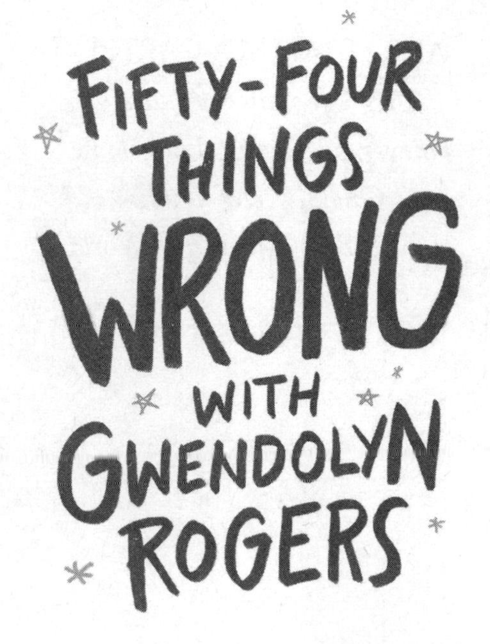
FIFTY-FOUR
THINGS
WRONG
WITH
GWENDOLYN
ROGERS

ALSO BY CAELA CARTER

*My Life with the Liars*

*Forever, or a Long, Long Time*

*One Speck of Truth*

*How to Be a Girl in the World*

*For my Sunshine*

*Who makes me happy*

*Regardless of the color of the sky.*

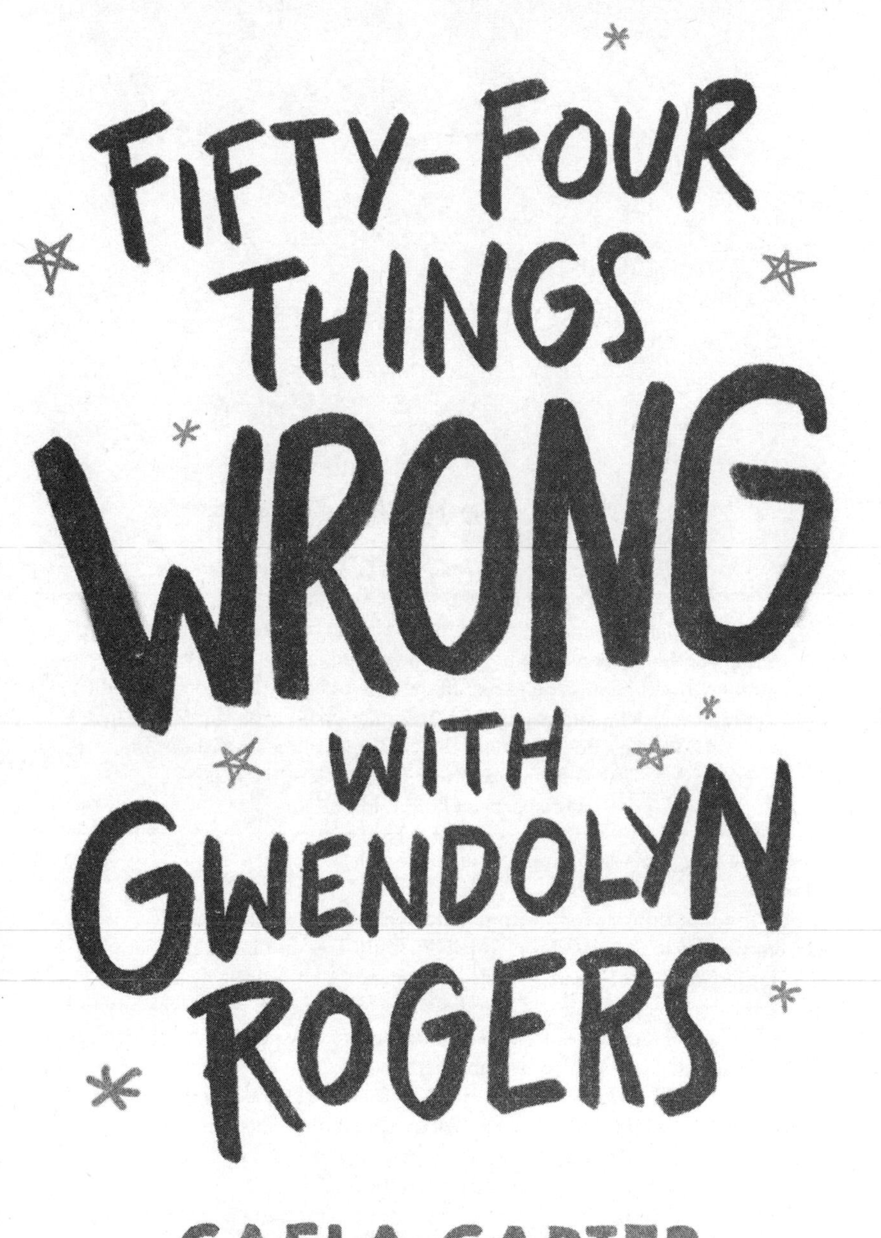


CAELA CARTER

Quill Tree Books
An Imprint of HarperCollinsPublishers

Quill Tree Books is an imprint of HarperCollins Publishers.

Fifty-Four Things Wrong with Gwendolyn Rogers
 For information address HarperCollins Children's Books, a division of HarperCollins Publishers,
195 Broadway, New York, NY 10007.
www.harpercollinschildrens.com

---

Library of Congress Cataloging-in-Publication Data
Names: Carter, Caela, author.
Title: Fifty-four things wrong with Gwendolyn Rogers / Caela Carter.
Description: First edition. | New York, NY : Quill Tree Books, an imprint of HarperCollins Publishers, [2021] | Summary: "A chronically frustrated eleven-year-old girl named Gwendolyn Rogers comes to realize she has an undiagnosed mental health issue and tries every way possible to get control of her emotions"— Provided by publisher.
Identifiers: LCCN 2020058531 | ISBN 978-0-06-299663-3 (hardcover)
Subjects: CYAC: Attention-deficit hyperactivity disorder--Fiction.
Classification: LCC PZ7.C24273 Fi 2021 | DDC [Fic]—dc23
LC record available at https://lccn.loc.gov/2020058531

---

Typography by Molly Fehr
21 22 23 24 25 PC/LSCH 10 9 8 7 6 5 4 3 2 1
❖
First Edition

# FIFTY-FOUR THINGS WRONG WITH GWENDOLYN ROGERS

1. Too demanding
2. Picky eater
3. Attention-seeking
4. Lazy
5. Will only do what she wants to do
6. Socially inept
7. Inattentive
8. Acts without thinking
9. Hyperactive
10. No filter
11. Overly emotional
12. Inflexible thinker
13. Impulsive
14. Constantly interrupting
15. Hard to redirect
16. Sneaky. For ex. eavesdrops
17. Rude/Impolite
18. Defiant
19. Doesn't respect others' space
20. Cannot manage transitions
21. Irritable
22. Talks too much
23. Talks too loud

24. Spacey
25. Picky about her appearance
26. Clumsy
27. Unable to multitask
28. Argumentative
29. Swears/Cusses
30. Fidgety
31. Poor sense of time
32. Obsessive
33. Unable to plan ahead
34. Often late
35. Temper tantrums
36. Constant complaining
37. Doesn't follow directions
38. Disorganized
39. Immature
40. Uncoordinated
41. Aggressive
42. Explosive
43. Doesn't listen
44. Irresponsible
45. Forgetful
46. Illogical fears
47. Whiny
48. Impatient
49. Reactive

50. Demonstrates a strong working memory but is unable to use it to her advantage
51. Demonstrates a large vocabulary but is unable to use words to diffuse her anger
52. Remarkably honest for someone who is sneaky
53. Demonstrates an understanding of others' feelings despite this not reflecting in her behavior
54. Above average intelligence but not so much as to be exceptional

# 1
# HEART SPLINTERS

"Cupcake."

My mom's soft voice and her hand on the back of my head startle me awake. I jump so high I almost hit the ceiling.

"You fell asleep with your light on again," Mom says, stroking my hair.

I wiggle my hand from where it was resting on my pillow and snake it down under my comforter until I feel the pages. *Still there. Still hidden.* My heartbeat evens out, and I'm able to talk to Mom in my regular voice.

"Sorry," I say. "I was reading . . ."

I pat the book next to me on the pillow. It's some corny book about middle school popular crowds and crushes, and I'd never read it, but Mom bought it for me at the school book fair so I keep it there on my pillow to distract from what I really read at night.

"It's OK, honey," Mom says. "But now you should turn

your light off. You get better rest that way."

"OK," I say.

Mom can't turn my light off because my bed is lofted, and she's standing on the ladder leading up to it. The reading light is above my head, attached to the other side of my bed. The lofted bed was the perfect solution when I started to get homework and wanted a desk in my tiny room. My desk and my chair and Mr. Jojo's tank fit perfectly beneath my bed, and there's still enough room by the window for Zombie and Marshmallow's aquarium. But it does make it difficult to get in and out of bed in the middle of the night.

"Turn it off, OK, honey?" Mom says. She sounds tired. Her eyes are red. She pushes her bangs off her forehead like she has a headache. Which she does. She always does. Because she cries. She always cries.

I make her cry.

She thinks I don't know because she waits until I'm in this lofted bed to start crying but I hear her while I read my list.

I hand Mom the book, which is how I pretend I'm going to turn the light off when she leaves the room, but luckily Mom never comes back to check if I actually turn it off.

"Will you tuck me tighter?" I wait until she's off the ladder to ask her so that I don't have to see the way the etches in her tired face get deeper when she hears the question.

"Oh, Gwendolyn, really? It's almost midnight." I make her so tired.

"It helps me sleep," I say.

I don't know how anyone sleeps the way people in movies and TV (and my mom) always seem to sleep. Like the blankets are resting on top of them and could slide in any direction at any minute.

Usually it takes longer to convince her, but Mom must realize she never gets away without tucking me in tighter because she climbs up the ladder again and reaches to the bottom of my mattress, pulling my sheets and blankets snug around my feet. She does the same with the top and folds it so the sheet is exactly under my chin.

I can still wiggle my toes a little, though.

"Tighter?" I say.

Mom sighs but does it. Then she kisses my forehead, and I try not to wince at the way her bangs brush the bridge of my nose.

As soon as she leaves the room, I pull my hand out from under the blankets and spread the pages in front of my face. I leave my light on. I hear Mr. Jojo running around in his cage beneath me. I love having a hamster. I love that someone is awake with me when I read this list in the middle of the night.

The pages are delicate because I shuffle through them constantly and I carry them with me everywhere, every day. I have to. Reminding myself is the only way I'll ever get better.

Tonight, the papers are warm and guilty from being under my blankets. I have to sneak them because, even though it was about me, I was never supposed to read that old IEP educational assessment report when the school mailed it home.

But I did read it.

Then I wrote a list.

Now I have a list.

And now I need the list.

Even though it's wrong and bad like everything else I do and everything else I need.

I wiggle to my side, careful not to let the blanket loosen too much, and start over from the top, reading until my eyes get heavy.

### FIFTY-FOUR THINGS WRONG WITH GWENDOLYN ROGERS

1. Too demanding
2. Picky eater
3. Attention-seeking
4. Lazy
5. Will only do what she wants to do
6. Socially inept

My eyes close. I'll start again at number 7 tomorrow night.

The next day, it's a regular normal day, and we're on the way to school, and Mom is talking. The mornings are always the best because I haven't had a chance to mess anything up yet. My list is folded up super tiny and tucked inside my shoe as always. I try to focus on the way it's poking into the arch of my foot. Sometimes when I focus on one thing—*bam*—then I can magically focus on something else. Today it's not working. I'm trying to pay attention, but Mom's words dance across my brain like brown and gray horses galloping in red and pink saddles.

"Oh, Mom!" I say, launching my head in between the front seats of our car. I like to sit in the middle of the back because that means I'm the farthest from all the windows, but I can see out of them all at the same time. "I forgot to tell you something."

"Gwendolyn, you just interrupted me," Mom says.

14. Constantly interrupting

22. Talks too much

"No, I didn't," I say.

28. Argumentative

Maybe I did interrupt. But there was so much going on in my brain before my mom started talking, it felt like she was interrupting me.

"Anyway, do you know what my brother said?"

Mom sighs. "I really need you to pay attention. What I was saying was important."

I don't answer her because what I have to say is important too. I imagine Dandelion. My favorite horse. The one I used to ride all the time. I imagine what her hair felt like when I would run a brush over it.

"What did Tyler say?" Mom asks finally. "And after you tell me, please listen to what I was saying."

"OK," I say. "You know Tyler is in PowerKids with me, right?

He does the summer camps too. Like me. And he said that this year there's going to be a whole week at Cruxman Farms for anyone who wants to learn to ride horses. He's going to do it and I want to do it too! Sign me up, OK?"

Mom gets quiet like she always does when I talk about Tyler. Which isn't fair. He's my brother even if Mom doesn't like it.

We turn right and the trees and fields we've been driving past disappear behind the buildings of downtown Madison. We're almost at school.

"Honey," Mom says. "I've told you I'm not ready to discuss this summer yet. We have to concentrate on this afternoon first. I need you to be on your best behavior in PowerKids after school today, OK?"

"And you get to brush them," I say.

"Brush what?" Mom says.

"The horses."

"We aren't talking about horses, G. We need to talk about this afternoon."

"You know I used to brush Dandelion," I say.

"I *really* don't want to discuss Dandelion," Mom says.

Bad memories flood my body making me shivering cold and chasing the good warm ones away. I don't know why she had to do that. Mom never lets me have the good memories without bringing up the bad ones. She knows I'll remember even if she doesn't bring it up.

50. Demonstrates a strong working memory but is unable to use it to her advantage

54. Above average intelligence but not so much as to be exceptional

Neither of us says anything for too long, and it gets colder and colder in the car.

"Well, I liked to brush her," I say finally.

"Gwendolyn!" Mom says, like I said something terrible. "We have to talk about PowerKids, OK? I need you to focus and—"

7. Inattentive

"I know, best behavior. I know. You say it every day."

Mom does say it every day. PowerKids is our after-school program, and in the summer, it turns into camp, or a lot of different camps, and if you're a PowerKid you get to choose which one you want to go to week to week to week. I've been a PowerKid for a long time because PowerKids ran the after-school program at my elementary school too. And I love it. I do love it. Even if I'm terrible at it. I'm also sometimes not a good student or daughter or person in general. But Mom mostly talks about PowerKids. I don't know why and I also don't ask her because I don't like to talk about the things inside me that jump and poke and make me not good.

Mom turns left and pulls around the outside of my school.

"I say the same thing every day but then I get calls—"

"I know! I'll be good today, OK?"

"How do I know that?" Mom asks as she parks the car in the parking lot.

I don't know how she knows that. I don't even know how I know that. But I do know that right now I'm not going to get in trouble today.

"Because . . . I heard you," I say.

"You heard me?" Mom says.

"Yes," I say.

"So you'll behave today because you heard me?"

"Yes!" I say.

"Does that mean you don't hear me other days?"

"Mom."

"Gwennie." Mom mimics my tone.

"Can I go to horse camp?" I blurt.

10. No filter. (That one means I don't watch what I say.)

Mom sighs. "Cupcake," she says. Then stops.

"What?" I say. "I want to go to horse camp. It's just one week of summer. Please."

Mom shakes her head and gives me a little smile. "I love you," she says. "No matter what."

I tilt my head at her. *I love you* is nice. But I don't know what the *what* is in the *no matter what.*

"Now listen to me. You know how to behave, right?"

"Right," I say.

Mom is always asking me if I know how to behave, and I do. Like if anyone gave me a test on it, like a math test, I'd get a 100 percent. But I sometimes don't behave anyway, and what I don't know is *why* I don't behave when I could totally get a 100 percent on any sort of behaving test. So when adults ask if I know how to behave, I just say yes.

I'd rather think about horses.

I spot a purple backpack in the group of students crowding around the school entrance.

"Tyler!" I call. Mom flinches. She'll say she's flinching because I'm being loud, but I know it's also partly because she doesn't want me to love my brother the way I love my brother.

"He can't hear you, Gwen. The car windows are closed," Mom says.

"I know," I say. Even though it's April, it's freezing and there's still snow on the ground. That's life in Wisconsin. I'm always asking Mom if we can move to Florida or Arizona, and she thinks it's because I hate the cold, but that's only a little bit of it. It's mostly because I hate losing my gloves at school every day and then having Mom yell at me because my gloves are lost again.

I watch a tiny, faraway Tyler run up the school steps and then back down. I open the car door and start to run.

"Gwen!" I hear behind me. "Gwen!" I turn. Mom is standing outside the car. "You forgot something," she says.

"Oh yeah," I say. I run back and throw my arms around her. A hug. "Bye, Mom."

"That's nice," she says. "But I also meant this."

She holds up my blue backpack. The one full of all the

homework I did yesterday. All the homework we fought about last night. "Oh," I say.

Mom sighs and shakes her head, and a little piece of my heart breaks off and falls, sharp, down my torso and legs all the way into my heels.

I disappointed her. Again.

"Have a good day," she says. "And behave!"

Then she gets in the car and she's gone.

The disappointment splinter is small this time. It was just one disappointed look. It's small enough that I can ignore it sticking in my foot as I run across the parking lot toward my brother. But I worry that my heart breaking apart so much is the reason I have trouble being a whole person sometimes. A good person. A person who acts like she would get a 100 percent on a behavior quiz.

I wish I could stop disappointing my mom. I wish I could stop getting in trouble. I wish I could be the kind of kid whose mom says yes right away when she asks about horse camp with Tyler or a hangout with Hettie.

But I'm not that kind of kid.

I'm a splinter-heart kid.

# 2

## ANGER AND HIS SHELL

At outdoor break a few hours later Tyler and I sit huddled under the big oak tree in the schoolyard. *Outdoor break* is the middle school word for *recess*. It means the school forces us to go outside for half an hour after we eat lunch. They used to even call it recess, Tyler says, but then a lot of kids complained about being treated like babies and being forced to play outside even in the freezing winter. Well, they still make us go outside and all they changed was the name, so I think I'm supposed to hate outdoor break like some of my classmates do, but I actually don't mind it.

We go to a charter school, which means they do things a little differently. Most of the kids from my elementary school go here, too, but Tyler went to private elementary school.

This has been my outdoor break routine—Tyler and the

big oak tree—since I first found out he was my long-lost brother in the beginning of fifth grade. In fourth grade, I spent recess with Hettie and her friends. It's OK though because I still spend most of PowerKids with Hettie because her other friends go home after school. Hettie is my only friend.

6. Socially inept

Kids are running in every direction around us, and Tyler is sitting on his heels bouncing up and down, and the bare branches above us are shaking in the wind making patterns on his face, and I can't hear what he's saying.

I close my eyes and build a glass wall. It's pretend. But that doesn't mean it's not important. I make it go from the ground behind Tyler's feet up to the tree branches. I make it a circle so it grows around me and Tyler and the tree and, sure no one else knows about it except me, but it fixes everything anyway because my brother and I are alone inside this glass tube with our tree, and all of the commotion is outside, and I can finally hear him.

"The best one is Midnight," he's saying.

I can hear him but I still have no clue what he's talking about.

7. Inattentive

"Will you redo my braids?" I ask him. Back in the fall he started doing that for me every day at outdoor break. At first, I didn't think he'd be able to get them as tight as Mom does, but Tyler loves to do hair and he's really good at it. He can almost always get them tighter.

25. Picky about her appearance

Every morning my mom folds my blond hair into twin French braids because that's the only way my head feels right. Otherwise it feels all loose and I can't concentrate without the pulling on my skull. I always have to tell Mom to redo them tighter and tighter, and she tells me we're going to be late to school or wherever we're going, and I tell her I can't go to school or wherever we're going with loose braids, and eventually she does them tight enough, and then we're late or almost late to school, and then, by the middle of the day, my braids are too loose again anyway.

5. Will only do what she wants to do

31. Poor sense of time

"Sure," Tyler says. He kneels behind me and I start to feel the tug of my hair pulling my ear closer to the top of my head. I sigh with relief. Tyler's own jitters calm down with the pulling and twisting so it's easier to understand him.

We haven't talked about it, but I've noticed: Tyler is like me. There's something(s) wrong with him too. He has the same things inside him poking and jumping and turning him into a bad kid all the time. He's a splinter-heart kid too.

Those bad pokey things—they must come from our dad. Neither of us have ever met our dad, at least not that we can remember. But he's still what makes us brother and sister.

"Did you talk to your mom about horse camp?" Tyler asks, excited.

"Yeah," I say. "It didn't go too well."

"It didn't?" Tyler sounds alarmed. He does this thing with his tongue where it sticks out the side of his mouth and sort of clicks. He always does that when he's nervous, and sometimes Hettie says some mean things about it behind his back, but I don't mind the clicking because he's my brother.

"What did your mom say?" I ask.

"I didn't get to see her yesterday," Tyler says. His mom works at the university like mine, although I didn't realize that until this fall. It isn't surprising though because it feels like almost every adult in this town works at the university. But I guess my mom didn't even know Tyler's mom also lived in Madison, Wisconsin, until this fall, when we ran into each other at Back-to-School Night and my mom's jaw dropped so far you could see all the way down her throat. She told me later that she never thought she'd see Ms. Christakos again. She told me that she didn't think I needed to know Tyler since she had never considered that there was a chance he could actually be in my life. She told me that she had no idea his mom was sort of her coworker for years.

My mom used a strange voice when she said all of this. And she spoke in shorter sentences than she usually does. It was weird.

The things that are wrong with my mom are different from

the things that are wrong with me. Which means my mom has a filter. Which means I don't know how much of that story is the absolute exact truth.

And even though our moms work in the same place, it's different because Tyler's mom works as a professor in the psychology department and sometimes ends up working all night long. They live in a big house with people Tyler calls *au pairs* and *housekeepers*, so I think she makes a lot of money. My mom works for the admissions department, and Mom and I live in a two-bedroom apartment that could fit inside Tyler's living room. I think that part makes Mom mad, but I like our apartment better than their big stone house.

"It doesn't matter, though," Tyler is saying. "I know my mom will say yes. She loves whenever I want to do anything outside."

"Really?" I ask. "She'll say yes no matter what?"

I can feel my hair go up and down as Tyler shrugs.

"Why wouldn't she?" Tyler asks.

"But . . ." I trail off. I don't want to say it. I don't think Tyler wants me to say it.

Before I can help it, the words are out of my mouth.

10. No filter

"But what about what happened yesterday?"

Tyler and I talk about animals and braids and I listen while he talks about outer space and dinosaurs and ninjas and video games. We don't talk about the biggest sign that he's my brother. We don't talk about things inside us that jump and poke and make us into bad kids.

And we aren't usual brother/sister. Not like my best friend Hettie and her younger brother, Nolan, who live in the same house and get on each other's nerves all the time, but who are also sort of like partners because they've been together for as long as anyone can remember. Tyler and I are siblings because of a stranger.

Tyler is in sixth grade and I'm in fifth, so he's a year older than me. But it seems like I matter to him as much as he matters to me. We both only had a mom, no one else in our family, until we found each other. Our moms know we love each other but they don't understand why it matters so much to have a sibling.

"What do you mean?" he asks. "What happened yesterday?"

I move my head against the pressure of the braid he's currently pulling on. "You know . . . at PowerKids?"

I'm talking about what I saw from the fifth-grade table. I'm talking about when Tyler purposefully slammed his foot down on Ms. Hayley's toes and then ran away when he was supposed to be playing chess.

His brain cracked.

When my brain cracks my mom says no to everything. Horse camp. Vacations. Hanging out with Hettie or Tyler. Dessert. My iPad. Everything.

Tyler's brain cracked but he still thinks his mom will say yes to horse camp.

Tyler shrugs. "She doesn't know about that," he says.

My face burns. "Ms. Hayley didn't call your mom?" I ask.

Ms. Hayley is like the boss of PowerKids and she always calls my mom. She always always always calls my mom.

Tyler shrugs. He changes the subject.

He doesn't like to talk about being bad. It's like being bad is just one thing about him and not everything about him.

There used to be other things about me too. And there still are, I guess. My pets. Hettie. Tyler. But the fifty-four things make it so hard to find any of the good stuff anymore.

"I'm going to that horse camp. It's so much better than the pathetic regular day camp option PowerKids does. Is that the one your mom wants you to go to?"

"Yeah," I say.

"Well you can't. You have to come with me."

"I want to!" I say.

The braids are tighter now and that feels good, but other things feel bad and I'm worried Anger is waking up. He's going to come out from his shell and ruin my day. He's red and triangular with big googly eyes and, when things are going OK, he sleeps in a white, circular shell in my left rib cage, but when they aren't, I can't stop him from waking up and poking his way out of his shell and shoving his pointy body all over my organs until I can't control anything, not even my own self.

"It's not enough to want to go," Tyler says. "Promise me you'll come."

"I can't. My mom didn't answer me. She just kept telling me to behave."

"Then you have to be good!" Tyler says. He's almost yelling at me as he snaps the final rubber band into place.

I think he maybe snapped it a little too hard.

*Poke. Poke. Poke.* Anger jumps inside me. My rib cage is on fire.

"Please," Tyler says, like he didn't hear any of what I said about it not being up to me at all.

Anger jumps faster. Harder. My insides are getting scratched up and achy.

The only way to slow Anger down is to speed up the rest of me.

I need to move.

## 30. Fidgety

I jump to my feet.

"I'll race you to the other tree," I say.

Tyler startles a little and I realize I was louder than I meant to be.

"Horse camp," he says. He never wants to run. At least not when I do. "What did Nina say exactly?"

Nina is my mom. I call Tyler's mom Ms. Christakos but he calls mine Nina. I'm still working on figuring out why but so far my eavesdropping hasn't answered that question.

"I don't remember *exactly*," I say.

"Tell me," he says.

*Poke. Poke.* I shake my arms and legs. I need to move. Now. "To the tree and back. Ready?"

Tyler can't see the glass wall I built in front of us, but I can. It's going to feel so good to run right through it and send shards of my imagination flying—sharp—through the schoolyard.

Tyler stands with me. He leans in so his face is right next to mine. We're siblings and you can see it, but you have to look closely. We're both white, but Tyler is half Greek and I'm not, so his skin is darker than mine. His hair is jet black and thick and sits in a pile of curls on his head while mine is blond and would be pin straight if I ever took it out of my braids. He has a higher forehead and I have a smattering of freckles all over my cheeks and chin. Our sibling-ness is in the smooth slope of our nose and the yellow specks in our hazel eyes. It's in the gap between our front teeth and the half dimple that shows up in our left cheeks but only when we're really happy. I like when Tyler stands close enough for me to count these brother clues on his face.

"She said something about after school, didn't she?" Tyler demands. Because he's not the only one who got in trouble at PowerKids yesterday.

I shrug. "I want to race," I say.

It happens with everyone. As soon as I really need to move, people insist on talking to me.

Tyler grabs my wrist. "Gwendolyn, you have to be good, OK?" His voice is pleading. "You know your mom won't let you go to horse camp or see me at all if you aren't good."

Something about the desperation in his voice makes Anger wiggle back into his shell.

I want to tell at Tyler that he knows about the creatures who live inside us. He knows I can't be good when I'm just plain bad.

But it doesn't matter if Tyler is a bad kid. Even if he stomps on people's feet, we still get to see each other. It's me that matters. I'm the one who has to be good so that we can be together.

I do a quick whole body shake to get out the worst wiggles. I manage to slip Anger back into his shell without him cracking my brain.

"I know. I will," I say.

I have to be good. I have to. For Tyler.

I'm still thinking about everything Tyler said later that day at PowerKids. I'm going to be good today. I just know it.

At free time Hettie asks if I want to play basketball like we have the past few days. I love playing basketball. But it's too risky. If I have the ball when free time is over, Anger gets so mad that I have to stop playing, and he might crack my brain. We need something safer today. I ask Hettie if we can do a swing-jumping contest like we used to in fourth grade. At first I'm afraid she'll say that's too nerdy or babyish because no one uses the swings here when in elementary school you had to wait hours just to get a short turn. But Hettie never says anything like that. She says swing-jumping is perfect.

We take turns jumping off the swings for a while, then we start just plain swinging. I love it. Inside my head I'm chanting: *No trouble, no trouble, no trouble TODAY.*

The words whoosh in my ears as the swing goes up and down and down and up. Everything is in perfect harmony for once, even me. My brain makes up the song and it falls into rhythm with the pendulum of the swing.

*No trouble. No trouble. No trouble TODAY!*

Up and down. Down and up. Up and down. Down and up.

I love the way the wind rushes past my face, pushing my newly tightened braids backward as my swing goes down forward. I love how the motion throws my braids up over my shoulders as I start the backward descent.

I love the weak April sun on my cheeks and the chain of the swing making indents into my palm. I love the feeling of blisters starting to work their way out onto the top of my skin.

I love the colors that rush past my eyes brighter with each swing. Green of the grass. Blue of the sky. White of the clouds. Yellow of Hettie's shirt.

I love Hettie's legs matching mine pump for pump. I love her voice chatting next to me about something and anything even though I can't hear the words right now.

Up and down. Down and up. Up and down. Down and up.

*No trouble, no trouble, no trouble TO—*

"Gwendolyn, NOW!" Ms. Hayley is yelling.

The words jam their way right into everything, like an ice chip that gets stuck in your straw just when you're getting to the sweetest sip of lemonade. The colors aren't as bright. The blisters start to hurt. My thoughts are jumbled.

Can't stop. Keep pumping. Keep chanting.

20. Cannot manage transitions

*Trouble. No, no trouble. Something. Today.*

The rhythm is gone.

"Gwendolyn! I told you three times already."

She's lying. I don't even know what she's trying to tell me. If she told me something three times, I would know what it was by now. Ms. Hayley is standing as close to my swing as she can without getting kicked every time I go forward. She seems like she's trying to step even closer but she can't because I don't stop swinging.

Right now everything is colors and wind and sun, and if I stop it will all just poof away, and I might poof away with it.

"NOW, Gwendolyn," she says again.

I manage to make my voice work. "Two more minutes," I say.

Two minutes means I can slow down. I can let the colors fade back to normal. I can let the wind gradually get weaker on my face. I can turn back into regular Gwendolyn, who doesn't fly, instead of having my wings ripped off.

"No," Ms. Hayley says.

"I'm supposed to get five more minutes!" I yell.

If Ms. Madeline were here, that's what she would do. She always gives me five minutes after telling me to get off the swing or stop whatever else I was doing. She knows that everything needs to change slowly for me, especially if I was just moving quickly. But Ms. Madeline is out sick today and Ms. Hayley doesn't know anything.

"I already gave you your five minutes. I told you five minutes almost fifteen minutes ago."

And she lies. She never gave me five minutes.

I feel the white shell behind my rib cage starting to rattle. Anger is waking up. I try to slow the swing but that makes Anger rattle even harder.

"Now!" she yells.

I keep pumping because I know if I stop he will definitely wake up and I don't want him to. I can't let my brain crack. Not today.

"Horse camp," I remind myself.

"What?" Ms. Hayley says, even though it's none of her business. "Gwendolyn, get down now."

I pump a little slower. "Horse camp," I whisper. "Just get

off the swing. You can do it."

"What?" Ms. Hayley says. "If you're talking to me I can't hear you."

"I'm not talking to you!" I shout. The words fly out of me. Anger throws them.

"Gwendolyn!" Ms. Hayley screams. If she would just be a little quieter, I could focus. I could do this. "Gwendolyn!" she says, even louder.

"I'm coming." I am. I'm coming the way I know how to. I was pumping like

PUMPpump PUMPpump PUMPpump PUMPpump

So I start instead like

PUMP pump PUMP pump PUMP pump PUMP pump

and next I will do

pump pump pump pump pump pump pump pump pump

and then I'll be ready to go inside. Ms. Madeline knows that. Ms. Hayley should know that too.

"Your legs are still moving," Ms. Hayley says.

Duh.

"I'm coming!" I yell back.

"Stop lying to me, Gwendolyn. This is unacceptable."

But I'm not lying. She's the liar.

Anger rattles his shell harder.

"Gwendolyn, I said *now*!" Ms. Hayley screams.

I pump, but more slowly. "I'm trying," I say.

"No you are not!" Her voice is high and desperate. Her face is red. "Get off that swing right this instant! This is unacceptable! You aren't listening!"

Anger breaks through his shell and digs his red pointy head between two of my right ribs and stabs me there so that it hurts and I have to yell.

"I'm slowing down. Duh! You can't just stop a swing, stupid."

"*Excuse* me?" Ms. Hayley says.

Anger's favorite meal is Other People's Anger. He's eating Ms. Hayley's now. He's sucking her anger right out of her brain like spaghetti. He's swelling between my ribs until they start to ache.

"If you're not off the swing by the count of three, I'm calling your mother," Ms. Hayley says.

Three? No. I can't be off this swing by three. I'd have to jump. I'd have to let everything go from moving to still.

I speed up, pumping faster. "No!" I yell.

"Yes!" she yells. "One."

"Stop it!" I scream. "Stop counting."

My legs go faster. They're supposed to be slowing down.

Anger sinks into them to make them go as fast as they possibly can.

"Two."

Anger jumps on my stomach.

"Stop it!" my voice screeches.

My legs pumppumpPUMP like Anger wants them to.

"Three!" Ms. Hayley yells.

Anger uses my stomach like a springboard. He vaults up my throat and lodges his pointy head into my brain.

Sirens sound inside my skull.

Then there's nothing except noise and speed.

*Crack.*

# 3

## THE MILLIONTH NEW PLAN

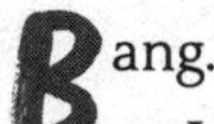

Bang.

I don't know how long the world was reduced to noise and speed. Anger has been controlling my brain. But now, pain rings through my arm and shoulder, and my body falls limp onto the ground next to the fence that goes around the outside of the schoolyard.

When my brain cracks, everything changes. Things feel different and look different and sound different. The world is louder up close and silent farther away. Everything around me seems so slow that I have to speed through it or I'll disappear.

Also, *I* feel like someone else. I don't remember a lot of what happens when my brain is cracked. Later, I'll sometimes remember part of it, but like it's a story someone told me a long time ago. Not like it's my own memory.

I look around. My muscles remember running. I ran so far I reached the fence at the side of the schoolyard. Ms. Hayley chased me the whole time. Now I'm on the ground. I fell off the fence. I must have been climbing it.

I look up at Ms. Hayley standing over me. I try to yell at her again. But that's the end of Anger. Sadness—blue, fuzzy, and blob-like—finally manages to coax him back into his shell. He spreads heavy and furry and hot over my arms and legs and back. My brain comes back together. Only Sadness can ever make Anger go back home.

There are tears. So many tears. For my shoulder. And my summer. And my badness.

"Gwendolyn," Ms. Hayley says. "Are you OK?"

I look up at her, through tears.

"Don't call my mom," I beg. "Please."

But, of course, she does.

At home, Anger is asleep. Sound asleep in his little white shell. I can feel it between my ribs, rising and falling rhythmically with his breath.

Sadness is awake. Sadness is not like Anger. He doesn't sleep. He's always alive and alert inside me, blue and solid, but sometimes he's the size and shape of a little marble, pinging around my body like a pinball: foot to hip to armpit to belly button to right knee to left knee. And sometimes Sadness spreads his fuzziness and heaviness, reaching through my stomach and crawling up my lungs. He'll stretch over my back and send warm, heavy tendrils down my arms and into my hands and fingers. He'll wrap his blue fur around my leg muscles. He'll envelop me until I'm unable to pick up my head. That's how my mom finds me in the kitchen: head on the table, arms hanging down between my knees, uneaten snack shoved off to the side (2. Picky eater). I should be in my room feeding Zombie and Marshmallow and playing with Mr. Jojo. And I will, later. I never forget my pets. But right now I can't do anything. Sadness is too heavy for me to move, even for Mr. Jojo.

Mom comes and pats my head. My braids become even looser and it makes my skin crawl, but Sadness is a thick layer between me and my skin, and I can't do anything about it.

"OK, Cupcake," Mom says. "We need a plan."

I don't move. This is not a surprising sentence. We always have a plan.

We make one plan, then another, then another. We meet with doctors and therapists who always make things worse. We rarely meet them more than once. Mom reads a book, then another book, then another. Mom knows more than the doctors. She comes up with one thing, then another, then another. The plans are supposed to kill Anger. To murder him. Each plan is supposed to leave him as a red triangular corpse inside me that will slowly disintegrate into my skin and then be shed with my dead skin cells.

Mom's plans never work.

"I have an idea," Mom says. She's talking too quickly. "I've been researching. I think if we tweak some things . . . Pick your head up, Gwendolyn."

"We don't need a new plan," I say into the table.

The current plan has two parts. They almost always have two parts. A part for me to do and a part for Mom to do. Or my teacher. Or PowerKids staff. This one is to help me "manage transitions." I stink at "managing transitions." The me-part of the plan is that for every day I don't have an "issue" around transitions, I get a cookie. Yes, a literal cookie. Or a Popsicle or a small dish of ice cream. But if I have an issue, no dessert.

I almost never eat dessert.

The adult-part of the plan is that they're supposed to coach me through transitions. They're supposed to give me warnings and talk me through how to move my body from one spot to another. This sometimes helps me but only if Ms. Madeline or Mom does it. No one else goes slow enough for me.

Plus, it doesn't help with the other fifty-three things that are wrong with me, which is why I still get in trouble with Mr. Olsen all the time, but I guess that doesn't bother Mom as much because he doesn't call her when I forget a pencil or only hand in half my homework.

"Not a whole new plan," Mom is saying, still talking too fast. "You're right. We haven't quite given this one a chance. But I think if we tweak it a little bit. Pick your head up, sweetie."

Mom's words are bouncing all over the place, almost

buzzing, almost happy. Sadness wants me to be still and quiet and go to sleep.

4. Lazy

"There's no point in a new plan if no one follows it," I say. My head stays on the table.

28. Argumentative

11. Overly emotional

21. Irritable

47. Whiny

"Huh?" Mom says.

"Ms. Hayley didn't give me a warning," I say. "She just said *stop swinging now*. She didn't follow the plan."

Mom sighs. Her words slow down a little and Sadness expands further inside me. I don't want to lose my mom's hope. No matter what, she's always hoping that I can be good.

"Ms. Hayley said that she did. She gave you a five-, three-, and one-minute warning."

"Well she didn't," I say. "She's lying."

"Hmm," Mom says. She's losing a little of the buzzing that a new plan sends through her. I think I took it away from her. I think I sort of killed her buzzing on purpose, even though I miss it now. "Maybe she did and you just didn't hear her."

"What's the point of a plan if I can't hear that it's happening?" I ask.

"We can't expect everyone to follow it perfectly all the time, Gwendolyn," Mom says.

My eyebrows furrow against the wooden kitchen table. "But *I* have to follow it all the time."

"You almost never follow it," Mom says.

"And I'm almost always in trouble," I say. Anger opens his googly eyes and stretches a little. He's waking up.

"Pick your head up," Mom says.

Finally, I do. I'm face-to-face with a spoonful of thick green liquid that smells like fake-mint mixed with gasoline. My stomach lurches.

"What is that?" I say. The disgust finally shrinks Sadness just enough for me to be able to move and speak like normal.

"It's food," Mom says, the buzz back in her words. "Fish oil. I've been reading, and we need to do a major diet overhaul. You're partly right, Gwendolyn, you know that? You're right that we can't make all these plans that count on everyone following them perfectly. Maybe we need a plan that depends more on you and me, huh, honey? So I think if we cut all sugar out of your diet completely and add some things like a multivitamin and some fish oil and maybe a few other supplements and really focus on nutrition that may help you curb some of your—"

"I can't eat that," I say. I interrupted her but if I didn't, I'm not sure she'd ever stop talking.

"Sure you can," Mom says. "The minty flavor is designed to cover up the fishy taste."

I lower my eyebrows at her. "Can't I just eat fish sticks?" I love fish sticks.

"No," Mom says. "No fish sticks. Nothing processed. Fresh, clean food from now on." She waves the fish oil spoon toward my nose. "I need you on board, Gwendolyn."

But I'm not on board. Eating is one of the only things Anger and Sadness and I all enjoy at the same time.

"There's more," Mom says. "I'm also thinking that the cookies weren't enough of a prize for you. What do you think?"

I open my mouth, but she keeps talking.

"And you can't eat them anymore anyway. Sugar and processed foods are wrong. I did a ton of research on this today. No more bad food. It's making it harder for you to listen and behave. According to food-and-kids-dot-com, fish oil and proper nutrition can help up to thirty percent!"

I have so much to say. *Proper nutrition* is starting to sound like starving. *Fish oil* smells like poison. *Thirty percent* is not that much.

"Help up to thirty percent with what?"

Mom sighs. "I don't know, sweetie. With whatever . . ."

She trails off. She doesn't say "with whatever is wrong with you" but I know that's the end of the sentence. She doesn't know that I know that there's something wrong with me. That I know there's fifty-four things wrong with me.

"Another thing." Mom opens her bag and pulls out a calendar.

"A calendar?" I ask. How is that going to help me?

"For each day that you don't have trouble in PowerKids,

we'll put a check mark on this calendar. If you have enough check marks when school ends, you get something you want. You choose."

"A prize?" I say. I can't stop my eyes from rolling. About eight hundred plans ago, when I was little, we had one that involved a lot of prizes. They were little stickers or stamps or those sticky hands you throw against a wall. Really stupid stuff that I didn't care about. And still, I got so mad every day that I didn't get to pick out of the prize bag.

"More like . . . a reward. Something big. Something you really want."

My ears perk up. I lift my chin to look at her.

"Take this," Mom says. She holds the spoon out again.

"I want to go to horse camp. With Tyler."

Mom slowly lowers the spoon.

"I don't know, honey," she says slowly.

I can feel Sadness shrinking quickly out of my arms and legs. He leaves a happy, zinging feeling in his wake.

"It's the only thing I want," I say. Even though I know Mom will say that's not true. At this moment, it is true.

"I was thinking more like a trip to the water park?" Mom says. "Or maybe a weekend camping? Or I take you and Hettie to the movies at the mall?"

I love those things. But I shake my head.

"Horse camp," I say.

"I was even thinking it could be something bigger," Mom says. "Maybe something you've been asking for for a long time." She really, really doesn't want me to really, really want to go to horse camp with Tyler but I really, really do. I don't know if it's the horses that scare Mom or if she just doesn't want me to spend that much time with my brother. And it's not because Tyler is a splinter-heart kid like me. It's only because Tyler's mom is also my dad's ex-girlfriend. I think that's something our moms have in common, so it should make them friends. But it doesn't.

"Like another hamster?" Mom suggests.

I do worry that Mr. Jojo gets lonely during the day when I'm at school, and during the night when I'm in bed. I hear him playing all night long, and I'd love to hear him playing with someone else. He deserves to have at least one friend like I do.

But I want horse camp more.

"No," I say.

"Or maybe . . ." Mom pauses and shakes her head like she's arguing with her own self. "Maybe even . . . a phone," she says finally.

"A *phone*?" Mom always says there's no way I can have a phone. Even when Thaís and Margaret, who used to be my friends, got phones. Even when Hettie got a phone. She doesn't just say no. She says *no way*. I'd lose it or break it or ruin it or do something impulsive and stupid with it. But if I had something as important as a phone, I know I'd keep it safe.

I think about being able to call or text Hettie whenever I

want. I think about telling Tyler he doesn't have to call my mom to talk to me anymore. Then I think about telling him I can't go to horse camp, but he can text me pictures of the horses he rides.

No.

"I want horse camp," I say again. "More than a phone."

12. Inflexible thinker

I stare down the green sludge on the spoon. I can do all of this for horse camp. I can give up sugar and fish sticks. I can swallow green sludge. I can kill Anger if I get horse camp in the end.

"You *do* have to be very motivated . . ." Mom trails off. "I guess, yes. Horse camp. If you get enough check marks, you get to go to horse camp." She pauses. Then adds, "With Tyler."

Sadness lifts the rest of the way out of me until he's a little marble rolling around again. Anger stops snoring so I can't even feel him.

I hold my nose and open my mouth.

The green sludge isn't even that bad.

Horse camp, here I come.

# 4

## GOOD MORNING, CONFIDENCE

That night I snuggle into my bed, and my mom comes in and pulls the covers tight. Luckily, she does the blankets perfectly on the first try. Then she sings "Good Night Sweetheart," kisses me on the forehead, and hands me the book I never read.

"Don't forget to turn your light out, OK, Cupcake?" she asks.

I nod and let the warm snuggly-ness fill me up.

39. Immature

Tyler says his mom never tucks him in anymore. He says he goes to bed whenever he feels like it, and sometimes it's before her and sometimes it's after. He sort of laughed when he found out my mom still tucks me in every night just like he sort of laughed when he saw our too-small apartment the first time he came over to hang out on a weekend. But I don't care. Tyler and I are the same but our moms aren't. Tyler gets vacations and Saturday night movies and weekend trips to the creamery at the university with his mom.

Some days bedtime is the only good moment I get with mine.

I didn't mind that Tyler laughed either, though. For all I know, he didn't actually mean to. Tyler's like me so sometimes he does things before he even knows he's doing them.

Mom leaves my room, and like always, I dig under the blankets and unfold the papers. I do it carefully because some of them are getting so thin I know they could rip easily, and if that happened, I'd have to sit and copy the list all over again—both sides.

Letters in my handwriting fill my vision. Black ink starts marching across the page. Even though I wrote these words, I always have to focus super hard to read them.

I start where I left off last night.

7. Inattentive

Because it's a good night, Confidence wakes up and steps in to interrupt the list. This is supposed to happen every night, but Confidence is a lot harder to wake up than Anger or Sadness. Confidence is a small stick figure that lives in the sliver between my brain and my skull, right at the top of my forehead. He moves and talks like a little soldier, and he's hunter green like a military uniform. Whenever my mom comes up with a plan that may actually work, Confidence wakes up and marches around declaring things.

"Not tomorrow!" he says as I read number 7. "Tomorrow at attention all day!"

He about-faces in the middle of my brain.

8. Acts without thinking

"Tomorrow we will think! Long before any action can happen! We will think as soon as our eyes are open!" He marches.

9. Hyperactive

"Tomorrow we will be hypo-active!" Confidence declares. "We will stun the world with how slowly we can act!"

10. No filter

"That's enough," Confidence says. "Tomorrow will be different. You can go to bed now."

And, for once, I listen. I turn out the light.

A few minutes later, though, I hear the *doo-dee-doo* sound of my mom calling someone on Skype. I know what I should do in that way that, if this were a question on a quiz, I'd get it correct.

*Q: What do you do if you hear your mom calling someone in the middle of the night?*

*A: Don't listen.*

While I'm thinking about how I shouldn't eavesdrop, I end up tiptoeing down my ladder and cracking the door to my bedroom open so that I can hear better. The light from the kitchen slices across my face, and I sit on the cold hardwood floor and lean my head against the doorway when I hear Marsha answer.

"Nina," she says. "Just let me step outside and I'll be right with you."

"No problem," Mom says.

Marsha is old so she's never remembering things like *mute* and *turn off your camera* when Mom calls. I can hear kids laughing behind her, a TV on loudly, two teens calling each other "bro." I imagine what my mom is seeing on her computer screen: chaos and noise and crowds. The opposite of our life.

Marsha is Mom's sponsor. I've listened to enough of these calls to sort of understand what that means. Mom calls her when she's had a tough day, and Marsha helps Mom make good choices.

They almost always talk about me.

"So what's up, kiddo?" Marsha says. It's quieter in her background.

I love that she calls my mom *kiddo*.

"I got called in again. To the school," Mom says.

"Ut-oh," Marsha says. "What was it this time?"

"Gwen tried to run away from her after-school program. They caught her climbing over the schoolyard fence."

I bite my lip so I won't start screaming the truth. Whenever I listen to Mom and Marsha at night, I have to work hard to keep myself very still and quiet because Mom never quite has the story right, and it's hard for me to let that go, even when I'm sneaking.

But I wasn't running *away*. I was just running. Then the fence got in the way.

"Golly. So what did you do?" Marsha asks.

Mom sighs.

"Same old, same old," Mom says. "Leaving work early. Taking a pay cut. Getting yelled at by the twenty-somethings who run this after-school program. I don't know . . . Nothing I do is working. . . . I already know what you're going to say."

I think I do too. I listen to these calls so much, I know everything about Marsha's voice. The smooth way it rises and falls. The calmness that rings through it even when she's surrounded by chaos. I've never seen her face, but I picture her with gray hair twisted into a bun and half glasses resting on her nose, like a cartoon librarian. In my imagination the cartoon librarian is nodding thoughtfully.

"Maybe you should think about which parts of it are in your control and which parts you need to let go of," Marsha says.

"Are you putting my *daughter* in the category of things I can't control?" Mom demands.

"Well she is another person," Marsha says. Like Mom forgot I'm a person. And sometimes I wonder if Mom does sort of forget that. Because sometimes I also sort of forget that. I think when I was younger I felt more like a person, a whole one. Now I feel more like a pile of problems. "Maybe this isn't the best afternoon plan for you and Gwendolyn?"

"I can't afford more help," Mom says. "PowerKids is subsidized. That's the only reason I subject us to it."

This is why I listen to these calls. If I didn't, I'd never know that Mom also blames PowerKids for what happened today. That she doesn't only blame me.

"And I know what you're going to say. But no. That's not an option. I'm not going to ask you-know-who for help. Not *her*."

*Her?*

"Hear me out. What if you ask for something small? An hour on the weekend?"

Mom snorts sarcastically. "Not from her."

Who is *her*?

"Rest would be good for you," Marsha says.

"Rest feels pointless when I have all this stress waiting for me at the end of it."

"That's when rest is the most important," Marsha says.

Mom huffs. She almost sounds like me. No wonder Marsha calls her *kiddo*.

"And it isn't even asking for help. Remember? She volunteered."

Who is she?

And why won't Mom let her help us?

Mom is silent this time.

Then "Grandma!" rings out from the background of Marsha's computer. "Jimmy won't read to me!"

"It's OK," Mom says quickly. "I'm OK. Go, go."

"Hang in there, Nina," Marsha says. "It works if you work it."

Then the computer makes more sounds and I know Mom has hung up, so I slowly close my bedroom door. I walk to the back of my room where the aquarium glows and watch

Zombie and Marshmallow swim in circles around each other.

They're so peaceful. They can't fight because they can't speak. Sometimes I wish my mom and I could live like that. Swimming around each other with no words or plans or fights or disappointments.

The next morning, all I can think about is getting today's check mark. On the way to school, my braids are a little too loose because I didn't want to be **25. Picky about her appearance** and ask Mom to do them again and again. And I don't hear anything she says in the car because I'm too busy telling my brain to slow down, slow down slowdown slowdownslowdown. So when I see Tyler and his purple backpack bouncing up and down the stairs to the school building, waiting for me, I don't lunge for the car door and launch myself out like I want to.

I lean into the front seat and give my mom a kiss on the cheek. She was talking. She stops as soon as I kiss her. My breath catches, and for a minute I'm afraid I interrupted her.

But she says, "That was nice, Gwennie."

"Have a good day, Mom," I say. Then I tell my hands to be still and ask myself if I have everything. My backpack. My gym shoes. There's nothing else.

I open the car door, forcing my muscles to move so slowly they hurt.

"Gwendolyn," Mom calls as soon as I'm outside the car. "You're forgetting something."

My heart drops to my feet.

There goes my check mark. There goes horse camp.

I turn around and she's holding my lunch box out the window. Suddenly it's a lot easier to move slowly. I trudge the few steps over to her and take the lunch.

"No check today, huh?" I ask.

This is so stupid because I never even eat lunch at school. And I'm definitely not going to eat whatever Mom packed today from the recommendations on food-for-impossible-kids-dot-com or whatever.

2. Picky eater

I lost a check mark over nothing.

"What, no! You can still earn a check today. Don't give up that easily," Mom says. She leans out of the car and laces her arms around my neck. "You don't have to be perfect, G. No one is."

That's a thing people tell me a lot. That no one's perfect. But from my view everyone around me seems so much closer to perfect that I can't see the difference between perfect and whatever they are.

"So I can break some of the fifty-four things?" I blurt.

"What are you talking about?" Mom asks. "Please don't break anything."

"No, they aren't like breaking things. Not like when I broke your glasses."

"Gwendolyn! Don't break anyone's glasses."

"That's not what I was talking about," I say. The fifty-four things list pokes the bottom of my heel. I'm wearing Mary Janes today, no socks. I'll come home with paper cuts on my feet, but it's worth it because I can't move as fast in these as I can in my sneakers, so they're an automatic slowdown.

Confidence, who is somehow still a little bit awake, butts in and says, "Speed up now, though!"

"Bye," I say without trying to explain more.

Then I run. I bolt. I'm faster than I've ever been in Mary Janes. I run so fast, I crash right into Tyler and his purple backpack.

"I've figured it out!" I scream.

23. Talks too loud

"Huh?" Tyler says, turning to face me.

He doesn't react to my volume, but still I rearrange my vocal cords and say in a regular way, "I'm going to horse camp. Also, will you redo my braids before school starts?"

While he braids my hair, I tell him about the plan Mom came up with.

"You can do that," Tyler says as he finishes fastening the last hair tie.

With my braids this tight, I believe I can.

After lunch and outside break, I slide back into my desk in Mr. Olsen's room and take out my science notebook. Our school is small so even though we technically switch classes like they do in most middle schools, I have Mr. Olsen over and over again for math every morning and for science every afternoon and sometimes for enrichment period too.

I dig in my bag. I don't have the pencil Mr. Olsen gave me this morning. My heart starts racing because I'm thinking about how I'm going to have to ask for one all over again.

I tap the kid in front of me. "Do you have a pencil?" I whisper.

"I gave you one yesterday," he hisses. It's probably true. Everyone in every single one of my classes probably thinks of me as Forgets Her Pencil Girl.

I turn to the girl next to me, but she shakes her head and rolls her eyes.

If I had friends in this class, maybe I could ask one of them to keep my pencil for me. If Thaís and I were still friends, I could turn around and ask her because she sits behind me. But we aren't friends anymore.

"As fifth graders, you are required to participate in the science fair," Mr. Olsen announces. He always starts class like that. Never a "good afternoon" or "arrange your desks so that you'll have what you need." He starts talking with no warning so usually by the time I realize I'm supposed to be paying attention, I've missed half of the important stuff.

"The science fair is a great school tradition here at Banneker middle. In fifth grade, we spend a lot of time helping you to prepare so that, in sixth, you are ready to apply the scientific method independently. The first step is to choose the subject matter you wish to study. It must be scientific, and it should be of great interest to you."

Lightbulbs go off in my brain. Animals. Animals are science-y, right?

"You will work over the next several weeks to complete all the related project components: the essential question, the traditional experiment using the scientific method, the written report, the visual demonstration, and so forth. Now because this is a significant amount of work and because science is almost always a communal endeavor . . ."

He's still talking but I can't listen anymore. The words are too big, and they're coming too fast, and I'm too distracted by all of my ideas. I imagine bringing home tons of furry and cute creatures and telling Mom I have to because it's for school.

7. Inattentive

24. Spacey

37. Doesn't follow directions

"So find your partner and start brainstorming," Mr. Olsen concludes.

Partner?

My hearts starts racing. I hate working with partners. I hate when someone else has to rely on my brain with its fifty-four problems. And what if my partner doesn't like animals?

Mr. Olsen projects a list of names onto the board and I scan for mine. And then I know that studying animals won't be a problem.

Next to my name it says *Thaís Gonzalez.*

Suddenly she's beside me. "Hi, Gwen," she says, chewing her lip like she's nervous, but I know she can't be because I'm the one who's nervous.

Thaís puts two papers down on my desk. They're blank graphic organizers. I guess Mr. Olsen must have explained what to do today while I was daydreaming about mice and hamsters and guinea pigs and maybe even a bearded dragon. I scoot over so Thaís can bring a chair up to my table. Around us kids start talking but I'm silent.

I haven't talked to Thaís in over a year. She's one of the girls who I thought was my friend until I read my IEP report. Before that, Hettie and Thaís and Margaret and I used to hang out all the time. We played different versions of tag at recess. We met up on weekends to draw horses in chalk in Thaís's massive driveway or make up new cookie recipes in Margaret's kitchen. In fact, if I had read that IEP report just a few weeks before I did, I wouldn't have believed the part where Mom said I had only one friend. But something happened at the beginning of fourth grade, and suddenly Thaís and Margaret weren't talking to me anymore. At first it looked like they stopped talking to each other, too, but now they're all together all the time: Thaís, Margaret, and Hettie. But Hettie is the only one who still talks to me.

"So do you have any ideas?" Thaís asks. She pushes her black hair out of her face. She always wears it down, and it's long, so it often gets stuck in her eyelashes or across her nose.

"No," I say, even though I had a ton of ideas before I got all nervous. "Do you?"

"Um . . . I was thinking, maybe, dolphins?"

Thaís loves all animals like I do. It's a thing you know about a person when you think you're their friend for years. I could probably suggest any of the other animals I thought of, but I don't. A dolphin is an animal so, even though it can't be a pet, I say, "OK."

Thaís writes *Dolphin* in the middle of her graphic organizer, then looks at me and waits for me to do the same.

"Oh," I say, "Let's just keep going. I don't know where my pencil is."

"She doesn't know where her pencil is!" Mr. Olsen's voice booms behind me. "Gee, that's surprising, Ms. Rogers, isn't it?"

I twist my neck to look up at him. My face burns. He always says we shouldn't be offended if he's sarcastic. That it's just part of his personality. But his eyes are too mean for me to believe that.

"*Here's* your pencil!" Thaís says suddenly. She shoves a mechanical pencil into my hand. This morning, Mr. Olsen gave me a yellow #2. This is not my pencil. Thaís smiles as I take it from her.

I write *Dolphin*.

Then, when Mr. Olsen is gone, I whisper "Thanks" to Thaís.

She smiles. "It's OK. I hate when he does that sarcastic thing. Do you want to know something cool about dolphins?"

I nod fast. Of course I do.

As soon as school gets out, Hettie runs up beside me and we make our way to the schoolyard together. Every day we meet Ms. Hayley and all the staff in the schoolyard before we go back into the building to start PowerKids.

"What should we do today at free time?" Hettie asks, all excited. Whenever she's around Confidence wakes up and starts marching.

My brain spins with all the fun things we could do.

Before I can answer, Tyler finds Hettie and me in the hallway.

"How's it going?" Tyler asks. "Are we still on track?"

I smile. "Totally," I say.

"On track for what?" Hettie asks.

"A check," I say, then turn back to Tyler and say, "Race you both!"

As we take off down the hallway, I hear Hettie call, "What check?" but she has to know about the calendar, right? Because I told her, right? Because she's my best friend.

She's still my best friend because a brother really, really isn't the same thing. Even a brother who doesn't live with you. Even a brother who you don't share parents with. I love Tyler, and I want to spend every minute with him, but he also makes me all jumbled and jealous, and I think I make him that way too. Hettie is different from Tyler and everything else in the entire world because things with her are simple and fun.

With Hettie, I'm a List of Things to Do instead of being a List of Fifty-Four Wrong Things.

So Hettie is super important to me. So there's no way I forgot to tell her about the new plan. Right?

"What check?" she asks again, catching me as we run out the back door of the school and into the schoolyard. Hettie is the fastest kid in the entire fifth grade, which is really unfair because she doesn't run half as much as I do. Usually when I tell her I need to move so let's race, she sits down. But now she's running and catches me. "What are you talking about?"

"The check for horse camp," Tyler says.

"It costs money?" Hettie asks. "We need the checks *today*?"

"Not like a money check," Tyler says. "Gwendolyn's check mark."

"Huh?" Hettie says.

"Horse camp," I say, "I told you." I hope she doesn't notice how I'm not quite looking at her.

Now we're standing on the stairs outside the back door to the school, and even though most of my body is still, my legs are moving, shifting back and forth and forth and back, because I still need to move, or actually I need to move *more*, because now I'm not sure if I *did* tell Hettie about the calendar and horse camp and all the things I should be telling her and, ever since I met Tyler, it's been harder and harder to keep track of what exactly I tell Hettie, and I know that hurts

Hettie's feelings, and it should because she's the good friend and I'm the one who's messing up, but I don't know how to—

"Race to the swings and back!" I yell.

This is allowed because PowerKids doesn't technically start for another ten minutes, even though most of my classmates are already finding their groups and lining up. But I'll do better all day if I run right now while it's allowed.

"Horse camp?" Hettie says.

"You can come too," Tyler says, shrugging.

"Ready, set, GO!" I say. I leap off the bottom stair in the direction of the swings. I can't tell if they're following me because I take off so fast and don't look back. If Hettie is following, she'll catch me.

I finally start to hear her breath behind me as I'm rounding the swings, but she isn't in front of me yet. This might be my one chance in life to beat Hettie McFee in a race.

I fly around the swings and bound through the schoolyard. I'm going faster than I ever have in my life. Everything around me is still but I'm a bolt of lightning. I fling my arms back and forth, and pump my legs, and only my body is awake. All the stuff inside it goes to sleep: Anger and Sadness and even Confidence and all fifty-four wrong things disappear because all I am is a pair of legs outrunning another pair of legs when

BAM.

I crash into a warm body and fall on the dirt.

I don't even look to see who I crashed into. I turn my head

and watch Hettie run past me. Tyler is jogging behind her. "No fair!" I yell. "I was beating you until—"

"Gwendolyn!" A familiar voice. Too familiar.

I look up at the body I crashed into.

"Mom?" I say. I let her help me up.

"What are you doing?" she asks. She's angry.

I open my mouth but for once no words come out.

"Ms. Hayley called and told me that I had to meet with her today at three fifteen," Mom says. "Now here you are running around like a maniac when you're supposed to be in trouble."

Anger wakes up, sudden and ferocious.

"I didn't do anything!"

"Why are you running when the rest of the kids are standing nicely?"

"I was running nicely until you got in my way," I blurt. My voice is way too high. It almost sounds like I'm crying, but I'm not. I swear (47. Whiny). "We're allowed to run before PowerKids starts. Right?" I turn to look for Hettie or Tyler to back me up but they're both gone. I look around and see groups disappearing into the cafeteria.

Why does this always happen? Whole movements of big groups of people seem to take place in a second when Anger is awake. Time stops making sense.

"Well, why did Ms. Hayley call then, Gwendolyn? Something must have happened."

"No!" I scream. "Nothing! I swear!"

Sometimes I swear nothing happened when something did.

And sometimes I blame someone else, like Ms. Hayley, when something is my fault. Or mostly my fault. But this time I'm right. Nothing happened. And they already called my mom.

"It's not fair!" I scream.

11. Overly emotional

"Good afternoon, Nina," Ms. Hayley says, suddenly behind me. I jump.

"What's going on?" my mom asks.

"Gwendolyn, you can go along to your group with Ms. Madeline, OK?" Ms. Hayley says. "Nina, we can meet in my office."

My mom's jaw drops. "Gwendolyn isn't in trouble?" she asks.

I hate how surprised she looks.

"Not presently, no," Ms. Hayley says. "But we want to have a talk with you about the incident on Wednesday."

"We've discussed that at length," my mom says. Wrinkles etch into her face. She's exhausted.

I know Ms. Hayley said to go and meet my group, but she only asked me once, and now she seems to forget I'm here, so I don't move. I need to hear this.

16. Sneaky. For ex. eavesdrops

Mom is still talking. "I had to take off work early. I would have appreciated a little more candor on the phone since this clearly isn't an emergency."

"We have some serious things to discuss. In my office," Ms. Hayley says.

"What kind of serious things?" Mom asks.

I make the mistake of turning my head back to Ms. Hayley to see how she'll respond, and when I do she says, "Go on, Gwen."

I move, slowly. It's easy to move slowly right now. And I do it so well I can still hear them.

"We wanted to give you some options. We don't like to remove children from our program before giving parents all the options."

Remove from the program?

"But Gwendolyn has become a safety risk. And we believe it's time for some proactive steps."

"You're talking about expelling her?" Mom says.

My heart stops. I freeze. That would mean no horse camp. That would mean almost never seeing Tyler. They can't do that.

"Well, we wouldn't call it that."

"It doesn't matter what you call it." Mom is almost yelling.

"We want to be able to help Gwendolyn succeed here, but we need some professional involvement . . ."

Professionals! No!

"I think she needs a formal assessment," Ms. Hayley concludes.

Not this again!

"You don't understand," Mom pleads, "We've been to almost everyone in the area."

"Oh, she has an IEP?" Ms. Hayley asks.

"No," Mom says. "We tried but it was a disas—you just . . . you can't do this to us."

"I want to work with you, Ms. Allen." Ms. Hayley sighs. "Please come to my office?"

I guess Mom finally listens because I can't hear them anymore.

This is part of the reason Mom's plans never work. Even when she comes up with a good one, some other adult comes along and messes it up for us.

I can't go to horse camp at all if I'm expelled from PowerKids.

# 5

## DIAGNOSIS INCONCLUSIVE

I know all about assessments. In the past two years, I've had so many full assessments and half assessments and mini assessments and formal assessments and informal assessments. I know they're pointless. Or at least they never help me.

Almost two years ago, my mom and I sat across from Ms. North, my third-grade teacher, as she went over my report card.

"Blue means she's meeting standards; purple means she's approaching standards; red means she's rather behind grade level. And green would mean she's exceeding."

I had headphones on, so I wasn't supposed to hear all of this. I had an iPad in front of my face, so I wasn't supposed to see. Ms. North had asked Mom not to bring me to the parent-teacher conferences, but Mom is a single parent who didn't have a choice and who also didn't know my headphones were on mute.

I quickly glanced at the card stock square in Mom's hands. The ink on it was black. The background was highlighted in different colors. It was almost all red and purple.

"I don't understand," Mom said. "You just called Gwendolyn bright."

"She is," Ms. North assured my mom. "Intelligence is not the problem."

The problem.

I knew before this moment that I wasn't normal, of course. But I'd never heard someone say, *the problem.* Not *what's my problem.* Not *difficult child,* or *handful,* or *distraction* or *in trouble.*

The problem.

Like it was separate. Something that existed outside of me.

Like when you trip, and it's so embarrassing because you look like a clumsy person who can't even walk, but then you realize your shoe was untied and that you tripped for a reason that's attached to you, but isn't actually you.

Before that moment I had mostly liked third grade. I didn't know about the fifty-four things, so if someone asked me to describe myself, I wouldn't even think about words like *good* and *bad.* I'd say things like *I love animals especially horses and hamsters* and *Recess is my favorite subject* and *Hettie is my best friend.*

When I thought of school with Ms. North, I didn't think about the work. I thought about my friends who sat at my table in the classroom, and I thought about how hard I could kick a ball in gym class. I thought about making Hettie and Thaís and Margaret laugh by using a funny voice when Ms. North called on me to read out loud.

In second grade, I'd been yelled at constantly. In first grade, I'd been yelled at constantly. At PowerKids, I was yelled at constantly every year. But Ms. North didn't yell. If I got out of my seat too many times or was too distracting, Ms. North would move me to the back of the classroom or hold me back from recess, but she never yelled and embarrassed me. I was happier in third grade than I was anywhere except at home or the stables. I was happy at school.

But I knew I was bad at it.

"I want to help," Ms. North said. "But we can't help without identifying the problem."

There it was again. *The problem.*

"What problem?" Mom asked.

"I wish I could answer that easily," Ms. North said. "I think it's best if we get Gwendolyn scheduled for an IEP evaluation."

I tore off my headphones. "What's an IEP?" I blurted. Mom jumped at the sound of my voice. But I'm sneaky, and I have no filter, so I think they should have both expected me to eavesdrop and then to interrupt them.

Ms. North also looked at me, startled. "An IEP . . ." she

started. Then turned back to Mom. "This is why I was asking if we could have this conversation in a manner a bit more . . . clandestine."

"But it's about me," I said. "I should get to know what you're saying."

"You know the word *clandestine*?" Ms. North sounded shocked.

"C-L-A-N-D-E-S-T-I-N-E," I spelled. "Yes."

Mom threw up her hands. "I can't," she said. "I can't come here without her, OK? I live far away from my family. I've never ever met a babysitter who can handle her. And I'm definitely not about to leave Gwendolyn alone."

Ms. North took a minute, then I guess she decided to keep talking.

"An IEP is an Individualized Education Plan," Ms. North said. "And I understand. I'm sorry I didn't think about how complicated that request might be before I made it."

"Like a plan for my teachers that's just for me and not everyone?" I asked.

First there was *the problem*. Now Ms. North had *a solution*.

"You think she has a learning disorder?" Mom said. She sounded startled. Not angry exactly but like the light was suddenly too bright in the classroom.

"I think Gwendolyn . . . What I think is that she needs more than I'm currently able to give her in the classroom. Students with IEPs receive services, individual attention. Some get extra time on tests or extra small group time to work on reading skills."

"Reading skills?" Mom said. She was so loud and spoke so fast compared to Ms. North. "Gwendolyn reads the newspaper over my shoulder in the morning."

"Amazing," Ms. North said. Then she pointed to the part of my report card devoted to reading. It was almost completely red. "But an IEP can help us understand why that talent isn't translating to the classroom."

"I want it," I said.

Mom brushed me off. "She needs to apply herself more maybe," she said.

I knew that was wrong. I immediately understood. I didn't notice it so clearly before, but it was true that it was somehow easier to read Mom's newspaper than it was to read the kid books in my classroom. That wasn't normal.

If we could solve the problem, whatever it was, would that mean school got easier? Everything got easier? Would that mean fourth grade would be better than third grade instead of turning back into second?

I didn't know then that this search for this stupid problem would take years. I didn't know that we'd never find it. I didn't know how much of myself I would lose searching for exact words for problems and solutions.

"IEPs are almost always worth it," Ms. North said. "Practically speaking there aren't any risks to getting evaluated."

I elbowed Mom. She ignored me.

"I've been to these conferences every year since Gwen was in kindergarten," Mom says. "And no one has said *IEP*. Every other teacher has said that Gwendolyn needs to apply herself more and stop goofing around. Improve her behavior."

"But what if we could help her?" Ms. North asked.

"How?" Mom said.

"I mean, what if Gwendolyn's behavior isn't difficult because she wants to be funny or she isn't applying herself? What if Gwendolyn's behavior is difficult because she doesn't know how to not be difficult?"

I stared at my third-grade teacher. It was like she had pulled back my skull and read directly from my brain. No one had ever said anything like that about me before.

"But Gwendolyn doesn't have any obvious boxes she ticks."

"To be candid, Ms. Allen, I think she does."

I sat up straighter. I wanted to fit into an obvious box.

"The thing is that an IEP assessment takes a long time," Ms. North was saying. "And although we're sitting in my third-grade classroom now, when you look at the wait-list and how long assessments can take, and how long it can take a team to truly implement the steps and interventions in an IEP . . . it starts to look like middle school is just around the corner."

Assessment.

I liked that word.

I tried to spell it in my mind. It made my head hurt but in a good way. I knew the word though. An assessment was a way to measure how something is doing. It's like a test but without the judgment. No failing or passing. I heard the word a lot in the detective shows Mom watched at night that I wasn't supposed to listen to: "Let's assess the situation."

"I'll think about it," Mom said. "Maybe you're right."

Ms. North was right. I already knew it.

By the time we actually started the assessment though, I was already in fourth grade, and everything about school was worse. I was constantly in trouble. I couldn't focus on anything the teacher was saying. Margaret and Thaís had stopped talking to me. Mom and I were fighting every day about my braids and my bed and my room and my behavior in school.

Hettie and Dandelion were the only good things about life.

Anger was constantly awake, shaking inside me, rattling my rib cage like the bars of a jail. The only place Anger ever slept was at the Millington Stables. I got to go there three days a week after school and on Saturdays. I'd bounce out of Mom's car and hug Ms. Kate, my instructor. Then I'd go about tacking up Dandelion. She was always happy to see me. She was my favorite horse, even though she was everyone else's least favorite. The only good thing about me was that I knew how to take care of Dandelion.

When I wasn't at the stables everything was awful. My stomach hurt. My head hurt. My heart hurt.

At the stables, a different part of me came alive. I followed directions. I was gentle with all the horses. Ms. Kate thought I was a "sweetheart." It was sort of like Ms. Kate didn't know the real me, and it was sort of like she was the only one who did.

Mom kept promising that she had filled out the paperwork and we were just waiting for an appointment. But I didn't believe her. I thought she didn't want me to have *the problem,* whatever it was. Even though I was sure I had that problem. I thought she didn't want to find a solution because that would prove that *the problem* existed.

Finally, I was taken out of class for a few afternoons in a row. I sat in a room with an adult I'd never met before and answered questions. They were mostly math and reading questions, with a few written and spoken questions about me. It didn't feel like the magical thing that could give us all the answers to the way I think and act. But, I thought, if it really was as amazing as Ms. North made it seem, I wouldn't be able to understand how it worked anyway. So I did the best I could.

Of course, the IEP assessment wasn't at the stables, so the best I could was pretty awful.

Then we waited again. It took weeks and weeks for the results to show up. This time I knew that it wasn't Mom's fault, but I still kept blaming her. I couldn't help it. It wasn't me yelling at my mom, it was *the problem* yelling at her. I thought the yelling would stop, and the headaches and the stomachaches would stop, and the getting in trouble at school and PowerKids would stop, and the not talking to Margaret and Thaís would stop. We'd get the solution and then everything would be different.

That year Mom used to pick me up from PowerKids or the stables, drive home, and then rest her head on the steering wheel for minutes or hours after we parked. While Mom sat in the parking lot, I would get out of the car, check the mail, and then go inside. I pretended I was doing a favor for Mom. I'd sort out all the junk and throw it away and leave the things that looked important on the table.

She'd say *thank you,* even.

It took weeks and weeks, but finally I found the envelope. In the top left—the return address—it said Department of Education. It was addressed to Ms. Nina Allen.

I knew better than to open it, even though I wanted to so badly it shook in my hands. I knew better than to even mention it. Somehow, for that day, I grew a filter. I stuck the envelope at the bottom of the Important Mail pile and went in my room to play with Mr. Jojo.

As I sat down to spaghetti and meatballs that night, I was sure my mom would say it. "Gwendolyn, you have: this." Some strange combination of letters that I could blame for the Anger in my chest and the Sadness in my limbs and confusion in my brain.

But Mom said nothing. Just passed me the Parmesan cheese.

All that night I bit my tongue with words. Extra, extra words. So many words. I talked nonstop about Dandelion like always, letting pointless words bury the questions I wanted to ask. Mom looked tired. I sat next to her while she watched the news and asked questions about what the reporters were saying. I tried not to notice the way her hair looked extra gray when she answered.

I waited.

*Don't mention it. Don't say assessment. Don't say results. Don't say IEP.*

I waited. I got in bed. I waited.

When I was sure Mom was in her room, I snuck into the kitchen. The envelope was still on the table but it looked bigger this time, pregnant with the information she had taken out and shoved back inside.

I held my breath.

I was about to have the answer.

I pulled the papers out. The stack was thick in my hands. I wondered how it was possible to need that much paper just to define someone's problem.

I found my name listed at the top. And my birthday.

Underneath it, in big letters, it said: *CLASSIFICATION.*

And next it said *INCONCLUSIVE.*

My jaw dropped and my hands started shaking, but my eyes kept reading.

*Gwendolyn displays some clear difficulties in terms of behavior and cognition and also some obvious talents. Her characteristics do not place her in any category according to the DSM-5 or the IDEA. Although she displays some behaviors typical of an individual with a learning or behavioral disorder, her strong capacity for working-memory and above-average intelligence mean that our evaluators did not find an accurate diagnosis, and we conclude she does not qualify under any of the thirteen IDEA classifications. We believe Gwendolyn is basically neurotypical and do not recommend she receive any accommodations beyond those typically given to every student in the classroom.*

Anger tore out of his shell fast and climbed up my ribs like a ladder.

They found no problem.

No problem.

No. Problem.

Ferociously I started to turn the pages of the assessment. I didn't care about getting caught anymore. I didn't think about what I was doing. I ate the words. Or Anger did. He gobbled them.

*Gwendolyn displays very little ability for emotional regulation . . .*

*Several times during the testing process, Gwendolyn became outwardly frustrated, easily moved to yelling, throwing objects, and tantrums . . .*

*Gwendolyn's mother described a laborious morning routine, which involves perfect twin French braids . . .*

Anger climbed up and down until he was exhausted. Sadness crawled into my fingers and spread slowly up my arms and through my chest.

*Gwendolyn has always been immature for her age according to her mother . . .*

*Gwendolyn's fourth-grade teacher describes her work as lazy and careless . . .*

*Gwendolyn has a best friend but despite that her mother and teachers describe a general social ineptitude. Her mother says she has only one friend.*

*I don't have a problem,* I realized.

*I* am *a problem.*

Sadness directed me. He moved my legs so I walked to the desk under my bed. He took out the notebook paper and the black pen. He sent my eyes through all the papers again. He directed my fingers to write down each problem I could find.

1. Too demanding, I wrote.

2. Picky eater

3. Attention-seeking

I wrote and wrote until I had filled out the front and back of two pieces of paper with fifty-four points.

I wrote a title at the top: Fifty-Four Things Wrong with Gwendolyn Rogers

Then I got in bed and read the list over and over until the sun came up.

# 6

## MOM HAS A PROBLEM

"An assessment, like fourth grade?" I ask Mom on the way home from PowerKids. "Or like the other ones? Like the doctor ones or something?"

My brain keeps telling me to shut up. Confidence, maybe, is telling me to shut up. He's telling me that Mom is mad, and that, if I know what's good for me, I won't keep asking questions when she's already mad because when people are mad it's super easy to make them madder, and, as someone with Anger living inside her rib cage, I should know that more than anyone.

"Can Ms. Hayley really make us do this?" I ask.

10. No filter

"No," Mom says. She turns in the direction away from our house. "That's not going to happen. That silly girl thinks she understands how things like this work, like she can just order an assessment and then magic! I'll be able to—"

"What did she mean by professional? Like a therapist?" I ask.

*Shut up! Shut up! Shut up!*

After the IEP didn't help, Mom made plans even faster than before. Some of them meant new, different assessments. We went to one therapist who decided I shouldn't be around horses until I could control myself. She thought taking away something that big would teach me my lesson, whatever that lesson was. She said if I really wanted to ride Dandelion enough, I'd behave better.

I missed Dandelion badly, so she was all I could talk about with the next therapist. He told my mom and I that he had the perfect solution: equine therapy! He said he often sent patients to the equine therapy program right at Millington Stables. He was so excited it was contagious. I asked him if that meant I'd get to ride horses again, and a little of his excitement disappeared. He didn't know. But I should at least get to be around Dandelion again. That was enough for me. I was pumped.

When I got to the stables for my first day of equine therapy, both Ms. Kate and Dandelion were nowhere in sight. Instead, I had to listen to the therapists. They didn't believe that I was already a horse expert. They told me I wasn't allowed to be near Dandelion because she was too difficult. I had to stay with the easy horses. And I wasn't allowed to ride any of them ever. I didn't hear what I was actually supposed to be doing because my brain had cracked, and I was screaming, and I had to be dragged out before I upset all the horses. So I was kicked out of equine therapy, and, according to that therapist—who broke up with us at the next session—Ms. Kate banned me from Millington Stables. Forever.

I learned two things from equine therapy: 1. I will always and forever miss Dandelion, and 2. I should never, ever trust a therapist.

Mom kept trying though.

Another therapist we went to wanted Mom to feed me baby food while she held the spoon. He said the problem was that we didn't love each other enough.

Another one came to our house and made rules up for every room and made my mom put me in time-out like a little kid every time I broke the rules. But time-out always woke up Anger and my brain was cracking and cracking so much, we quit.

Another therapist made a rule that Mom and I weren't allowed to talk to each other between the hours of 8:00 p.m. and 10:00 a.m. He said we were codependent. He thought we loved each other too much.

I don't think any therapist is a good idea at this point.

"You weren't supposed to hear Ms. Hayley," Mom says.

"I know," I say. "But I did."

16. Sneaky. For ex. eavesdrops

Mom keeps driving down a winding road that's leading us somewhere that's not our house.

"Are we going grocery shopping?" I ask.

"Do you think I have the money to shop right now?" Mom says. The words are sharp and make me jump. But pretty quickly she says, "I'm sorry, Gwendolyn. I'm not angry with you."

Mom is always worried about money. I don't like to think about it because she worries about me most and about money second most. I'm always looking for ways to make Mom less worried, and it seems like every time I fail I get more and more expensive for her.

"She doesn't know what she's talking about. I can't get another assessment done in a matter of weeks. We've been on the waiting list for this Nessa person for months now. And I don't want to go to anyone else. From what I hear she's the best and I'm so sick of therapists who make things worse."

Mom isn't talking to me, really. She's talking to herself. And I know that. But I still say, "Me too."

"But I can't have you home all summer or come up with thousands of dollars to send you to some private camp, which you could get kicked out of anyway. Does she think I can afford a private neuropsychological evaluation out of pocket?"

"A what?" I say. That word sounds terrifying.

"We're completely stuck," Mom concludes.

"A what?" I say again, even though I know she isn't hearing me. I say it in my brain. *Neuropsychological evaluation.* Twelve syllables. I'm sort of afraid of big words I can't spell.

"So I think you know where we're going."

"Huh?" I say.

I have so many questions. What is a *private one?* Why can't we afford it? And where are we going?

"I'm sorry, G." I see Mom shaking her head in the rear-view mirror. Her black bangs swing over her eyebrows. I think she likes that feeling. She always does that when she's upset: swings her bangs so they tickle her eyebrows. I think bangs-on-eyebrows is for my mom what the tight braids are for me. But somehow she can't understand my tight braids.

Mom takes a deep breath then says, "I shouldn't have said all that. I don't want to speak to you like you're an adult before you're ready."

Whoa! Did Mom just lose *her* filter?

"Does Ms. Hayley think I have a problem?" I ask, hopeful. I would think Ms. Hayley, of all people, would dismiss me as just fifty-four wrong things without anything else attached to me.

Mom doesn't understand what I mean. She's still shaking her head, and I think her filter is still gone because she says, "Of course she does! You tried to run away. You threw your shoe at her. Last month you threw a milk carton into the ceiling fan and sprayed the whole school."

I try not to giggle. The last example doesn't even belong with the other two. I didn't do that one because I was angry. I did it to be funny. Hettie sort of dared me after I dared Hettie to dare me, and then it really made her laugh.

"Of course you have a problem," Mom says.

She says it wrong but I don't correct her.

I don't *have* a problem.

I *am* a problem.

We pull into a big parking lot. The sign at the entrance says *Greater Madison Area Methodist Church.*

"Oh!" I say. "You're bringing me to a meeting?"

"I thought I told you that," Mom says. Then she does another quick eyebrow tickle. "I'm sorry. I had to miss my meeting this afternoon to get to school early to meet Ms. Hayley. But now I need one. Even though this one is always so uncomfortable with—never mind. I brought you some carrot sticks and your iPad and headphones. You can hang out on the bench outside the door and watch YouTube, OK?"

I used to get a cookie whenever Mom brought me to a meeting. Since I'm only allowed healthy, boring food and green sludge and chewable vitamins now, I guess that's what the carrot sticks are for. I want to complain about the cookie, but I can tell Mom is upset so, somehow, I don't.

Mom is lucky. Mom isn't a problem. She isn't fifty-four things. She just *has* a problem. Or she had one.

Mom's extra lucky because her problem has a simple solution: stop drinking.

She found that solution, and Alcoholics Anonymous, a long, long time ago. Before she was even pregnant with me. She hasn't had a single drink the whole time I've been alive. She tells that to a lot of people because it's a big accomplishment even if I can't understand why because, you know, I haven't had a single drink in the entire time I've been alive either. But it's a big deal for my mom because she has a disease called addiction.

My dad has that disease too, but he never found a cure, and that's why I don't know him. It's crazy to me because the problem is so obvious and so is the solution. Alcoholic? Stop drinking. It's nowhere near as complicated as what I'm going through, and he still couldn't do it. Maybe he *has* a problem and he also *is* a problem.

I curl up on an old church pew that's in the basement outside the meeting room, put on my headphones, and watch horses gallop across my screen.

I miss Dandelion. My brain does the math. I haven't seen her in over three hundred days. It won't be the same this summer since PowerKids horse camp is at Cruxman Farms, not Millington Stables. So Dandelion won't be there. I'll have to ride other horses. I hope another kid figured out how to take good care of Dandelion. I hope another kid knows that just because she's always veering and trying to eat the grass and whinnying when you want to gallop, doesn't mean she's not lovable. Being around other horses will probably make me miss Dandelion even more.

But, still.

I have to get to horse camp.

When Mom comes out of her meeting approximately seventeen horse videos and eleven carrot sticks later, she sits next to me where I'm sprawled across the old pew and rubs my back.

"I'm sorry about before," she says. I immediately close my video and sit up to look at her. Mom's post-meeting apologies are always the best.

People are strolling out of the meeting room and passing our little bench. They hold steaming Styrofoam cups of coffee and pat each other on the back and laugh, even though some of them have red eyes like they were just crying. I wish there were other people with the exact same fifty-four problems I have who could pat me on the back and laugh and understand me.

"I lost it for a minute and started talking to you like you were an adult. That's not fair. It's something I have to keep watching out for as you get older. Just because you're the only other person in the house doesn't mean I get to vent to you, OK?"

"OK," I say.

"How about we stop for some food? I think the new salad place around the corner will have something on your meal plan," Mom says.

"OK," I say. But since my filter is still broken the words fall out. "What about the assessment?"

Mom puts her arm around me as we stand and start climbing the stairs to the parking lot. "That's a grown-up thing, Cupcake. That's why you weren't supposed to hear it. You don't need to worry about an assessment."

"But you said you can't afford it," I point out.

"That's grown-up stuff, Gwen," Mom says. "Let's enjoy some kid stuff."

"And the waiting list for the good therapist is so long, and there's only a few weeks left until camp."

"I got this," Mom says. "Really."

We walk outside and the sun is finally shining. It's warm enough for me to not miss my lost mittens. I unbutton my coat and turn my face to the sun.

"I'll see you soon, Nina," someone calls. Then someone else. I keep my face tilted up as we walk to the car. A lot of people call friendly goodbyes to my mom.

I wish she would go to afternoon meetings more often. She's always able to see the things past fifty-four when she comes out of a meeting. She likes me better after meetings. It's probably only because she likes everything better, but I'll take it.

Then I hear someone say, "I'm so glad you pulled me aside, Nina."

I feel my mom stiffen beside me and she wiggles her bangs over her eyes. But she makes her voice cheerful when she says, "Thanks again!"

"I'll see you Sunday," the woman calls back.

I turn my head in the direction of the voice. It was so familiar. I see black hair twisted into a tight bun disappear into a blue minivan.

"Was that Ms. Christakos?" I ask.

"Can't answer that," Mom says, letting out a relieved sigh.

"What's Sunday?" I ask.

"Not today. Now let's go."

The questions won't stop popping out of me at dinner even though I know Mom isn't going to answer them.

Mom makes a game of it and says every time I repeat a question she gets to take a sip of my seltzer. I don't mind because, even though I love lemon-lime seltzer, it's one of the only things in the world that Mom doesn't put a ton of limits on.

By the time my fancy salad is ready at the pickup counter, half my seltzer is gone.

Maybe if I rearrange the words, I'll get some information out of her. "If that *was* Tyler's mom," I try, "if she *had* been going to your meetings before now . . . why wouldn't you have told me?"

Mom doesn't steal seltzer this time. "Do you know what the word *anonymous* means?" Mom asks.

"Yes," I say. "A-N-O-N-Y-M-O-U-S . . . It means without being known."

"Right," Mom says. "That's a pretty big part of Alcoholics

Anonymous. So even if you saw someone you knew, or think you saw someone you knew, I can't confirm that to you or explain anything. Because we get to keep our secrets at AA. No one tells the world about me being there either."

"Oh," I say.

That works. I understand. A lot of rules are stupid. Like how it's a rule at school that I always have to remember my own pencil even though the school is full of pencils. That's a dumb rule.

But this anonymous rule isn't. I'm not an alcoholic so I'm not supposed to ask about the meeting.

If Ms. Christakos goes to that meeting that means she doesn't go to Mom's usual meeting. Because Mom usually goes in the mornings. But still, how long has Mom known that Ms. Christakos is in AA? Did she know that before Back-to-School Night?

And why did Ms. Christakos sound so happy to see my mom when Mom always seems so uncomfortable around her?

After a few minutes Mom says, "Gwendolyn, it looks like I have to work this weekend. Would you like me to call Ms. Christakos and see if you can hang out with Tyler while I go to work on Sunday?" She has a goofy smile on her face so I can see she's trying to ask without breaking the anonymous rule of AA.

"Yes," I say, matching her goofy smile.

Inside, I'm surprised. Shocked. I've been to Tyler's house

before, of course, but only because he's invited me to come. And he's been to mine for the same reason. Our moms never seem to talk to each other at all.

But I'll take any Tyler-time I can get.

# 7

## TYLER HAS A PROBLEM

I knew about Tyler before Back-to-School Night. Of course. Mom doesn't just forget to tell me huge things like You Have a Brother.

I sort of know the whole story, and I sort of don't. It goes something like this.

My dad was Tyler's mom's boyfriend first. Then he was my mom's boyfriend. He met my mom at a meeting but neither of them were finished with their problem yet. Then Mom found out Dad was going to have a baby. That was Tyler. Then Mom got finished with her problem. And then she found out she was going to have a baby, too. That was me. When Dad didn't work on recovering from his own addiction, she told him to get straightened out or leave. He left. She thought he left for rehab, which is why she gave me his last name when I was born. But it turns out he just left.

He left Tyler too. But I don't know if Mom knew that before Back-to-School Night.

Before then, Tyler almost didn't seem like part of the story. He was a footnote. It was like, *this is how you came to be here, Gwendolyn.* It was like, *Gwendolyn, don't pay attention to all those cartoons with two perfect parents who are in love and decide to have a baby on purpose.* It was, *Gwendolyn, don't even think about wanting to know your dad because he has a terrible disease.* It was *Gwendolyn, it's hard to explain.* It was, *you'll understand when you're older.*

*Oh, and Gwendolyn? There was another baby too, somewhere. Somewhere you have a brother.*

I guess Mom may have known the whole time that *somewhere* was in Madison, Wisconsin. I guess she might have known he was only twenty-five minutes away my entire life. She didn't technically lie. Madison is a *somewhere.*

The night of Back-to-School Night, I trudged behind Mom through the main door of the school. It was the first Friday in October and I should have been at the stables.

Mom didn't understand why I was walking so slowly. She didn't understand why Sadness had stretched his furry self into my legs and wrapped his long fingers around my heart.

"Come on," she said as I shuffled behind her down the hallway toward the school auditorium. "We're going to be late."

That didn't matter. We were always late. Mostly because of me.

31. Poor sense of time

"Come on!"

Mom didn't know I had opened the informational flyer about Back-to-School Night when it came in the mail. She didn't know that I read it even though I wasn't supposed to (16. Sneaky). She didn't know I'd seen where it said, "Please do not bring students or other children unless no other childcare can be arranged."

Before those dumb therapists, other childcare could be arranged.

I used to be able to go to the stables and ride Dandelion or help Ms. Kate almost any time I wanted.

"Gwendolyn, hurry," Mom said. She'd say she wasn't yelling but there was an edge to her voice that made Anger rattle in his cage.

I took a step closer to her. "Why does it even matter?" I asked. "We aren't that late. Some people are later than us."

Just as I said that, we heard a voice behind us. "Nina?"

Mom twirled around and her jaw almost hit the floor. It was Ms. Christakos, but of course I didn't know that.

"Does Gwendolyn go to Banneker Charter Middle School?"

Mom nodded but didn't say anything. Mom was staring at the woman hard. I stared too but I didn't recognize her.

"How does she know my name?" I whispered. "Who is that?"

Mom shook her bangs like crazy until her face started to look a little more normal. "Oh my goodness!" Mom said, finally. She sounded cheerful but I knew it was fake. "Is that Tyler?"

The woman nodded. "I . . . wow. That's Gwendolyn . . ." She trailed off.

I looked slightly to her side. There was a boy there. Short, skinny. Black hair that almost covered his face. He shifted his weight from foot to foot and kept his eyes on the comic book in his hands. Something about robots.

Later I would know that Ms. Christakos had planned to leave him home, but he had thrown a big fit and she didn't think she could trust him alone for an hour. Later, I'd find out he was a bad kid, like me.

"So . . . they go to the same school now . . ." the woman said.

"Who goes to the same school?" I asked, staring at the boy. He didn't look up from the comic book.

I knew a second before she said it, I think. I think when I looked at him I knew but I can't be sure because Mom said it pretty quickly.

"Gwendolyn . . . this is Tyler. Your brother."

It turns out Ms. Christakos was sort of exaggerating when she said "See you Sunday" after the AA meeting on Friday. All day Saturday I had imagined that they would have a nice greeting. I thought maybe Mom would come in with me and drink an iced tea with Ms. Christakos while Tyler and I were in his room. That *See you Sunday* sounded so friendly, I thought maybe things were changing.

On the drive to Tyler's, Mom does not sound friendly. She comments under her breath about how big their house is. She mutters about how different things are in this part of town. I don't know if she knows, but I hear her. I see the way she barely looks up from the steering wheel when we're in Tyler's driveway. And I've heard her say those things when she's on Skype at night too.

16. Sneaky. For ex. eavesdrops

"Bye, G," she says in a normal voice. "See you in a few hours."

She doesn't even wave to Ms. Christakos.

She has to work because she has to take a day off next week, but I totally forget I meant to ask her why she has to take a day off next week until I'm all the way out of the car and she's backing down the driveway.

45. Forgetful

"Gwendolyn! Gwendolyn!" Tyler bursts out the front door of his house past his mom and sloshes through the melting snow to give me a hug.

"You're only wearing socks," I point out, looking at his feet. They're soaked.

"Oh yeah," Tyler says.

"Tyler," his mom says from the doorway, shaking her head in a way that would shatter my heart. But Tyler is laughing.

We walk through the slushy yard even though it would make more sense to walk down the driveway to the stepping-stone path. Tyler's house looks huge to me but maybe it's normal. Maybe that's why Mom is so jealous of it. I think there are three bedrooms, maybe four. The outside is made of stones all the different colors of the earth, and a fancy chimney rises right out of the middle of the roof. It's a pretty house, like something out of a fairy tale, even when it's surrounded by gray snow and sludge. But I wish I could tell Mom, yeah it's pretty, but I wouldn't want to live in it. I don't like the idea that Mom and I could spend a whole day in the same house without ever hearing each other. I guess I could tell her that, but I don't think it would matter. Mom would just keep on hating Tyler and his mom and everything that they have that we don't.

I almost walk right past Ms. Christakos (7. Inattentive 17. Rude/Impolite), but at the last second I turn around and remember to say *hi*.

"Nice to see you, Gwen," she says. "Why don't you and Tyler go up to his room while I get lunch ready?"

I don't tell her that I just ate breakfast. I follow him through the front hall and up a set of stairs to his room. It looks like someone came into it and emptied all of his drawers onto the floor. I mean, there's a lot of nice stuff in his room but it's everywhere.

I've been here before. His room always looks like this. I always try to stop myself from commenting. I never succeed.

10. No filter

I step over balled-up socks and wrinkly T-shirts to join Tyler at his desk in the back of the room. A blue laptop buzzes on the desk. Tyler's own laptop. He has his own phone too.

It feels like I'll never get any of that stuff. "How do you tell which clothes are clean?" I ask.

Tyler shrugs. I know my questions are rude but he never seems to mind. "I throw dirty clothes on the floor. Clean ones are on the dresser." He nods to the dresser behind us, which does have piles of clothes on it that look a little more folded than the stuff on the floor.

"Oh," I say.

"And guess what?" he continues, as if what he's about to say is part of the same thought, but since I've known him for a while now, I know it's not. He doesn't even keep talking. He just clicks his tongue and points to his computer.

The website shows a rotating picture. First a little boy standing next to a horse. Then a girl riding hunt-seat style, her ponytail flying behind her under her helmet, then the logo. Millington Stables.

The pictures make my muscles ache. I fall into the chair next to Tyler.

"My mom signed me up!" he declares like it's the best thing in the world. "I start next Sunday."

"Why?" I hear myself ask.

"To get ready for horse camp."

"Horse camp isn't at Millington." I'm not sure where the words come from. I can't hear Tyler's answer. I just see the pictures rotate. Happy kids who get to ride horses and saddle them and brush them. Happy kids who get to be with

Dandelion. Happy kids who aren't me.

I think my heart stops beating.

Every single day, I try so hard not to think about how I want to be there because, when I think about Dandelion, both Sadness and Anger grow and grow inside me like water balloons. I start to swell and bloat with emotions. It makes me bigger and bigger until I feel like I might burst into a thousand little Gwendolyns that get lost all over Tyler's messy room.

"Gwen," Tyler says, shrinking me back into myself. "Did you hear me?"

"No," I say.

24. Spacey

"I said, maybe you can do it with me? Riding lessons? Sunday mornings?"

"No," I say. I should probably pretend I'm thinking about it. I should probably say *I'll ask my mom* or *it looks expensive* or *I don't have a ride*. But—

10. No filter

"I used to go there."

"You did? When?" Tyler asks.

Before my brain can keep up, my mouth is moving with the truth. "All the time. Three days a week after school and on Saturdays, and I had this favorite horse named Dandelion, and I would ride her, and she was actually really hard to ride, but I was good and I could do it, and then—I miss her."

My brain catches up to my mouth and stops me.

"You know how to ride a horse?" Tyler asks, shocked.

"Yes," I say. "Don't you?"

"No," he says. "Why didn't you tell me?"

"Why didn't *you* tell *me*?"

Tyler shakes his head. "Anyway . . . did Dandelion move away or something?"

"No," I say.

"Then what happened?" Tyler asks.

"I just . . . I can't go back," I say.

I'm afraid I'm going to cry. Memories are flooding me. My muscles soaring. Dandelion's stink in my nose. My legs stiff around her saddle. Her nose nuzzled into my palm after a good trail ride.

"Kids! Lunch!" Tyler's mom calls.

Tyler looks like he wants to ask a thousand more questions, but somehow his own filter wins. "I'm sorry," he says. "I hope you can go to horse camp and then you don't have to be so sad about it anymore. I have to learn to ride horses though, if you already know. So that we can see each other there. Otherwise I'll be with the beginners and you won't."

He's talking fast, like his mouth is running away from his brain, which I understand. So I nod and blink so the tears won't fall, and then I follow Tyler out of his room and down the stairs.

It makes sense. I do want to be with Tyler at horse camp. If Tyler has never ridden a horse before, they'll definitely put us in different groups. So I tell myself it's OK that Tyler gets to go to Millington Stables. I tell myself it's a good thing. I manage to keep Anger locked away.

Lunch at Tyler's is not like lunch at my house. No cold cuts and wheat bread and mustard. Instead there's roast chicken breasts with lemon slices on top and grilled vegetables with a mustard glaze and couscous. The first time I came here I asked if Tyler's mom was a chef. He laughed and said no, but she watches cooking shows for fun.

I couldn't think of anything my mom does for fun.

Everything Ms. Christakos has prepared is even approved by boring-foods-for-bad-kids-dot-com, or whatever, so I pile up my plate. Tyler's mom and her friend are there too, and we all carry our food from the kitchen to a table in a totally different room.

As soon as we do, Tyler's mom says, "Oh, I forgot."

Then she has to stand up and walk all the way through the room and into the kitchen to get the thing she forgot. I file this away as another reason our apartment is better than this house. Our living room and kitchen and dining room are all one room. The walk to something you forgot is way shorter.

When Ms. Christakos returns, she has a small blue pill in her palm. She hands it to Tyler, who quickly washes it down with a swig of fruit punch like he's done it a thousand times before.

"What's that?" I ask.

"It's Tyler's," Ms. Christakos says. That is the answer to a different question. I didn't ask *whose* it was, I asked *what* it was. Ms. North used to say that adults sometimes answer the wrong question because they don't like the right one, which makes no sense to me because I don't know why they can't just say "I don't want to tell you." It takes too long for my brain to remember all that, and by the time I figure out that Ms. Christakos answering the wrong question probably means she doesn't want me to know what I'm trying to know, I've already asked "What for?"

10. No filter

"My meds," Tyler says.

"For what?" I ask.

Ms. Christakos starts to say, "I'm sure you've taken medi—"

But Tyler interrupts and says, "ADHD."

I drop my fork so loud it clangs on my plate and then falls onto the floor. My cheeks burn. I dive after it and then slam my head into the table on the way up.

26. Clumsy

"Tyler!" Ms. Christakos says like he wasn't supposed to tell me.

"What?" Tyler says. "Gwen's my sister. She's allowed to know."

"You have ADHD?" I ask. My brain fills with something. A few somethings. I'm fascinated. It turns out my brother has one of the problems I used to think I might have before we found out that I don't have a problem at all, and I just am one.

"Yeah," Tyler says. "Without the meds, I get real crazy."

"You cure it with medicine?" I ask, dropping my fork again.

"Yeah," Tyler says.

"It's not exactly a cure, Tyler," Ms. Christakos says.

Tyler shrugs. "Whatever . . . They make me more . . . normal."

I'm also jealous.

That's why Tyler's mom doesn't get called every time he messes up at PowerKids.

That's why he gets to go to horse camp and I probably don't.

That's why he's allowed at Millington Stables with Dandelion.

Tyler *has* a problem.

And his problem is just as easy to solve as Mom's.

One small blue pill and *boom*. He's normal.

Will we ever find a way to make me normal?

That night, I curl in bed around my list and read.

27. Unable to multitask

28. Argumentative

29. Swears/Cusses

30. Fidgety

31. Poor sense of time

I didn't do anything too terrible today so I'm surprised when I hear the *doo-dee-doo* of Mom Skyping Marsha. As usual, a cacophony of noise fills our apartment when she answers. And as usual, my brain lists all the ways I could prevent myself from overhearing and give Mom her privacy while at the same time my body crawls out of bed and moves closer to the door so that I can hear more clearly.

"Nina, give me a second," Marsha says. "Or . . . Well I have five minutes now, and then I could call you back."

Somewhere on her end a dog barks. I imagine the dog running up to the cartoon librarian. He'd be big and black with a strong jaw. The kind of dog that people who don't know better would be afraid of.

"It'll be quick," Mom says. "I wanted to let you know that I did it. I took your advice. I reached out for help."

Help? What kind of help? I thought she was at work today.

"Congratulations!" Marsha says. They both laugh. I have no idea what's so funny.

"It feels awful to admit that I'm . . ." Mom trails off. "Not in control," she concludes.

"Well, you're more in control than you used to be." Marsha says this like it's a joke and, sure enough, Mom laughs again. She always laughs with Marsha. It's half of why I eavesdrop.

"Yep. True," Mom says. "There was a time I had no control over anything."

I know it's not the same, but whenever Mom talks about how she used to be, she sounds like me. She talks to Marsha about being helpless. Being scared. But unable to control her own actions. I think of me climbing the fence at PowerKids. Me forgetting my pencil. Me fighting with Mom.

"Even if it doesn't feel great, I'm proud of you," Marsha says. "I know how hard it can be to accept help. But sometimes you have to. Even if you aren't crazy about the source."

"I know," Mom says.

What help?

"And don't discount small miracles!" Marsha adds.

"I'm not even sure this qualifies as a *small* miracle," Mom says. "Feels like my higher power got sick of hinting and decided to hit me over the head instead."

They laugh again and, since I can't understand any of this anyway, I decide to go back to bed. I hang onto Mom's laugh and repeat the sound-memory in my brain as I fall asleep.

# 8

## TYLER IS MY BROTHER

On Wednesday, Thaís pulls her chair up next to mine again and smiles. I missed Mr. Olsen telling us to sit with our partners so it takes me a second too long to smile back at her.

17. Rude/Impolite

"Science is all about questions," Mr. Olsen is saying. He's using his big voice, which he uses when he thinks he's saying something super wise that will make us all lean forward in our seats and let him pry our minds open. I don't understand half of what he's saying though because his big voice distracts me from the actual words, so I never lean forward in my seat, which may be part of why he hates me.

"So that is the first component of your science fair project. The essential question. What is it about your subject that makes you wonder?" he's asking.

Thaís leans forward. She's always leaning forward for the big voice. She's always raising her hand and turning in her homework and remembering *please* and *thank you* and is good at all the fifty-four things I stink at.

"Discuss with your partner and do not stop until you have a profound, demanding question written at the bottom of your graphic organizer. That is what you will spend the next few weeks answering. You will not rest until you do."

Before I can stop myself, my hand is in the air.

"Yes, Gwendolyn?" Mr. Olsen says. Sarcasm is back. He says my name like it's boring.

"What's a profound and demanding question?" I ask.

I need to do this project right. I can't mess it up because I'm working with Thaís, and she never messes anything up. I don't want her to get a bad grade because of me.

"By profound I mean deep and—"

I cut him off. I don't mean to. But he's misunderstanding me again.

"I know what profound means," I say. "P-R-O-F-O-U-N-D. Deep, intense, insightful."

Mr. Olsen pauses. I think he's debating whether to correct me for interrupting him. He hates it most of all when we interrupt the big voice. But instead he says, "If you store a dictionary in your head, why are you asking?"

The class giggles.

Anger rattles my ribs.

"I mean, how can a question be demanding?"

"Ah," Mr. Olsen says, switching back to the big voice. "A demanding question is one that will not leave you alone until you have the answer. It crawls around your head at night. It taps you on the shoulder in the shower. It begs you to solve it and you can't rest until you do."

And then I understand completely what a profound and demanding question is. I've been working on one for years.

*What is wrong with me?*

But how could someone ever have a profound and demanding question about dolphins?

Thaís shifts in her seat beside me. I had almost forgotten she was there. I should probably stop talking. She's probably embarrassed to have a partner with so many questions.

My mouth keeps moving anyway. "Can you give an example?" I ask. "From science?"

Mr. Olsen freezes. He shakes his head, which is a sign I'm making him impatient, but I also know he's about to tell us to get to work, and I can't get to work because I don't know what the work is.

"It seems like the question of what is a demanding question is a demanding question for you, Ms. Rogers."

"Huh?" I say. I'm 23. Talks too loud. Everyone is laughing at me again.

"Can anyone give Ms. Rogers an example?" Mr. Olsen asks the class.

The laughing stops suddenly. I look around. I'm expecting lots of hands in the air, but most people are looking at their desks. Maybe I'm not the only one who doesn't understand.

"OK, OK," Mr. Olsen says. "I'll give you some examples

from the history of science. Write these down."

Around me, my classmates pick up pencils. But of course I don't have one. I sit still and listen.

"For William Harvey in the 1600s, the profound and demanding question was *How can the blood that is in our feet reach all the way to our heads?* And Robert Hooke could not rest until he answered the question *What is the building block of all living things*? Which is why he discovered the cell in 1665. Of course we can all guess that for Benjamin Franklin, the profound and demanding question would have been *How can we harness that power that slashes the sky during storms and use it for human advantage?* And more recently, in the 1920s, Georges Lemaître could not stop asking *How did this begin?* Which is why he came up with the Big Bang Theory."

I have a thousand things to say.

How can we write something like this about dolphins?

Even if we can come up with a profound and demanding question about dolphins, how can we possibly solve it when we're kids in landlocked Wisconsin with no money or transportation?

How do you know if a question is profound and demanding or if it's just annoying to you?

And why were all those scientists men?

But I don't get a chance to ask any of these because Mr. Olsen turns to me and says, "Ms. Rogers, I told you to write these down."

"I know," I say.

"And yet you aren't writing," he says.

"I don't have a pencil," I say.

He drops his hands. They had been flying everywhere as he gave us those profound and demanding questions. Now they rest on my desk, like a challenge.

"I gave you two yesterday!" he says. He sounds angry.

I shrug.

"OK, everyone, get to work. Gwendolyn, meet me at my desk, please."

I whisper "sorry" to Thaís as I slide out of my seat and go to the front of the room.

"This pencil situation is getting ridiculous," Mr. Olsen says. "You may have one today, but from now on you must have a pencil at the start of class or you'll lose five percent on whatever graded assignment is next."

"Five percent? Just for forgetting a pencil?"

"Today is the one-hundred-and-fifty-eighth day of school," Mr. Olsen says. "And you see me at least twice a day. So I'd say that's over three hundred and sixteen missing pencils."

"But—"

Mr. Olsen cuts me off. "Unless you'd like to discuss this with Principal Dickens right now?"

My face burns. Anger wakes up hot and lodges himself into my throat.

*Horse camp, horse camp,* I remind myself. I won't let Anger take over.

I sit back down next to Thaís.

"You OK?" she whispers.

I don't answer.

6. Socially inept

At outdoor break, I sit in front of Tyler behind our imaginary glass wall as he does my hair. The braids are almost perfect, but I still feel gross. I can't stop thinking about how Tyler swallowed that little blue pill. If I had a little blue pill like that, maybe I would remember my pencils. Maybe I wouldn't yell when Mr. Olsen is sarcastic with me. Maybe I'd be perfect.

"Guess what I did yesterday?" Tyler asks.

"Tighter," I say.

He drops my hair to start over, which feels worse.

"Guess what I did?" he says again. "After PowerKids?"

"Do it really tight this time," I say.

"Guess," he says. He pulls the first three strands of hair together and the world gets a little more clear.

"What did you say?" I ask.

"You didn't even hear me?" Tyler pulls the next piece of braid but I can already tell it's too loose. He's distracted.

"I need to get a check mark," I say. "Make it tighter."

"What do your braids have to do with check marks?" Tyler asks. He keeps braiding but it's too loose.

"I can't lose my pencil," I say. "Tighter, please."

Tyler drops my hair and then pulls it as tight as it can go, which sort of hurts, but also feels perfect. Then he says, "Please! Guess what I did yesterday."

"What did you do yesterday?"

He drops my hair completely. It's loose around my shoulders. The wind is blowing and it's tickling my face. It's itchy and flowing. My hands shake. I'm so distracted I almost don't hear what he says.

"I met Dandelion!"

Anger has been in his shell for days, eating and sleeping and eating and sleeping. He's gotten bigger and bigger each time I locked the shell and didn't let him out.

Now he explodes so suddenly, he sends shards of shell flying all through the schoolyard. He's escaped. He's all over my body, bruising up my organs, making me lose control.

"That's not fair!" I scream. I whip around, yanking my hair out of Tyler's hand so fast he has strands of blond in his fingers when I turn to face him. "That's the most unfair thing I ever heard!"

Tyler falls backward, like my words are strong enough to knock him over. It feels good to see him fall like that so I keep yelling.

"You get help. You get medicine. Now you get Dandelion? You have everything and all I have is all the problems and a cracked brain."

"What are you talking about?" Tyler whispers.

He's not getting back at me, which should mean Anger calms down. But I also know that the only reason Tyler isn't getting mad is because he gets to have a little blue pill while I have to deal with Anger all by myself.

"You! You're stealing all the good stuff from me!"

"Stealing?" Tyler says.

"First you stole ADHD. Now you stole Dandelion! I bet you stole our dad too!"

Tyler gasps. We don't talk about our dad. It's almost like a rule.

Suddenly there's a shaky hand on my arm. I whip around and come nose-to-nose with Hettie. My arm almost swings to hit her but somehow some part of my brain makes it stop.

"Gwen?" she whispers.

I'm shaking. I can't believe I almost hit my best friend just because I'm mad at my brother. That has to be some sort of fifty-fifth problem I don't have a name for.

Behind me I hear Tyler say, "I didn't steal anything." Then, quieter. "I don't know him either." His voice wobbles. I think he might be crying.

I sort of want to give him a hug. I sort of want to make sure he still loves me now that he's seen how bad I am. Or part of how bad I am.

But I keep my eyes on Hettie.

She says, "Do you want me to do your braids?"

I nod. I didn't even realize it but I'm crying too. Tears are falling down my face and into the collar of my T-shirt so fast it's like a faucet has turned on. We leave Tyler sitting in the mud and go over to the picnic tables.

"Are you OK?" Hettie asks.

"Yes," I say, even though I'm lying and she knows it.

I don't usually lie. I'm really bad at lying because my mouth is faster than my brain. But no one ever wants the real answer when they ask how you are, so when you say *good* or *yes* or *I'm OK*, that's not even a real lie.

Hettie is different.

"No you aren't," she says, twisting the hair on the top of my head into something that's like a braid but way too loose.

"Tyler gets to see Dandelion," I say. "And I never will again."

"Oh," Hettie says.

"Yeah," I say.

"I know you miss her," Hettie says.

"I really do."

And now I miss Tyler, too. I'm still mad at him but also, I miss him. It's so hard to be someone with fifty-four problems and a big red angry triangle inside her.

Hettie finishes one braid and starts the other. I can't tell her it's too loose because we only have a little bit of time left in outdoor break, and Hettie isn't that good at braids anyway.

"So are you and Tyler in a fight now?" Hettie asks.

I shrug.

"Are you going to start hanging out with me after lunch again?"

I shrug again, but also the tears turn back on. I don't want to spend outdoor break with Hettie and Thaís and Margaret, who aren't my friends anymore. I want to spend outdoor break with Tyler, and PowerKids with Hettie. Or not really. Really, I want to spend outdoor break *and* PowerKids with Hettie, and I want to just, like, live with Tyler. I want Tyler to be a given, so much in my life that he annoys me, the way Hettie's brother, Nolan, annoys her. I want Tyler to be family in a way that means I don't have to worry about losing him.

"We could race, or oh! We could work on our free throws so we're ready to play basketball against the boys in PowerKids," Hettie is saying.

"I don't want to turn back into a girl who doesn't have a brother," I sob.

Hettie's face falls and lights up at the same time. Like she just realized something, but the something she realized is very sad.

"Oh, Gwen. I'm sorry," she says. "It's going to be OK, though. You don't have to spend outdoor break with me. Tyler will forgive you."

I wipe my eyes and take a few shaky breaths as she finishes my second braid.

"You know Tyler sees you like I see you, right?"

"Huh?" I manage to say. "How do you see me?"

Hettie snaps the last rubber band in place and sits beside me.

"Just . . . you," Hettie says. "How you really are."

How I really am is a problem. I'm fifty-four bad things. I thought Hettie and Tyler were two of the only people who didn't see me how I really am.

The bell rings and we have to go to class. Hettie says, "Race you!" Which is perfect. I run after her, my legs pounding to get closer to hers. My braids are too loose but hopefully running and Hettie will keep Anger inside me, even without his shell.

Later that afternoon, Hettie and I walk into the cafeteria for PowerKids, and I'm feeling a little better. We gather with the other fifth graders at one of the long cafeteria tables for afternoon meeting. One of the good things about PowerKids is that a lot of it happens the same way every day. First afternoon meeting, then art appreciation or coding, then free time outside, then homework hour, then dismissal.

As I slide into the seat next to Hettie, I glance over to the sixth-grade table to see if Tyler is looking for me. He almost always smiles at me as soon as I come into the cafeteria for afternoon meeting. But today I don't think he will.

Tyler isn't sitting in his usual spot. I scan the cafeteria and then I find him in the back, talking to Ms. Hayley. Ms. Hayley always sets up at the very back of the cafeteria where she can watch all the groups. She spreads her papers and computer and stuff out on the long table like it's her own personal desk.

Ms. Madeline starts our afternoon meeting, but I'm not paying any attention. I'm watching Tyler and Ms. Hayley. Tyler looks angry.

Ms. Hayley throws her arms over her head. She's out of

patience, which makes sense. She doesn't have a lot of patience to begin with.

Tyler leans closer to her. I can't hear him but I can tell by the way his body is tilted and the way his mouth is moving that he's being rude.

Ms. Hayley points toward a corner. I can't hear her either but I can tell she's ordering Tyler to go sit on the other side of the cafeteria alone, which means he's in big trouble.

I lean toward them, trying to hear.

16. Sneaky. For ex. eavesdrops

I've lost track of anything happening at afternoon meeting. Usually Ms. Madeline asks a question and everyone goes around and gives an answer. Which means I should whisper to Hettie so she'll repeat the question for me like she does almost every other day (7. Inattentive). But instead I lean across her lap, trying to hear Tyler and Ms. Hayley.

Ms. Hayley is still pointing at the chair in the corner. I can see it clear as day when Tyler says, "NO!"

Will Ms. Hayley finally call his mom? Will he get Dandelion taken away too?

Finally, Tyler turns fast and it looks like he's going to walk to where she was pointing. Then he stops. He holds out his arm and sweeps it across the table. Ms. Hayley's papers fly and then her computer lands on the linoleum with a bang.

Now everyone is watching them. Everyone is silent.

Tyler laughs. I know that laugh. I know he's not happy even though he's laughing because sometimes I laugh when my brain is cracked, and when that happens, I'm never happy. No one except me can ever tell that it's not a happy laugh, though. The same thing will happen to Tyler. Ms. Hayley will think it's a happy laugh. Ms. Hayley will think Tyler is a terrible person who does awful things and thinks it's funny.

Ms. Hayley will finally call his mom.

Tyler storms out of the cafeteria toward the bathrooms and I watch Ms. Hayley and her cell phone.

Anger is jumping, joyful. Tyler will be just like me. He'll have to go home early. His mom will take away his riding lessons. Dandelion will be all mine again . . . even if I can't see her.

After a minute Ms. Madeline says, "Gwendolyn, did you want to add anything to our discussion today?"

Anger dances in my chest. I watch Ms. Hayley's hand move toward her phone. *Call her. Call her.*

"Gwendolyn?" Ms. Madeline tries again.

Ms. Hayley's finger lingers over the phone for half a second, then she picks up a piece of paper instead, leaving the phone where it was.

I stand. Anger launches himself up my throat and into my brain.

I run across the cafeteria and stand right in front of Ms. Hayley. Usually she's bigger and taller and stronger than me but Anger has puffed me up so that I'm the size of an elephant.

"You have to call his mom!" I demand.

"What?" Ms. Hayley says. "Gwendolyn, please sit down."

A part of my brain tells me Ms. Hayley looks tired. I don't care.

"No," I say. "You have to call Ms. Christakos. Now!"

"This isn't your business. Please go sit down."

"It is my business," I insist, my head growing taller than hers. She may not realize it but I'm towering over her. Anger has made me that powerful.

"It quite simply is not," Ms. Hayley says, like she's talking to someone normal and not the angry superhero I am.

"You always call my mom! You need to call his mom!"

"Gwendolyn, go back to your group. Your mother and Tyler's mother have nothing to do with each other." She's still rearranging her papers. She can't even be bothered to look at me.

"Yes they do," I say.

"How so?" Ms. Hayley asks, like I'm exhausting.

"He's my brother," I say.

Now Ms. Hayley looks up, confused. "Your brother?"

"Call his mom."

"He's not your—"

"Call his mom!" I yell.

"You have the same last name but—"

"Call her. Now!"

"His mom is working and he's not your—"

"You call *my* mom when *she's* working."

"Exactly . . . you have different—"

"CALL HIS MOM!"

"Stop lying!" Ms. Hayley yells. "You two are *not* related."

Before it happens, I see everything flash before me. The smart part of my brain sees it all. Horse camp flashes and disappears. All good things flash and disappear. Lunch at Tyler's: gone. PowerKids: gone. My mom loving me: gone.

It still happens.

"Tyler is my *brother*!"

*Crack.*

# 9

## A BAD KID

When Mom arrives, she puts her arm around me. Tyler is outside playing basketball like nothing happened. They didn't call his mom of course.

We walk over to Ms. Hayley so Mom can sign me out. "For your edification," Mom says in the snooty voice that only comes out when she's defending me for something that I definitely shouldn't have done, "Tyler is Gwendolyn's paternal half brother."

Take that, Ms. Hayley, I think, wiggling my head. My braids are too loose.

Ms. Hayley looks at Mom, her eyes as hard as marbles. "She threw my computer at me."

"She did?" Mom asks.

As soon as Ms. Hayley says it, my muscles sort of remember. The swing of my joints as I pulled the computer back. The release when I let it go. My body remembers but my brain doesn't, not really. I know I had thoughts. I know they were there because my brain was screaming them right up to the moment of the crack. I know I probably threw that laptop to see if Ms. Hayley would call my mom and not Tyler's even if we did the exact same bad thing. But I still don't remember deciding to do it.

Now Ms. Hayley doesn't have to apologize for trying to take away my brother. Why is it that adults get away with doing something awful just because I also do something awful?

Mom signs the paper and we leave. She doesn't say anything until we're in the privacy of our car.

"What happened?" she asks.

"Ms. Hayley told you," I say.

"I mean, *why* Gwen? Why did you throw her computer? What's wrong with you?"

Fifty-four things. Everything.

Mom sighs from the front seat. "I don't see how you can be around horses if you're throwing computers."

Even though I knew she'd say something like this, Anger ramps up again. He starts running laps around my heart, ready to springboard back into my brain if he needs to.

"Horses don't even use computers!" I wail.

"I think you know that's not the point," Mom yells. "The point is that you need to control yourself."

"But I can't!"

I buckle my seat belt. My braids are too loose. I rub my head on the back of the seat, trying to give my body a feeling that I can focus on. It's a thing I do when my braids aren't working. I create friction on my head another way so that I can still concentrate a little. I rub my head fast enough that the fabric starts a tiny burn on my neck. It almost makes up for the braids.

"Stop doing that," Mom says, but I don't.

After a few minutes she adds, "Let's start over. What happened? Why did you get so angry?"

*Rub, rub, rub.*

"My braids were too loose," I say.

25. Picky about her appearance

"Good grief, Gwen. You threw a computer because your braids were too loose?"

I shrug. I can control myself better when my braids are tighter, so yes.

"Don't shrug." Mom glances at me in the rearview mirror. "Speak! What happened?"

I rub my head again.

"It's not fair that—" I start.

"I don't want to hear that word," Mom interrupts.

"Well you asked," I spit back. I keep rubbing my head.

"Stop shaking your head," Mom says. "Listen to me. You can't go throwing computers and then claim life isn't fair for you."

I rub my head harder. Faster. "Every time Ty—"

"I asked you to stop doing that," Mom says. "Sit still. Pay attention."

"Rubbing my head helps me pay attention!"

"Gwendolyn!" Mom says. Now her voice is high and fast.

"I'm trying to answer you!" I say, still rubbing. Can't she see that I am paying attention? I'm totally focused. "Tyler gets to—"

"Stop comparing us to them." Mom is even louder than before. "And stop that thing with the seat. You're driving me crazy!"

Mom hasn't yelled like this in a long time. I need her to see why I got so angry. I need to answer her question.

"But he—"

"Gwendolyn, stop!" Mom says.

"Then stop asking me questions if you don't want the answers!" I explode.

"Fine."

Mom doesn't say anything else. Neither do I. I keep rubbing my head on the seat though. I know it's making Mom angry and, even though she'll never believe me, I'm actually trying to stop moving my head like this.

I just can't.

The next morning I tiptoe into the living room, scared to see if Mom's still mad. She's drinking coffee and scrolling through her phone. She's not in her typical pantsuit and ponytail. She's in jeans and a T-shirt.

Oh no. Did she have to take the day off? Am I suspended from PowerKids?

"Hi," I say. "Are you . . . going to work like that?"

"No," Mom says.

"Am I . . . kicked out of PowerKids?" I ask.

"No," Mom says. "You're suspended for the day. But you picked a good day to mess up."

"Huh?" I say.

"You weren't going to be there today anyway," Mom says. "Today is the first day of your assessment. You're skipping school and PowerKids so we can meet with Dr. Nessa."

"Oh," I say. Then, because I have 10. No filter, I blurt, "How did we get off the wait-list? And is this why you had to work this weekend? Wasn't the wait-list, like, super long?"

"Just eat your eggs, Gwen," Mom says.

A few hours later I'm in a glass-walled room full of diplomas announcing the achievements of Dr. Nessa Anderson. This is already different than my IEP assessment. That one happened in an empty classroom in my school. Today, we're in a big fancy building in downtown Madison. There's a lobby filled with games and magazines for kids and a coffee machine and even a cooler with snacks and drinks. I eyed the cookies and juice when we walked in, but managed to just take a water and stick to my meal plan. Even though, if the meal plan were working, we wouldn't be here.

"You OK, Gwen?" Mom asks. She slides an arm around me. It feels good to have her close to me again.

"This is the person you think can actually help, right?" I whisper to my mom. She's sitting next to me. She's not on her phone or anything. Her bangs are dancing on her face but her wrinkles aren't as deep.

She nods. "Fingers crossed," she says. "Dr. Nessa is supposed to be the best."

Now I'm nervous. This feels like some sort of last chance.

Once we go into her office, Dr. Nessa sits across a table from my mom and me and explains everything we'll be doing today: a whole bunch of tests and talking to try to figure out how my brain works. Mom doesn't have to stay. She can wait in the waiting room or leave and come back.

"And then what can we expect? After the tests are concluded?" Mom asks.

Dr. Nessa looks at her. She had been looking mostly at me. "A lot of times children present with a clear diagnosis," she says. "But even when they don't, we brainstorm strategies to help them be successful. Are there strategies you've used before?"

"Oh, yes, believe me," Mom says, rolling her eyes. "I think I've tried them all."

That's when I realize Mom doesn't actually trust that Dr. Nessa is the best.

"Are you trying any interventions currently?" she asks.

"Oh," Mom says, surprised by the question again.

None of the other therapists ever surprised her. It was always like she knew more than they did from the start.

Mom tells Dr. Nessa about the calendar with the check marks and our diet plan.

"You do your research," Dr. Nessa says.

Mom smiles. "You could say that."

"Gwendolyn benefits from your commitment, Nina. You can count on that. I can lend you a book or two if you're interested in some further reading."

"Really?" Mom says. "You're not going to discourage me from doing my own research?"

"Of course not. But for now, while we're assessing, it's probably best to drop that intervention plan."

"Were we doing something wrong?" Mom asks.

"It wasn't *my* idea," I blurt. Mom shoots me a look and my face turns red.

"No, no," Dr. Nessa says. "Nothing wrong. It could be a great plan. We just don't want it to influence the data. Let Gwendolyn go back to eating as normal. Throw away the calendar or give Gwendolyn automatic checks until the assessment is over."

"And do what?" Mom asks.

"We'll wait and see if these tests reveal anything."

Mom looks worried. "Wait and . . . do what? What do we do while we're waiting?"

Dr. Nessa smiles. "Live. Let the thinking and solving go. Just for a few weeks."

"Oh," Mom says, but it sounds like she doesn't know how to do that. She doesn't know how to wait. To live.

I understand how she feels. How am I supposed to earn

horse camp if there's no calendar?

But before I can put that question into words, Mom is out of the room and Dr. Nessa is talking to me alone.

She seems nice. I don't want to waste her time.

"You don't actually need to do this," I tell her. "It's OK with me if we just pretend you did your job. Because we already know."

"What do we already know?" Dr. Nessa asks.

"I already had an IEP assessment. So we know I don't have anything that you can help with."

Dr. Nessa nods. "I see," she says.

She's the prettiest therapist I've ever met. She has perfect skin and an Afro that fluffs out from behind a hot pink scarf that's tied around her head like a headband in a way that's wonderful and even and loose and somehow all that looseness on her head isn't driving her insane. She has big black plastic-rimmed glasses that frame her eyes and almost hide the little silver stud in her left nostril, but I still see it. She has on a floral dress—black with red and pink flowers printed on it. She looks like it's so easy to wear. Everything about her is so easy. She could never understand me.

"I should tell you, I already knew that," she says. "In fact I've seen the IEP report."

My eyes go wide and Anger tries to peek at her, the tip of his pointy head poking out of his shell. "What?" I ask. "When? How?"

"I asked your mom for any information she already had before we agreed to an assessment," Dr. Nessa said. "I'm aware you've already had an IEP meeting and that it wasn't exactly productive."

"Then you know," I say, probably too loudly (23). "You know that I don't have ADHD or dyslexia or autism or any of the other things. You know that for me it's different."

"And how is it for you?" Dr. Nessa asks.

"I don't *have* a problem," I say. "I'm—"

I want to say *I'm bad.*

I want to say it because it's true. I want to be able to say it the way I might say *I'm blond* or *I'm a girl.* I want to say it and not have Dr. Nessa—or anyone—say *No you're not.*

Or, *You're not bad Gwendolyn, you just do bad things!*

Or, *You're not bad just because there are fifty-four things wrong with you.*

I don't want it to be true but it is true so I want to be able to say it. I want to be able to say *I'm bad.* And the only thing I want to hear back is *You're still lovable.*

Dr. Nessa doesn't make me finish.

"IEP evaluations can be valuable for some kids—"

"Like Tyler," I say.

"Who's Tyler?" Dr. Nessa asks.

"Tyler's my brother," I say. "He's not like me though. He has ADHD and so he gets to take a pill for it, and then everything is fine, and he can do anything, and PowerKids never calls his mom."

Dr. Nessa's eyes flutter like she's thinking a lot of words and forcing her filter not to say them.

"I see," she says. "We're here to talk about you, but that is good information because ADHD often runs in families."

"It does?" I ask. "Like brothers and sisters have ADHD together?"

"Sometimes," Dr. Nessa says. "And you should know that your brother's medication probably helps him, but it doesn't make everything magically better. There's no magic for anyone."

Maybe. But if siblings often have ADHD together, I bet they often get cured together too.

Then Sadness takes a big full stretch through my guts because I remember.

"It doesn't matter, anyway," I say. "We already know I don't have ADHD. Or anything else."

"I'm not sure we do know that," Dr. Nessa says. "What we know is that your IEP evaluation did not determine conclusively that you have any known neuropsychological difference. But IEP evaluations can miss a lot of things."

"They can?" I ask.

Dr. Nessa nods. "Have you seen your IEP report, Gwendolyn? Or have you just heard about it?"

I close my mouth before I answer. I'm careful with my words. "I just heard about it," I say. I manage to lie.

Dr. Nessa looks relieved.

"The thing about IEPs . . . and all evaluations . . . and

basically everything in the world . . . is that they're more helpful for certain groups than others," Dr. Nessa says. "I'm going to use ADHD for an example, not because I believe you have ADHD, but because the research is the most vast there. IEP evaluations across the nation tend to overestimate the ADHD tendencies of boys and underestimate them of girls. Furthermore, they lean significantly toward overdiagnosing ADHD in Black boys in particular and underdiagnosing it in girls of every race. Do you understand?"

My brow wrinkles.

"So those tests only work for white boys?" I blurt. "That's not fair."

"It isn't quite that simple . . . but you're right that it isn't fair." Dr. Nessa smiles, but not like what I said is funny and not like she's having fun. She smiles like she wants to show me that she likes me. "If it feels hard to understand, that's because it's complicated. It's not because your brain is having trouble with it, or because you're young, or because you aren't neurotypical. The way that race and gender intersect with every single thing in society is a twisted web of confusion that some of us are constantly working to untangle."

"Oh," I say.

"The part I want you to understand right now is this: if studies have said that tests can be biased against certain groups, that means these tests aren't perfect. And if they aren't perfect, you shouldn't consider their results the absolute truth, OK?"

*The tests could have been wrong.*

There still could be a diagnosis out there for me. And if there's still a diagnosis, there also might be a cure.

Dr. Nessa continues, "You know, when I talk to your mom and read that evaluation, I see that some of your talents maybe aren't being fully used. Some of the things about you that make you great are going unnoticed. And some of the things you struggle with maybe don't have to be as hard."

"You think there are good things about my brain?" I ask. It sounds stupid because it is stupid. Every adult is going to say *Yes, there are great things about your brain.* It's like the rule of being an adult to say those things.

Dr. Nessa says exactly that: "Of course!"

But then she adds something better. Something that sounds almost science-y. "You know all neurological differences only cause struggles because the world is built for and by mostly neurotypical people. It's another part of the same web that confuses everything along with race and gender. But the world needs all sorts of brains, and people actually do best when different types of brains work together. So your brain, no matter if we find a diagnosable difference or not, is an important puzzle piece in the way it fits with the brains around it. We need to help you harness those differences instead of being held back by them." She pauses. "Do you understand?"

My mouth moves before my brain knows what I'm going

to say. "I don't quite know what that means, but I like the way all those words sound."

Dr. Nessa smiles. "I think if you pay attention to the brains around you over the next few days, you'll see what I mean. You'll find ways that you fit together perfectly."

I can't help smiling back at her. Without meaning to, I'm doing it. I'm hoping.

"But be patient, OK?" Dr. Nessa is saying. "Give it all some time. I can help many kids who come to see me, but it takes time."

And that's the problem. I don't have time.

Horse camp is only a few weeks away.

That night I hold Mr. Jojo in my hand and lean against the cracked-open door while I listen to Mom in her bedroom. She's talking to Marsha. Mr. Jojo runs over my fingers and pauses to sniff the top of my thumb. His nose is so tiny compared to Dandelion's, but the way he smells my hand and pokes around looking for treats reminds me of her.

I love Mr. Jojo and Zombie and Marshmallow, but they aren't horses. I want to be on a horse again. I want to feel the wind on my face, and the powerful muscles pounding beneath me, and the way the horse trusts me to lead her to the right place, and I trust her to keep me safe.

Mr. Jojo is different. It's up to me to keep him safe. And I love that job. But it doesn't make missing Dandelion any easier.

I don't even know how to ask Mom about horse camp now. The calendar is in the garbage. Twelve check marks earned for nothing. And for once Mom doesn't have a new plan.

But I need one. I need something to help me stay on track right while we wait for Dr. Nessa to fix me.

"This one seems different," Mom says to Marsha. She's talking about Dr. Nessa.

"See what happens when you accept a little help, Nina?" Marsha says.

Mom laughs. "Well, I'll believe it when I see it."

"I understand. But you can't force Gwen to behave in school."

"Hey, I know the Serenity Prayer," Mom says. "I've worked the Twelve Steps. Twice."

Twelve Steps.

Mom keeps talking but my brain snags on those words.

*Twelve Steps.*

I've heard about them before, of course. I've heard a lot about AA my whole life because it's so important to my mom. But I've never really focused on the words themselves. Twelve Steps. It sounds like directions. Like a Lego set. Like a recipe.

My mom's problem is different than mine, but she uses so many phrases that feel like they belong to my brain.

*out of control*

*helpless*

*scared*

I tune back in to my mom saying, "It works if you work it."

AA and the Twelve Steps worked for my mom because she has one problem, and it's one a lot of other people have. I have fifty-four problems that only I have. But if they're similar, maybe they can have the same solution.

Maybe the answer was right in front of me all along.

I'll cure myself with the Twelve Steps! I'll become a good kid. I'll get rid of Anger and all my badness. I'll be perfect like my mom.

All I have to do is follow the directions.

I'm so excited that as soon as my mom's light is out, I sneak to the kitchen where my iPad is charging and look up Step One.

*We admitted we were powerless over alcohol—that our lives had become unmanageable.*

P-O-W-E-R-L-E-S-S: without ability to influence

U-N-M-A-N-A-G-E-A-B-L-E: impossible to control

I read the step out loud but replace the word *alcohol* with *Anger.* And *we* with *I.*

"I admitted that I was powerless over Anger—that my life had become unmanageable."

Then I get out an old notebook and write it down on the first page.

Step One: I admitted that I was powerless over Anger—that my life had become unmanageable.

I read what the website says about how to do the steps. It says I should keep track of my progress by sharing how I'm doing at meetings and with my sponsor. Since I can't go to meetings and I don't have a sponsor, I'll use this Top Secret Notebook.

Then I read about Step One. It says there's three ways to do it. You can talk about your alcohol problem in a meeting. Or you can share it with your sponsor. Or you can share it with a trusted friend.

Directions. I'll follow directions.

It seems almost too easy.

I don't read Step Two. I'm going to do them slowly. Mom's always saying, one day at a time.

For me, it's one step at a time.

# 10

## JIGSAW BRAINS

Mom drops me off at Hettie's on Saturday morning, which is perfect because I'm going to do Step One with her.

I was thinking that the person I admit my anger to should probably be Tyler because (a) he understands the Twelve Steps and might know why I'm telling him and (b) he is also a splinter-heart kid.

But the website said tell a *friend*. Not a brother. And I want to do things perfectly.

I haven't seen Hettie since school on Wednesday when my brain cracked at PowerKids because I spent all day Thursday and Friday with Dr. Nessa. I haven't been to Hettie's house in a long time. I used to come here almost every weekend, but one time this winter my brain cracked when I was here, and I haven't been back since. I don't remember why my brain cracked, but it did. It wasn't the worst crack ever. I yelled at Nolan, which is really not cool because he's only six years old.

I never would have done that with my put-together brain.

I don't know everything that happened because, sometimes, after my brain cracks, Mom rescues me, and then we just move on. I don't always want to hear about it, and sometimes Mom is too exhausted to tell me.

All I know is that I haven't been invited to Hettie's in a long, long time, and no one explained to me what changed or why I'm suddenly allowed to be here again. I stand on Hettie's doorstep with my cheeks burning. I don't know how to look at Hettie's mom. She probably hates me now. She probably should hate me now.

Hettie's house is a whole house, so it's bigger than my apartment, but it's not as big as Tyler's house. There's only one floor and Hettie and Nolan share a bedroom. But they have a huge front yard and a huge backyard with a brook running through it. I've missed it here, even though I don't want to be here now. Those feelings are jumbling me up.

Luckily Hettie is standing next to her mom, bouncing from toe to toe when the door opens.

"Gwendolyn!" she says. Then she asks the question she always asks whenever I appear anywhere in her world. "What should we do today?"

"Let's find them!" I say.

I rush through the front door and sprint through the living room, through the kitchen, and out the back door without even looking at Hettie's mom. That's good because looking at her might crack my brain. I don't know why but sometimes when I look at someone who I know sees the fifty-four things, and who I know can't see any fifty-fifth or fifty-sixth or seventy-second thing, I get so angry right away. All I want is for that person to see me as something else. Something good. When I look at them and know all they see is something bad, I remember that I am bad. And being bad wakes up Anger. And then Anger is huge inside me and reaching toward my brain, and sometimes I crack from just looking at someone who thinks I'm trouble. I know it's polite to say *hello,* or *thank you for having me,* or at least nod at Hettie's mom, but it's better that I didn't have to.

17. Rude/Impolite

"What are we looking for?" Hettie calls, running behind me.

The sun is out again and we're both in sneakers that are muddy three steps into her huge backyard. Our hoodies fly behind our backs like capes, and that's what I love about Hettie: she makes me feel like I can fly. She loves my ideas. She loves my games. She doesn't care that my brain cracks sometimes because she likes all the places it leads her.

I stop running when I reach the graying piles of snow next to the brook.

"Right!" Hettie says, and I know she's remembering how, in December, her mom took Nolan and Hettie and me to McDonald's and, when we got home, we pulled on boots and coats and hats and buried our Happy Meal toys in the snow by the brook. We were pretending they were buried treasure.

"We need the map!" Hettie declares.

"Right," I say. I forgot all about how we made a map so we'd be able to find the treasure again when the snow melted.

We run back to the house and luckily Hettie is faster because she remembers to slip off her muddy shoes before we walk into the kitchen. I would have run right through and accidentally sprayed mud all over. Then Hettie's mom would never let me come back.

## 45. Forgetful

We walk in damp socks through Hettie's kitchen and down the hallway to her room. Nolan is watching TV in the living room so it's just the two of us. Thank goodness. One way to make sure I don't end up yelling at a six-year-old again is to never be in the same room as a six-year-old again.

"The map's still in my top desk drawer," Hettie says, turning to shut the door to her room.

I walk over to the desk. I don't know why she's closing the door. I want to find the map and get right back outside. I don't like being in this house. It's making me too nervous that my brain will crack again. You would think that when I know my brain might crack, I'd be able to keep it together better. You would think that it's like how, if you're walking on an uneven sidewalk, you're extra careful so you don't turn an ankle, but if you're walking on a regular sidewalk and there's suddenly a crack in it, you aren't being careful, so you're definitely going to turn an ankle, even though there were a lot of cracks in the first sidewalk and only one in the second. But my brain cracks aren't like sidewalk cracks, and the more I think about them the more they seem to happen.

As soon as Hettie closes the door, I realize the moment is here.

I don't open her desk. Instead, I look her in the eye. "I have to tell you something," I say.

She freezes like she knows it's serious. "OK," she says.

The words burst out of me, whole and smooth and loud (but not 23. too loud) and perfect: "I ADMIT TO YOU, HETTIE MCFEE, THAT I AM POWERLESS OVER MY ANGER AND MY LIFE HAS BECOME UNMANAGEABLE."

My breath stops. Or I'm holding it. I think I'm holding it. I'm scared about what she'll say.

She waits, like she's making absolutely sure I'm finished. When I don't add anything she says, "Now?"

All my breath comes out. "Huh?"

"Are you feeling angry now?" she asks. "At me?"

"Oh," I say. "No. Of course not."

Hettie shrugs. "OK," she says. "Do you want to find the map?"

That was . . . anticlimactic. I should do something. Or say something else. Or Hettie should be saying something else. Some part of this should be harder.

But I did everything the website told me to do. So after a minute, I shrug back and turn to Hettie's desk. . . I open a drawer and there's a map right on top. But it's on yellow paper. It's drawn with pink marker. I've never seen it before. It's a different map. I slowly pull it from the drawer as Hettie walks over to stand next to me.

"Oh," she says.

"This isn't the right map," I say.

"I know . . ." Hettie says.

I want her to keep talking, but she doesn't. She knows me very well. She knows if she stands here silently my mouth will start to fill in the blanks even if my brain doesn't want it to.

"Where did this one—"

"I made it with Thaís, OK?" Hettie says, fast.

"Thaís Gonzalez?" I ask.

"I . . . she came over a few weeks later. And I was missing you."

"You were?" I never think about someone missing me. It sort of feels like Hettie disappears when she's not in front of me. I mean, I miss her sometimes, but I don't think about her out there, existing, while I'm missing her. I don't think about her doing things without me. Like making treasure maps with Thaís Gonzalez.

"Yeah," Hettie says. "My mom suggested I should try to have a different friend come over." Hettie shrugs. "Don't be mad."

I look up, startled. My brain is busy but Anger isn't. He's

silent and still in his shell.

"Mad?" I say.

I'm not mad that Hettie has other friends. I know someone needs more friends than just me, the Fifty-Four-Wrong-Things Girl.

Hettie doesn't have to be 6. Socially inept just because I am.

"Yeah . . . I'd probably be mad if, when our moms said we couldn't spend the weekends together, you were off playing with someone else."

"You would be?"

It's so weird to think something would make someone else angry when it doesn't upset me at all.

"Yeah, Thaís and I hid some toys but . . . she didn't get into it. She wasn't as fun."

That reminds me about what Dr. Nessa said yesterday.

"You think I'm fun? Is that why we're best friends?"

"You're the most fun person I know!" Hettie declares. "Do you forgive me?"

"Yeah," I answer. "Wait. No. I can't forgive you."

"What?" Hettie squeaks.

"I mean, I can't forgive you because I'm not even mad," I say.

"Really?" Hettie looks so relieved. She bounces on her feet.

"I know you're friends with Thaís. I'm glad you have other friends."

Hettie takes Thaís's map out of my hands and puts it down. My brain keeps repeating the way she called me *fun*. I'm smiling.

"Thaís misses you too, you know. And Marty. The stuff that happened with her was so . . . and for a while everything was . . . ugh."

"Stuff happened with Margaret?" I ask, then I remember I'm supposed to call her Marty.

"Marty," Hettie says. "Yeah. You know what I mean." I don't know what she means. But she doesn't explain, and I don't ask her to because she starts saying something even more interesting. "But Thaís and Marty aren't mad at you. Just FYI. They still think you're fun and funny. They miss you. None of us really understands what happened. But everyone knows it's not anyone's fault."

"Really?" I say. "They miss me?"

I think about Thaís in class. Whispering that she hates how Mr. Olsen talks to me. Bringing me a pencil because she knows I'll forget. Are those signs she misses me?

"Of course, Gwennie. No one is as fun as you," Hettie says.

She starts looking through a different drawer and that's good because it's easier to ask this next question to the back of her head than it is to her face.

"Hettie . . . do you think I'm fun *because* my brain is weird?"

Hettie looks up quickly and squints at me. "Your brain is weird?" she asks.

"Um, yeah," I say. *Duh.*

"Oh, I didn't know that," Hettie says. Then she pulls out the map we made in December. "I found it. Let's go!"

I run like crazy back through Hettie's house to our shoes

and then to the brook. But she beats me, like always. And like always, I don't mind.

Dr. Nessa is right, I realize. At least when it comes to Hettie. Hettie's brain is normal and mine is not and we fit together like puzzle pieces.

I'm back at school on Monday. I have to meet with Dr. Nessa one more time, but she didn't have an appointment for a few days, so I'm back at school in the meantime. At outdoor break, I decide I'll hang out with Hettie. I didn't see Tyler on Thursday or Friday because I was with Dr. Nessa. I didn't see him over the weekend because I spent it with Hettie. I don't remember exactly what happened on Wednesday because my brain cracked, but I'm pretty sure Tyler was mad at me. He probably still is.

"Race around the swings!" Hettie yells when we get outside. We take off running, but then I stop.

There he is, under our tree, like he's waiting for me. My brother. The snow has finally melted from the entire schoolyard, and the ground is damp, but he's sitting on it anyway like he doesn't care if his jeans get wet. He has a few blades of grass in his hand. He's braiding them like he's waiting for my head to show up so that he can braid something that makes sense again.

Hettie stops running and walks back to me. She watches me watching Tyler. "It's OK. Go talk to him," she says. "I'll hang out with Thaís and Marty."

Then she's gone and for the first time I realize I don't know what Hettie and Thaís and Marty have been doing at outdoor break all year while I've been building glass walls for Tyler and me.

I walk toward him slowly.

He looks up. "Hey," he says.

He drops the grass.

I feel around in my body for Anger or Sadness or Confidence. They all seem gone. Even Sadness must have shrunk so much I can't detect him. That's good because I don't want to be any of the fifty-four things right now. I want to be the in-between stuff or the fifty-fifth thing or something, anything, but bad.

"Hey," I say.

I fall to my knees beside him. They're immediately wet and for some reason it feels good. I sit all the way down in the grass and feel the wetness crawl up my jeans.

"Do you want me to do your braids?" he asks.

"Yes," I say. He's already started untangling the one on the right before I remember to say, "Thank you."

17. Rude/Impolite

I'm supposed to say I'm sorry, but I can't figure out how. I'm sorry that I threw Ms. Hayley's computer, but that's a weird thing to say to Tyler, who also threw her computer, and I'm not sorry I yelled about it when they called my mom but they didn't call his.

"Are you still mad at me?" Tyler asks as he starts my braid, nice and tight.

"No," I say.

It's not Tyler's fault that he has ADHD or that Ms. Hayley only calls my mom or that he's allowed to see Dandelion but I'm not.

"I know you didn't steal Dandelion," I say finally. The closest I can come to sorry. "Are you mad at me?"

"Did you know Dandelion is the ornery-est horse at Millington Stables?" Tyler says.

"I don't think ornery-est is a word," I say. "But I love the word *ornery*. O-R-N-E-R-Y. Tough to please, grumpy."

"Like us," Tyler says.

Then he freezes. His hands hold my hair tight so I'm able to think about what he just said. Everyone called Dandelion *ornery*, not *bad*. Maybe they mean the same things. Maybe we're finally going to talk about this.

"Is your mom ornery, too?" Tyler asks.

I forget he's braiding my hair for a second and shake my head no. The braid falls out of his hands, but he starts over like he doesn't care.

"Neither is mine," Tyler says. "It must have been . . ."

"Him," I conclude for Tyler. I know he was trying to say *our dad*. He knows that's who I mean, too.

"Yeah," Tyler says. "Do you think he had—has ADHD?"

I remember Dr. Nessa saying that ADHD runs in families.

"Maybe," I say.

Then we can't say anything. And maybe this is why we can't

talk about being bad kids. And maybe this is why I always want to be around Tyler all the time even though he makes me angrier than anyone else lately.

Maybe it's because there are no words for blank spaces. The story of us is just exclamation points and question marks.

"Anyway, you were right," Tyler says. "Ms. Hayley should have called my mom too."

My jaw drops. "What?" I say.

I feel Tyler shrug by the way my hair goes up and down.

"I told my mom about the whole thing."

"*You* told your mom?" I ask, shocked.

"Yeah, I always tell her when I mess up like that," Tyler says.

I'm too stunned to talk. What is the point of PowerKids never calling your mom if you just turn around and tell her everything anyway?

Tyler keeps talking. "She said people aren't always fair to girls like you. That they aren't always fair to boys like me either, but that it's harder for girls like you to get the help you need."

"Girls like me?"

"Girls with ADHD."

"Your mom thinks I have ADHD too?" I ask.

"Don't you?" Tyler says.

"No," I say. "I had the whole IEP thing. They said I don't have it . . . I don't have anything. But now I'm—"

"You seem like you do," Tyler interrupts me. He snaps the last rubber band into place. "But I'm glad you don't. I hate

ADHD. Anyway, want to run?"

"What's it like?" I say. "What's ADHD like? What's the pill like?"

Tyler shrugs. "It's just . . . me. I don't know. Want to run?"

I don't. I want to keep talking about how we're the same. I want to hear more about why he thinks I have ADHD like he does. I want to hear all about his blue pills and how they make him less "real crazy." I want to hear what it's like to have something fixed, and if he really thinks I can have something fixed about me too.

I want us to find another way to try to talk about our dad, even if we still can't.

But I can see Tyler's hands are shaking a little bit. Maybe that's because Tyler doesn't like to talk about this stuff.

Tyler needs to move.

"To the swings and back!" I yell.

Then I take off. He leaps after me.

He doesn't even know we just busted through a glass wall. But I can tell it was good for him.

At home I sit at my desk and take out my Top Secret Notebook. Mom is making pork chops with rice and salad, and the tangy and sweet smells fill our whole apartment.

I write the date at the top over where it says Step One: I admitted that I was powerless over Anger and that my life had become unmanageable.

Then I stand and wander over to Mr. Jojo's cage. I let him climb onto my hand and up my shoulder. I take him over to Zombie and Marshmallow and watch them swim in peaceful circles.

Then I remember I'm supposed to be writing in my notebook.

Even when the assignment comes from my own self I'm

4. Lazy

and

27. Unable to multitask

and

24. Spacey

Mr. Jojo runs across my desk as I write.

Step One: Check. I told Hettie about Anger. I guess I admitted it because "admitting" just means "telling." It seemed too easy but that's probably because it was Step One.

Then I turn the page and boot up my iPad to look for Step Two. There it is, looking all bold and simple like the first one. I copy it onto the next page of my notebook.

Step Two: I came to be aware that a Power greater than myself could restore me to sanity.

But it isn't all bold and simple. This one is a lot harder.

The website says that "a power greater than myself" often means God, but it doesn't have to mean the traditional version of God. People come up with a lot of different higher powers to turn themselves over to. The important thing is to really believe in whatever the power is.

I've overheard enough of the AA meetings and the phone calls between Mom and Marsha to know that the higher power is a super important part of the Twelve Steps. But I don't go to church or pray or know what I do and don't believe when it comes to God. It feels like this step should have seven hundred mini steps first about trying out every different religion and belief system until you figure out what you actually believe in. But horse camp is only a few weeks away. I don't have time to find a whole religion.

Mr. Jojo runs over my notebook and I pick him up and bring his nose to mine for a kiss. He wiggles against the tip of my nose and I giggle.

"I wish you could be my higher power," I say.

He wiggles again.

"But I can't take you to school with me. Isn't that silly?"

I set him down, and he climbs back up my arm. Maybe some people think hamsters can't feel love. Not the way a person can. But I know Mr. Jojo loves me just like I know Dandelion loves me. When I'm with them, it's easier to hide Anger and shrink Sadness and wake up Confidence.

I tap my pen against the paper as Mr. Jojo tries to wiggle under my shirtsleeve.

I wish I could ask my mom what her higher power is, but I don't want her to know about the Top Secret Notebook.

"Gwendolyn," she calls. "Dinner, honey."

Confidence is marching around in my brain. Mr. Jojo must

have woken him up before I even realized it.

"Answer her!" he commands.

"OK," I say.

Usually I forget. Usually I hear her call for me but I keep doing what I'm doing without answering her until she has to come and get me. And by then she's annoyed because she worked hard on dinner, and I don't even appreciate it, and it's cold, and it's not as good as it would have been fifteen or twenty minutes ago if I just came the first time she called me. And then we're fighting. So just that one word "OK!" makes Mom say, "Thank you so much for answering me."

Confidence starts marching even faster as I stand up. "Thank you for making dinner," he makes me say.

"Oh, Cupcake!" Mom says, all bright and happy. "You're welcome!"

Maybe the Twelve Steps have already started working.

And, with that, I rush back to my desk and scribble because I have it.

My higher power is Confidence!

# 11

## GOLDEN, GLITTERY GWENDOLYN

The next morning I sit at my desk in Mr. Olsen's classroom pulling on my braids. He's yelled at me twice this morning already. I'm afraid my brain will crack if I mess up again.

It's one of those terrible times when another teacher has come to talk to him, and he's standing right in the hallway—I can even still see his brown docksider shoe holding the door propped open. But before he walked out, he was in the middle of a sentence, which means he didn't leave anything for us to do while he stood out there.

Having nothing to do is really bad for me. My body tries to fill the space all at once, and whenever that happens I do something I'm not supposed to, then someone yells at me, and then my brain might crack. So I'm sitting at my desk trying to fill up my body so it doesn't fill up the space around me. I pull on my braid. I tap my feet on the ground. I wiggle my back against the chair.

Around me, kids are talking. A few have gotten out of their seats. I don't know if they're breaking the rules because Mr. Olsen didn't give us any rules. I don't know how long he's been whispering in the hallway. Maybe minutes. Maybe hours.

I haven't taken my eyes off the sole of Mr. Olsen's brown shoe. I need to keep looking at it to remind myself that he's still there and that I need to stay at my desk.

But then I hear my name.

"Gwendolyn?"

There's a body next to me. I turn and glance before looking back at Mr. Olsen's shoe.

It's Thaís.

"Gwen?" she repeats.

It's hard to know how to answer her because she doesn't talk to me. Not unless we're working on our science fair project, and that isn't what we're doing today. Every other day she sits behind me and we don't say anything to each other.

"Gwen?"

Words in my handwriting appear before me over and over . . .

6. Socially inept

6. Socially inept

6. Socially—

"Hey, are you OK?" she asks.

I look at her, then back at Mr. Olsen's shoe. Then back at her because that's what an un-socially inept person would do.

I bounce my feet harder and speak.

"I'm fine. Are you OK?"

She lowers her eyebrows. "I'm fine. But I said your name three—never mind. I wanted to give you this."

She hands me an envelope. The paper is purple. My name is written on the front in sparkly gold ink.

"What is it?" I ask.

"An invitation. To my birthday party."

"What? No," I say.

23. Talks too loud

10. No filter

"Oh, OK. If you don't want to—"

"Wait! I mean, yes," I say. "Sorry, I misheard you. I want to come obviously it's just that—"

My brain catches my mouth, and I snap it shut before I can say, *It's just that I don't go to birthday parties. Other than Hettie's, I haven't been invited to a birthday party since we were all little. Kids don't usually invite a girl like me to a birthday party now that we're in middle school, and you don't have to invite the whole class.*

"I have to ask my mom," I say.

Thaís smiles. "Of course."

Phew! I said the right thing.

"You're funny, Gwen. I hope you can come."

"Ms. Gonzalez."

My eyes go wide, and I jump three inches in my chair. Mr. Olsen is back in the room, and I didn't do what I had promised myself I would. I lost focus. I stopped looking at his shoe. I didn't hear him come back.

"Who gave you permission to be out of your seat?"

He uses the sarcastic voice, and I'm starting to wonder if *sarcastic* is just a sneaky word for *mean*.

"Sorry," Thaís squeaks. She scrambles into the desk behind mine. She ignores the kids who chuckle.

And then it's over.

My heart is still thumping, but Mr. Olsen moves on. I wasn't out of my seat so he didn't even say my name. Thaís isn't 49. Reactive or 11. Overly emotional, so she went back to her desk without making it worse.

My hands are opening my book and searching my bag for a pencil.

I did it.

I'm not in trouble.

It's hard to believe, but then Confidence wakes up and starts marching. "I got you," he says. Step Two is working.

And I'm invited to a birthday party.

I can't find a pencil as usual, and Mr. Olsen is on the other side of the room helping Mike Clark, so I have to wait to ask to borrow one.

My hands keep moving though. Like my mouth, they're working before my brain can direct them. Quiet as can be, I slide the invitation out of the envelope.

*Thaís's Eleventh Birthday Sleepover*

It's a sleepover!

"Ms. Rogers," Mr. Olsen says.

I drop the invitation into my backpack before he can see.

"Can I borrow a pencil?" I ask, fast.

"I supposed I could have guessed that." Mr. Olsen sighs but hands me one. "Five percent," he reminds me.

I don't even care.

The next morning I'm out of school one last time to finish the assessment. The last thing Dr. Nessa has me do is a reading test, which is really easy because I'm alone in the room and my braids are still tight. I finish before she even comes back into her office. When she does, I'm sitting there pulling on my braid and tapping a pencil with one rhythm and my feet with a different one.

"Well, Gwendolyn, that's the last thing I had for you. I think you can go to school this afternoon. Your mom should be here to pick you up any minute."

"That's it?" I ask. I can't believe it. It was so much easier than the IEP assessment. I mean, it was longer and there were more tests and the questions were harder. But it was also easier because Dr. Nessa let me take breaks and always backed off a long time before my brain cracked if I was getting upset.

"That's it," she says, gesturing for me to follow her back into the lobby of the office. When we get there she asks if I want a snack.

I don't answer. Instead, I blurt, "Do you think I have something?"

10. *No filter*

"I know I'm not supposed to ask that." The words won't stop rushing out of me. I ask Confidence to stop them, but he doesn't. He's asleep or something. My mouth is still moving. "I know I have to wait months and months to find out if there's a thing. Something real. Like my brother has. I have to wait and see if it's a thing with, like, a name and medicine, or if I'm just bad—I know I have to wait. Other kids probably wait easily. But I'm bad at waiting. It's one of the things. I'm impatient. I'll wait though. I know I'm not supposed to be saying any of this."

"Hold on," Dr. Nessa sounds surprised. She holds up her hand like a stop sign. "You have a few misconceptions. Do you know what a misconception is?"

"Yes," I say. I spell the word. "It means I'm wrong."

"It's so interesting how you spell words when I ask if you know them."

I shrug. "You don't really know a word if you can't spell it, right?"

Dr. Nessa looks up and to the left, then back at me. "Well I'd say a person can know a word without spelling it, but I'm not sure that's true for you and who you are, Gwendolyn Rogers."

She gives me that smile again. The one that isn't quite

laughing at me. That almost looks like she's enjoying me.

"So first, I'd like you to know that it will not take months for you to see me again."

"I'm going to see you again?" I ask. I was imagining another envelope in the mail.

Dr. Nessa smiles. "Yes. Soon. I'm waiting on a few papers from your teachers. Then I'll write a full report. I'll meet with your mom first, then with both of you, and we can go over my conclusions and recommendations."

I take a deep breath.

"And it won't be months?"

"No," she says. "Days. Maybe a week."

I nod. She won't be able to sound as mean as those IEP papers if I'm sitting here on her couch when she tells me everything that's wrong with me.

"And what's more, I want to remind you that this is actually a first step, OK? This is how I try to catch up and get to know everything I can about you from the start. This is not the ending."

"But what if I don't have anything?" I say.

"Oh," Dr. Nessa says. "You know, I think I can answer your question now. I don't like to think so much about a diagnosis as you seem to want to. They can be useful. Sometimes they can give patients a sense of identity and community. Sometimes they can help with boring stuff like insurance forms and payments. But what I like to think about is how my patients' brains work. How I can help them bring out their talents and cope with the things that hold them back."

"Oh," I say. Because that sounds like she's not going to tell me now or ever if I have something. Something real. Something with medicine or some other kind of solution.

"And so I think I can answer the root of your question. Today. Diagnosis or not, your brain, and how it works, is real.

I stare at her.

"Like anyone else's brain, it has strengths and challenges. You have been so tangled in the challenges it can be hard to even find the strengths, let alone use them."

I'm still staring.

"Life can get easier, Gwendolyn. With or without a diagnosis. I can help. I know I can."

For once, I have no words.

Confidence is awake. Wide awake and running more than marching.

"Do you understand?"

I do.

This is bigger than horse camp.

Someone finally gets me.

I get back to school in time for outdoor break.

"So, what do you think?" Thaís is standing over Tyler and me. She just walked right up to Tyler and me and our tree like the glass wall that I built isn't even there, which I do know it's not, but it's still weird to have her inside it. I can't hear what she's saying either because only half of my hair is braided.

"What?" I say.

"I know I only asked you yesterday but we . . . my mom . . . she needs the total number. Did you ask your mom? Can you come?"

I have been thinking almost constantly about this birthday party. About that purple envelope with the gold *Gwendolyn* on the front. About the fact that someone wants me in her house, at her party, making her birthday more special. I've been thinking about what that invitation means about my brain and how it's a puzzle piece in a whole world of brains.

But somehow the purple envelope is still in my backpack. I haven't asked my mom. I didn't even look at what day the party is.

38. Disorganized

24. Spacey

6. Socially inept

"Yes, I can come. I can't wait!"

13. Impulsive

That night, after I finish my homework, I pull out my Top Secret Notebook. I sit in front of Zombie and Marshmallow and watch them swim as I write.

Step Two: Check! Confidence is a good higher power. The website said that trusting God would make good things happen. I found my higher power, then got an invitation and Dr. Nessa said she can help me. It worked.

I open my iPad and turn the page in my notebook to write down the new step.

Step Three: I made a decision to turn my life and will over to ~~God~~ Confidence as I understand him.

I go to bed thinking that Step Three seems a lot like Step Two.

# 12

## DIAGNOSIS CONCLUSIVE

The following Friday, I'm back in Dr. Nessa's office. I'm sitting alone in the lobby. My homework is on my lap but I'm not looking at it. Instead I'm watching through the glass wall as Dr. Nessa and my mom sit across from each other at the big wooden table where I took all of those tests. I watch as their heads bend over the same piece of paper. Maybe that's the paper that will help me.

I can't stop the alphabet soup from running through my brain:

ASD

SPD

ADHD

OCD

ODD

PDA

ABCDEFG

I understood what Dr. Nessa meant when she said that even if there aren't specific letters for my brain, even if she can't give it an easy title, she can still help me.

But I want a set of letters anyway.

1. Too demanding

2. Picky eater

3. Attention-seeking

4. Lazy

5. Will only do what she wants to do

6. Socially inept

7. Inattentive

*On and on . . .*

It would be so easy to have a way to explain them all.

*Oh, I'm bad at remembering my pencil. That's because of my ABC.*

*Oh, I'm only comfortable if I have super tight braids in my hair. Otherwise it's too hard for me to pay attention to anything. That's because of my DEF.*

*Oh, I'm always doing only half my homework and not the other half. That's because of my GHI.*

And it would be even better if I got a little blue pill that made all of those things go away.

After what feels like forever, Dr. Nessa opens the door. "Gwendolyn, come on in." I sit down in the chair next to my mom, and even though I don't do or say anything, Mom reaches over and pulls the back of the chair so that it's right next to her. She puts her arm around me and I snuggle in close.

I'm eleven, and that number sounds like I'm too old to sit all curled up with my mom in someone's office like this. But it also feels like love, so I don't care if I'm too old. Mom seems to like it too.

39. Immature

Maybe Number 39 is one of those things Dr. Nessa was talking about. Maybe it's sometimes good and comfortable and loving to be immature.

With Mom's arm around me, I don't even think about my braids.

"Thank you for being so patient, Gwendolyn," Dr. Nessa says.

Even though 48. Impatient.

"I want to be sure I discuss everything with you as well as with your mom. I didn't say anything to her that I won't say to you now, OK?"

I nod.

"I know you're looking for a concrete answer, and so I'm going to tell you that I do have what I think is a very solid diagnosis for you."

My heart speeds up. The letters!

"However, I want you to understand that psychological issues are not the same as, say, strep throat. There are no standard methods that work for basically everyone. What happens next is a series of trial and error. And anything I do needs to be agreeable to both you and your mom, OK?"

I barely hear what she's saying, I'm so excited. I try hard to keep her words in my brain but they slip out quickly. Still I say, "OK."

"So, Gwendolyn, I am diagnosing you with ADHD."

"YES!" I say.

10. No filter

Mom backs away from me. Maybe only a centimeter, but I feel it. Like me having ADHD is something she doesn't want to be too close to. Except that makes no sense because Dr. Nessa told her before she told me, so Mom knew about the ADHD before she put her arm around me.

It was the *YES* she didn't want to be close to.

I zero back in on what Dr. Nessa is saying. ". . . unusual reaction. Do you want to tell me what that diagnosis means to you?"

"It means I'm like—" I stop myself just before I say *Tyler* because I know that will make Mom inch even farther from me. "Like other kids I know. And it means I have a reason for being the way I am."

"Ah," says Dr. Nessa. "That sounds like a relief, huh?"

"Yes," I say. "And it means I can take a pill and get fixed."

"Well—"

I interrupt Dr. Nessa before she can say more because I don't want to hear all about how a pill can actually only do so much, and how it's going to be trial and error, and how there's no magic that fixes ADHD.

"Maybe not, like, fixed. But there's pills that can help me. So, there's something to help me that I can't mess up. You know, like the calendar? I was so afraid of messing that up," I say to Mom. She backed up more, sometime when I didn't notice. Her eyes are wide as she looks at me now. "Sorry," I say to her. "I know those plans are supposed to help. And maybe that weird diet was helping. I mean, Thaís Gonzalez did invite me to her birthday party."

"What?" Mom says. I realize then that I forgot to tell her. I realize that even though I'm excited, I never showed Mom the invitation.

"Yeah," I say. "I have an invitation."

Then I file the party away for later. I promise myself I'll come back to it with Mom after we leave. Even though I know I promise myself those things all the time and then don't do them.

"Anyway, those plans are hard. And I like the idea that there's a thing I can do that's not hard. Swallow a pill. I like that maybe there's something that can help me without me having to put in all the effort. Something that can maybe help more than the thirty percent that the green sludge—fish oil, I mean—is supposed to."

Mom and Dr. Nessa are quiet for a moment.

Then Mom says, "Well, at least we always know how Gwendolyn feels." She says it like a joke and they both laugh. But I also think it isn't a joke. It might be another of those good things about my brain. Everyone always knows how I feel.

"How do you know about ADHD medicine?" Mom asks me after a few silent moments go by.

I swallow. "Tyler takes them."

"Oh," Mom says.

"So, Gwendolyn, it's important that you know that there are some ways to treat ADHD that don't involve medications, OK?" Dr. Nessa says. "Your mom and I have been discussing—"

"No!" I say. Anger has woken up suddenly. There's fire in my chest.

"Those are strong meds, Gwen," Mom says. "And medication isn't something to play with."

"I don't want to play with it," I say, too loud.

I shake Mom's arm the rest of the way off me. I didn't want to do that. I wanted her to be the one who moved it. But my skin is burning where she's close to me.

"Medicine that's unnecessary—"

"How can it be unnecessary if I have an actual disease?" I say.

"ADHD isn't exactly a disease," Dr. Nessa says. Both of us barely hear her.

"A doctor says I need it," I say.

"Medication would help but I didn't say you need it," Dr. Nessa says. I realize my mom and I hear different halves of that sentence. I hear *would help.* Mom hears *don't need it.* But I know I need anything, anything that would help.

"It's not like you hate medicine. You give me Tylenol when I have a fever," I say.

"That's because Tylenol brings down fevers more effectively than any other interventions," Mom says.

"And this medicine helps ADHD more than any other interventions," I cry.

"No it doesn't," Mom says. "There are plenty of other—"

"Nina, if I may." Dr. Nessa interrupts Mom a little more forcefully than I'm expecting. "I want to be clear with Gwendolyn. Here, we tell her the truth. Always. The truth is that while it's not as simple as Tylenol and fevers, stimulant medication is the most effective way of improving executive functioning for most individuals with ADHD," she says. "However, your mom is right that it's also the most risky. And there are other proven interventions."

"What other things are there?" I ask. Or more like demand.

"Well, your mom is right about diets and supplements," Dr. Nessa says.

"No," I say.

"And reward charts. Structure. Schedules. Exercise."

"That's all so hard!" Anger is more active than Sadness right now, so I'm surprised when I figure out I'm crying.

"Gwendolyn, Cupcake," Mom says, moving to put her arm around me again.

"I'm so tired," I say. I shout. But I guess shouting is OK right now. For some reason, even though I'm shouting, they both seem to be listening to me. "I'm so tired of trying so hard to be good. I need help. I need some sort of help that doesn't mean a whole lot more trying."

When Mom talks, I realize she's also crying, which surprises me enough that Anger shrinks just a little.

"I'm in recovery," she says to Dr. Nessa. "You know . . . addiction is hereditary . . . something like Adderall really scares me."

This is so unfair for a thousand reasons. Mom is in recovery, so I can't get the help I need? Mom messed up with alcohol, so now I can't have medicine? Mom's one problem means I can't solve all fifty-four of mine?

Dr. Nessa nods. "I understand."

Once again we're back to me being the only person who no one understands. Even when Mom is wrong. I know she's wrong.

"Tyler's mom is in AA too and he gets to take them."

"Gwendolyn!" Mom's looking at me like she's shocked. Like my brain just cracked. I rewind fast through the last few seconds, and no. I'm angry and emotional and loud, but no brain cracking.

"What?" I say.

"Remember," Mom says, hushed. "It's Alcoholics *Anonymous*."

"So?" I say. "Dr. Nessa doesn't know Tyler and his mom."

But Dr. Nessa is looking down at her lap, uncomfortable. Her fingers fidget there. She shifts in her seat.

"Do you?" I ask her, still loud and demanding because the realization that I messed up is coming on slowly.

"I can't answer that," Dr. Nessa says. She keeps talking but I don't hear her.

I think about the past few weeks.

PowerKids was going to kick me out and we couldn't do anything about it because we'd been on the wait-list to see Dr. Nessa forever.

Then we suddenly got an appointment.

Right after Mom ran into Ms. Christakos at that AA meeting.

Right after our moms randomly arranged for me to spend Sunday at Tyler's house.

Right after I heard Mom and Marsha talking about some mysterious *her* who had offered to help. Whose help Mom didn't want to take.

What if the *her* is Ms. Christakos? What if Ms. Christakos is the person who's been trying to help Mom and me?

What if she did help us and that's why . . .

I look up at the wall behind Dr. Nessa. Her diploma hangs there: University of Wisconsin, Psychology Department. Where Tyler's mom works.

*Tyler's mom got me off of Dr. Nessa's long wait-list.*

Dr. Nessa must be Ms. Christakos's *friend.*

Ms. Christakos is the reason I can even see Dr. Nessa. She's why I'm still in PowerKids. She's why I even have a sliver of a chance at riding a horse this summer.

And I just betrayed her!

"Oh no. Oh no," I say, my voice shaking. "You *do* know her!" Tears are threatening my eyes. Sadness is big and hot and furry and itchy and makes my skin red. The shame version of Sadness. "Oh no!"

*Tyler's mom is in AA too.*

How could I have said that?

ImpulsiveAttentionSeeking ActsWithoutThinkingNoFilter

"She was helping us?" I ask my mom. "Why would she help us when she hates us?"

"She . . . she doesn't . . . hate us," Mom says.

"Well she's going to hate me now. I can't believe I—"

"It's OK," Dr. Nessa says. "I can't . . . I can't confirm anything. I can't explain . . . but it's OK. I promise."

"No," I say. "No it isn't."

I can't believe that Ms. Christakos was the one who helped me. More than Ms. North or the IEP team or Mr. Olsen or Ms. Hayley or anyone who ever told me they were trying to help me. Ms. Christakos never said any of that, but then she actually did help me. And then I *hurt* her.

"It's OK, Gwen. It's OK. Dr. Nessa is sworn to confidentiality because you're her patient," Mom says.

"That's right," Dr. Nessa says, like it's just dawning on her. "I can't tell you if I know her, but I *can* say that I can't tell her or anyone else anything you said because you are my patient."

C-O-N-F-I-D-E-N-T-I-A-L-I-T-Y. It means a secret that is so important to keep, telling it is illegal. It means she can't tell Tyler's mom that I told her the thing I wasn't supposed to tell her about Tyler's mom.

"Even though she's the one who helped us get off the wait-list?" I ask.

Dr. Nessa smiles. "If it were true that someone referred you to me, I would still be bound by doctor/patient confidentiality, even when it came to that person."

I take a deep breath. I'm still embarrassed that I said that, but I'm glad Ms. Christakos will never know.

"But, listen, Cupcake. You have to stop comparing us to them, OK?" Mom is saying. "We're different. I know he's your brother . . . but they aren't us and we aren't them."

He's my family though.

So he sort of is us.

Or me and Tyler are our own *us*.

I manage not to say it. I know it's not what my mom wants to hear. But I don't get how she can still look so angry when she talks about them, even when Ms. Christakos did this big thing for us.

"I'm so tired," I say again. "I would need that medicine

whether Tyler was my brother or not."

"I'm sorry, Gwen. I didn't see how hard this is on you," Mom says. "But the meds . . ." She trails off.

"I think we hear what you're saying, Gwendolyn," Dr. Nessa says. "I hear you saying you need something that's easy for you to do. That our first step in treating ADHD should be easier than a restricted diet or reward chart."

"Yes," I say.

Mom nods. "Let's work on that then. It doesn't need to be medication, does it?"

"No," Dr. Nessa says.

"What else could it be?" I ask.

But Dr. Nessa doesn't answer. She doesn't have an answer. She says she has to think about it, which I know means that most kids who have ADHD get to take the medicine as the first step, and it's so unfair that I have to use some other first step that will be less popular and probably will still be harder than swallowing a pill, even if Mom and Dr. Nessa promise it won't be. I'm crying again when Dr. Nessa says we're out of time.

When we get to the car, my eyes are still red and puffy. My head is pounding. My hands are shaking.

I can't wait to be a grown-up. I can't wait to be untied from Mom's issues so that I only have fifty-four wrong things to worry about and not also addiction.

I strap myself into the middle of the back seat, lean my

head back against the headrest, and close my eyes. They still sting from all the crying.

"OK, Gwen, let's see if you can find it," Mom says. She puts on her seat belt but doesn't start driving.

"Find what?" I ask.

"Remember? The invitation? To Thaís's birthday party?"

"Oh yeah!" I say. I can't believe I keep forgetting about something that means so much to me. I lean over my lap and dig in my backpack. TBH, my backpack is gross (38. Disorganized). It's full of really old papers that I never remember to take out and old bits of pencils and stuff. It's not full of moldy or smelly stuff, like old food, because I know I'm terrible about keeping my backpack clean, so I never put anything like food inside it, ever, at all. But somehow even paper and pencils start to stink when they've been folded up in a backpack for long enough.

I find the purple envelope pretty quickly. I hand it to Mom without opening it. My name shines in gold on the front.

Mom smiles and slides the invitation out of the envelope. The smile disappears fast. "Gwen," she says. "This is a slumber party."

"I know," I say. I could have sworn I told her that.

"And it's today!" Mom says. "It starts in two hours."

"What?" I ask, shocked. I guess I never thought beyond how awesome it was getting an invitation. I never looked at when it actually was and put it on the calendar.

"Cupcake, you can't go to this," Mom says.

"No," I say. The tears that were there a minute ago come back, more quickly than before. "I have to."

"But we don't have—"

I want to let Mom finish her sentence because I know that's the not-bad-kid thing to do, but I can't.

14. Constantly interrupting

"I told her I'd go!" I say. "I can't just not show up."

"You told her you'd go?" Mom asks. "You RSVPed without asking me?"

"Well . . . She asked, and I had forgotten, and I was going to talk to you . . . I have to go, Mom."

Mom sighs. She's shaking her head. Her bangs are going crazy dancing on her eyebrows but it doesn't seem to be making her feel any better.

"I have to," I insist.

"You haven't packed," Mom says. "You don't have a gift or a sleeping bag."

"Let's go get one," I say.

"Honey, you're exhausted. And that was a really hard meeting. And I think we both need some rest and—"

"Please, Mom! I'm sorry I didn't tell you. I'm sorry I didn't look at the date. I'm sorry I forgot. I always forget everything and this . . . this day. It can't also be the day I don't get to go to the first birthday party that I've been invited to for years. Please, Mom. Please."

Mom shakes her head again and then the shakes go into her arms and fingers and legs like her whole body has to shake out how much of a disorganized mess I am.

"OK," she says. "Let's go to Target."

# 13

## LETTER FRIENDS

A few hours later, Mom and I stand on the doorstep of Thaís's mansion. Maybe it's not a real mansion but it looks like one to me. There are so many windows. I'm sure I'll get lost.

On my shoulders, I have Mom's backpack (mine was too gross) stuffed with pajamas and clothes for tomorrow and my toothbrush and everything else I need. Mom packed for me so I know it will all be there. Under my right arm, I have a brand-new, rolled-up teal-and-black sleeping bag. Under my left arm, I have the at-home pedicure set I bought for Thaís's birthday present. Mom wrapped it in the car so it's a little messy (but way better than if I had wrapped it), and it has a big purple bow right over the part where she messed up from rushing. My braids are tight on my head because for some reason Mom did them and redid them until they were perfect without me even asking. Maybe because I have ADHD now.

Maybe having a disorder that people understand will mean it's easier to get what I need.

Except medicine. Of course.

"Make sure you say please and thank you, OK?" Mom is whispering. "And don't forget to greet Thaís's parents. And don't stay up all night, OK? And make sure if you're up late that you remember to lower your voice. And make sure that you leave room for the other kids to talk, too, OK? And don't forget to say happy birthday right away."

I'm nodding along to all the reminders even though this is sort of like asking me if I know how to behave. I'd get 100 percent on the Sleepover Behavior Quiz too. I hope that this is different than PowerKids. I hope that knowing how to behave means I actually do behave tonight.

*Confidence, please help me.*

The buzzing inside me turns from nerves to excitement. My first sleepover.

And something—anything—to think about besides the fact that Mom won't let me have those blue pills.

Ms. Gonzalez opens the door. I immediately smell melted cheese and grease and hear my old friends laughing.

"Gwendolyn!" she says. "You're the last to arrive."

I knew I probably would be because we're thirty minutes late.

31. Poor sense of time

"The girls are in the back. Follow the sound of their voices. We were just about to serve the pizza."

I step inside the door, forcing my muscles to move slowly. I turn and look at Ms. Gonzalez. "Thank you for having me," I say.

She smiles. "Aren't you polite," she says.

I can feel Mom's body relax behind me.

"What time should I pick her up tomorrow?" Mom asks.

"Oh right," Ms. Gonzalez says. "My oldest has a basketball tournament tomorrow. We have to leave at ten, so if you could pick her up any time before that, that would be great."

*Ten,* I think. *Ut-oh.*

I turn to look at Mom. I know she has a meeting at ten on Saturdays. She usually lets me sleep in and goes by herself every Saturday. It's the only time she leaves me home alone. I thought I'd be able to stay at Thaís's until lunchtime. I guess Mom did too. I half expect her to say I can't sleep over after all. She hesitates, but then smiles and nods.

Maybe she'll skip the Saturday meeting? Even though I know it's her favorite. She's been going to it for as long as I can remember.

Mom waves and walks away. I watch for a second, then I hear my name being called behind my back.

"Gwendolyn's here!"

"Hey, Gwen."

"Yes! Now everyone's here."

"Gwendolyn!"

My name has never sounded so beautiful. Before I follow their voices, I pause. I tell Anger and Sadness to go away, just for today. I tell them not to think about Dr. Nessa or Mom or what happened in that office, or Tyler, or ADHD, or blue pills, or anything.

Then I say, "Hi. Happy birthday, Thaís!"

My legs are running, even though running inside in someone else's mansion is probably not a great idea. My voice is too loud, like always.

But no one seems to notice.

When we finish our pizza, Margaret and Thaís pull out their phones. Hettie has hers out too for a second before she looks at me and remembers I don't have a phone.

"Well, what should we do?" she asks.

It takes me a minute to realize she's looking right at me. Even though it's the question she always asks me, I guess I didn't think she'd ask me here.

"I don't know," Margaret says.

"Let me think," Thaís says.

But they don't say anything. They don't even look up from their phones.

My brain is on fire. I have about fifteen ideas. But I don't know if I should say them.

The sleepover is just the four of us. The same four who used to be together all the time in fourth grade and earlier. It feels good but a little weird to be back here, sitting and eating pizza with a group of friends like I never was 6. Socially inept in the first place.

Thaís taps her foot on the floor. Margaret rocks in her chair.

Marty, I remember. I'm supposed to call her Marty now. I can't remember when that changed or why she stopped going by Margaret.

Hettie picks up her phone too, then puts it back down.

What's the point of a sleepover if we're just going to sit here?

"What do you want to do?" Hettie asks again, only this time she says it more like "What do *you* want to do?" and I can tell the *you* is me.

"Um, I got Thaís a pedicure set," I say. Then my face burns because I know I'm not supposed to walk into a birthday party and announce the present before the birthday girl even gets to open it.

6. Socially inept

13. Impulsive

10. No filter

But because I'm all those things my mouth keeps on filling the room with words, even though my brain knows I should stop.

22. Talks too much

"It has a little foot bath and a massager that you rub on someone's feet and, you know, those things that look like an *E* with too many branches that you put between someone's toes to paint them? And little lotions, and a whole ton of different nail polishes. Anyway, I know I shouldn't have said all of that because it ruins the surprise for when you open it but . . . we could give each other pedicures?"

"Cool!" Thaís says.

"Yeah!" Hettie says.

Then they both freeze and look at Margaret. Marty. Her cheeks are a little pink. "I don't . . . I don't think I want to paint my nails. Anymore. I mean, I could. But it doesn't feel like something I want to do."

"OK," Thaís says.

"But um . . . I could still do the foot bath?" Marty says.

"No," Thaís says firmly. "Let's come up with something that works for everyone."

All three of them are chewing their lips, thinking, and my brain is still on fire with ideas, but my face is also on fire now because I can tell I said something weird, even though Thaís said *cool* and Hettie said *yeah*.

Then I remember that back in Hettie's room when she told me that Thaís still thinks I'm funny, and that everyone still wanted to be my friend, she also said something about the *stuff that happened with Marty*. I'm supposed to know about the *stuff that happened with Marty*.

It's too quiet in here, and I'm too embarrassed so more words tumble out of me. I hope Confidence is awake.

"We could play spoons. Remember that old card game? Or we could play ultimate spoons, which is a game I made up that's just like spoons except the spoons are hidden all around the room, so when it's time to grab a spoon, you have to go look for it. I mean, I made it up, but I've never actually played it. But I think it would work. Or we could play ultimate ultimate spoons, which is when they can be hidden anywhere in the house. We could also play ultimate Uno, if you have Uno cards, Thaís. That's when you play Uno except each player can't look at their last card until you only have one left. It's, like, way harder. I've played that one with my mom, but it would be fun to try with more than two people. I mean, they aren't real games. Ultimate spoons or ultimate ultimate spoons or ultimate Uno. I just thought them up. You know? We could also play sardines. That's like hide-and-seek except opposite because there's one person who hides and everyone else looks for them, and then, if you find them, instead of tagging, you hide with them until the last person finds them. But I've also been thinking that game could be fun if you made it so that when the last person finds everyone she immediately runs away and hides. Then everyone else has to look for her. So it's like never-ending sardines, you know? Or we could make up our own game, maybe?"

Everyone is looking at me. Six big eyes stare at my face. My words are burying us all.

"I don't know, maybe all that's dumb. But sometimes I think there's a way to make a game more fun by adding to it or changing it so there's not like a winner or a loser or whatever. But also we could, you know, watch YouTube."

It's silent for another minute. I'm so hot I'm sweating and I think I'm going to melt like a Popsicle so that I'm just a puddle of Gwendolyn staining this chair.

But then Marty says, "Let's do all of that!"

Hettie says, "Yeah!"

And Thaís says, "I'll go get the spoons. And the cards. And Uno. But let's start with never-ending sardines!" She jumps up from her chair and then freezes and says, "This is going to be the best sleepover ever!"

It's easy during the games and the cake and the movie not to think about what happened today with Mom and Dr. Nessa. It's even easy when we all put on pajamas and crawl into sleeping bags on the living room floor and start to whisper. It's easy when Mr. and Ms. Gonzalez appear over and over to tell us to be quiet, but no one is quiet.

But when the lights are out and everyone except me is breathing deeply, all the worries come rushing back into my head. Every time I close my eyes, I see blue pills.

Suddenly there's a whisper above all the measured breathing around me.

"Is anyone still awake?"

I sit up before I can even think about it. I look around for the owner of the voice.

Slowly another body appears on the other side of the room. Marty.

She wiggles around in her sleeping bag until she finds her green glasses and slides them onto her face.

"Oh, Gwen," she whispers. She runs her hand over her hair. I remember when she was little and nervous she used to twist her curls. No more curls now, though. Her hair is short, almost like a crew cut. "I can never sleep at sleepovers."

"Me neither," I agree before I even know what I'm saying. But I guess it's true because this is my first-ever sleepover, and I haven't slept at all.

"Want to talk on the couch?" Marty asks, pointing.

I nod. Inside my head, I look for Confidence. My higher power. He's awake.

Marty adjusts her glasses, and we both crawl out of our sleeping bags and tiptoe over to the couch.

We settle ourselves, facing each other. Marty is wearing an old baseball shirt, the kind that's white but the sleeves are blue and three-quarters length. And a pair of blue boxers. Her hair is fanned up at the forehead. I forget when she got this haircut, but it looks good on her. I don't know how she keeps it fanned up like that, even when she's been in a sleeping bag.

"I'm glad you're here?" she says, as if it's a question.

"You are?" I say.

"Yeah. You're so fun!"

*Fun* sounds like the opposite of 6. Socially inept.

I try the word out in my head.

*Gwendolyn is fun.*

55. Fun

"When you're not here everyone stays on their phones the whole time."

"Well I don't have a phone," I say. I wonder if that's what makes me fun.

"Yeah, but also," Marty says, "Hettie and Thaís usually end up spending all this time giggling about boys and looking at their pictures online and . . . well, you know. I'm not into that. I'm glad you figured out how to be cool with me."

"Cool with *you*?" I say. Who wouldn't be cool with Marty?

"Yeah, you know, since I came out as NB last year."

"You came . . . oh!"

This is the *stuff that happened with Marty.* This is what I'm supposed to know. But what is NB?

"It was really hard for a while, TBH," Marty says. "I mean, I thought it would be easy for you guys, but . . . then Thaís was all confused about how to have a best friend who's not . . . who is . . . you know, like me. And you only wanted to hang out with Hettie. It took Hettie a while to get used to it, and it took Thaís longer, and you . . . well, Hettie swore you didn't have a problem with me, but I know it's a lot for people to figure out. Especially when people are busy with their own lives. And you are, of course. I know you found your brother and all that, and that's been good for you. I'm happy for you about that. It just . . . well . . . it makes sense that you didn't really have time to think about how to still be friends with me once I came out as NB. And sometimes that hurts my feel—"

"No!" I say, too loudly. I freeze for a second to see if Hettie and Thaís wake up, but I don't even have time to fully check. I don't even have time to ask what NB is. The words need to get out of me—now. "I stopped hanging around because *I'm* socially inept. It didn't have anything to do with you,

Margaret." I shake my head. 45. Forgetful. "Marty."

"Socially inept?"

"Marty. Marty. Marty. I'm sorry. But see? Socially inept," I say.

Marty shrugs. "People still accidentally use my old name a lot. I know it was an accident, and you corrected yourself. That's the important part for us."

"Us?"

"You know, NB people."

I have no idea what she's talking about, but I can tell I'm supposed to. I'm trying to figure out a way to ask what NB is when she says, "What do you mean you're socially inept? I haven't heard of that before."

"S-O-C-I-A-L-L-Y space I-N-E-P-T," I say. "It means I don't know how to have friends."

*"What?"* This time Marty is so loud it could probably wake up everyone. But our friends still don't move. "Who told you that?" Marty asks.

"The teachers," I say.

"I'm sorry, *what*?" Marty says again. "I don't think that's a thing. That sounds . . . mean."

I sigh and try to sort through everything in my mind, to start at the beginning without letting my whole brain fall out of my mouth.

"I had an IEP assessment," I say. "In fourth grade. And I wasn't supposed to read it, but I did. And it said I'm socially inept. It said I only had one real friend and couldn't maintain any other friendships."

Marty's eyes are wide. Her head is shaking. "No," she says.

"Yes," I say. "That's what it said."

"No. No, no, no." Marty's head goes back-and-forth, back-and-forth like she can't believe it. "That can't be what happened. They told you you didn't have any more friends than Hettie, and you believed them?"

"Um . . . yeah," I say.

"But *we* were friends," she says quietly.

"I thought so too," I say. "I thought we were but then no one was talking. I mean, none of us were talking to each other, and no one told me why. And when the IEP report said we weren't friends and . . . I thought . . . it made sense because . . ."

This is confusing, though, because the IEP report also said I don't have ADHD, and now Dr. Nessa says I do.

Marty doesn't seem to hear me. She says quietly, "I always thought it was because of me. Because I'm . . . different."

"I'm the different one," I insist.

"No," Marty says. "You're fun. You're perfect. And so am I. I'm just NB."

"What is NB?" I ask, finally.

"You don't even know what it is?" Marty asks, louder. "All this time I thought you didn't want to be my friend. Just because I was being myself. But it turns out you don't even know?"

My mouth opens, but for once there are no words. I shake my head.

"It means I figured out I'm not a girl . . . I'm still sort of figuring it out."

A lightbulb goes off for me. "Like trans?" I say.

"No," Marty says. "It turns out gender identity is a spectrum. Like a number line. Like you know how Mr. Olsen was saying there are infinite numbers between one and zero?"

I nod.

"It's like that. Like there's male on one side and female on the other and a whole lot in between. Trans means you belong on one edge, even if some people think you should belong on the other. NB means nonbinary. It means I belong somewhere in the middle. Not everyone uses the abbreviation. A lot of people just say nonbinary all the time. But I like NB because it's easier to text."

"Oh," I say. "How do you spell it?"

Marty tilts her head at me like that's an odd question.

"See?" I say. "I'm weird."

"N-O-N-B-I-N-A-R-Y. Binary means when there are only two choices for something. So nonbinary means, like, not fitting into either of those two choices. And you aren't weird, Gwendolyn."

"Wait . . ." I say. "Wait."

My heart is beating faster. Anger is stirring a little bit in my ribcage. But I'm not angry at Marty. I'm angry at myself.

"It's OK if it takes you some time to get used to it," Marty says.

"No, it's not that. It's . . . that means changing your name was really important," I cry.

"Oh," Marty says. She looks away from me, toward our sleeping friends. "Yeah."

"And I kept messing it up," I say.

Marty opens her mouth. Then closes it then shrugs.

"I didn't know," I say. "I thought it was just a new nickname or something. And remembering things like that is hard for me. So I didn't . . . I didn't know. But this is different. This is important. I'm not going to mess it up again."

Marty's eyebrows go up. "A lot of people still mess up and deadname me," she says. "At least you correct yourself."

"But I'm not going to correct myself anymore because I'm not going to do that. Ever again," I say.

Marty smiles. "I believe you, actually," she says.

"What else do I need to know?" I ask. "I don't want to make any more mistakes that seem small to me but are actually big to you."

"Um." Marty squints behind her glasses. "I guess . . . I might switch my pronouns one day."

"Your pronouns?" I say.

"Wow," Marty whispers. "I haven't told anyone that yet. It's weird to say out loud. For now, I'm sticking with she/her. But I might switch to they/them. It's just something I think about."

I nod. "I'll be ready," I say. I have a lot to learn about being friends with someone who is NB.

"That's kind of amazing," I say.

"What?" Marty asks.

"Just . . . you. That you knew that much about yourself in fourth grade. Like enough to tell all the adults they were wrong about you. You knew something so real and strong and . . . I mean, I'm always waiting for an adult to finally . . . I don't know . . . I want someone else to teach me how to be, you know? I'm waiting for a therapist or a teacher or my mom or a test to tell me who I am. But no one can figure me out. And you . . . you figured yourself out. And then you taught all of them how you *get* to be."

"I never thought of it like that," Marty says.

I smile at her. I'm impressed. I'm jealous. I'm so happy that we're sitting on this couch.

"So wait . . . What happened with your IEP?" Marty asks.

"Huh? Oh, nothing," I say. "But then I had another meeting with a real doctor and it turns out I have ADHD."

I freeze. That's the first time I said it out loud. It feels good. To sum everything different about me up in a few letters.

"You do?" Marty asks. "When did you find that out?"

"Today," I say. "Like right before this party."

"Wow! Today? That's huge," Marty says. "How do you feel about that? About having ADHD?"

I smile. "I like having the letters. Like you."

"The letters?" Marty says.

"NB. ADHD. They're different but they both come with letters."

"They're easy to text!" Marty declares.

"Yeah! We're the letter friends."

Marty giggles. "Letter friends. I like that. So why did you see a new doctor today?"

It's choppy and weird but I end up telling Marty about Dandelion. And finding Tyler. And my brain cracking at PowerKids. And all the awful doctors and therapists. And Dr. Nessa. And how I'm dying to go to horse camp.

That's when she interrupts me. "I'm going to that camp!" she says.

"What?" I say. "You aren't in PowerKids."

"Not for after school but I am for summer camp," Marty says, excited. "So is Thaís. Maybe she'll sign up for the horse camp part too."

My heart speeds up in a way that's both good and bad. I imagine that week and it's almost too perfect. Horses. My brother. Lots of friends. All day, every day, for a whole week. It seems too good to be true, and also so close to being possible I can taste it on my tongue.

"Wouldn't that be awesome?" Marty is saying.

"I really hope I don't mess it up," I answer.

"You won't," Marty says. But she doesn't know. Because even though we could have been, we haven't been friends for two years.

And she doesn't know that Mom won't let me have the one thing that could really really help me get to horse camp.

Those little blue pills.

# 14

## A GOOD KID IN THE MAKING

Mom is the first parent to ring the doorbell the next morning before Mr. Gonzalez has even served us the pancakes he's making. I ask Confidence to help me get out the door without waking up Anger, even though I'm hungry and exhausted. He does.

"So how was it?" Mom asks as we walk to the car.

It's finally really spring. I hear some birds singing and I can't see any snow. The morning smells good, like the freshness of new sunlight. But I'm exhausted from not sleeping.

"Good," I say.

"Good?" Mom says. "That's it?"

"I'm tired," I say.

The other words that would typically burst out of me swim sluggishly around my brain.

*They think I'm fun.*

*They want to be my friend.*

*They're all going to go to horse camp.*

"Really tired," is all I can say.

And suddenly Mom laughs. It's a sort of beautiful bell ringing. I haven't made her laugh like that in a long time. "I remember that. The post-sleepover exhaustion."

I don't answer. I'm too tired to use my jaw. Our red car looks hazy in the Gonzalezes' driveway, and I don't know if that's because I'm so tired my eye muscles are giving out or because the sunlight is new and there's a fogginess to the morning.

I climb in the back seat and strap in like usual.

"You can sleep when we get home," Mom says. "But we aren't going right home."

She turns around and hands me three things. One is an egg and cheese sandwich on an English muffin. I take a bite before even looking at what the other things are.

My iPad.

Headphones.

"I'm going to your meeting?"

I watch the back of Mom's head as she nods. "I'm sorry, but you know how important this one is to me, Gwen. I never miss a Saturday morning."

"I know," I say. "It's OK."

I'm almost asleep in the car when we get there. We walk in, and Mom leaves me on the bench with my headphones and iPad and her backpack still packed from the party.

Saturday mornings are Mom's favorite because the meeting

is small. It's just a handful of women who meet together. Afterward they go out to breakfast, and Mom says they talk and talk. Even though I never see them, except on the rare times Mom takes me to this Saturday meeting, I think they might be her best friends.

I put on my headphones but I don't turn on YouTube videos of horse trainers like usual. Instead I put on my happy playlist, take my notebook out of my backpack, and open my iPad to the Twelve Steps site.

I think Step Three worked! I didn't understand it, but I kept talking to Confidence and asking him to be in charge and—bam—the sleepover was fine! Marty even told me some important stuff. I didn't mess up once.

I manage to get the words on the page but my eyes keep closing as I write. I close my notebook and pause my music because I don't want any noise in my head. I can hear a little of what's happening on the other side of the door. I know I'm not supposed to listen because of the whole anonymous thing, but I'm too tired to watch YouTube or even to move so I curl up on the bench and put my head in a nest of my arms.

I fall asleep for a while, but when I hear my mom's voice, I wake up.

She isn't talking to me. She's talking to the meeting.

"She has ADHD," my mom is saying. "It's funny. You'd think most kids would consider that bad news. But when the doctor told her, it actually made my kid happy."

She's talking about me. That has to mean it's OK to listen, right?

"I think she's that desperate for help. And then, immediately—there in the doctor's office we were in another fight. She wanted the medication. Stimulants. You know, like Adderall? Yeah, that's scary. I'm terrified of pills like that. I mean . . . it's not an Advil, you know? She's only eleven. And she's my daughter—so she's predisposed to addiction, right? It's—well, the thing is that after the doctor's appointment, we got in the car and it turned out she was supposed to be going to a sleepover. Like, right that minute."

I don't usually hear my mom talk like this. Almost everything about her voice is different. It sounds deeper. Fuller. Somehow both more and less patient than when she's talking to me. Like patience is irrelevant right now. When she's talking to me, she's almost always either losing her patience or trying to hold on to it.

"And the thing is, my kid, she was *dying* to go. She had nothing: no sleeping bag, no gift. She hadn't mentioned the sleepover, though she'd had the invitation for days. But she really, really wanted to go. Part of me was thinking, you can't want to go that much because if you did, you wouldn't forget to tell me about it, right? But in that moment . . . that wasn't true. It hit me, you know? That it's not about motivation. That even though she wanted to go to this party she had still messed it up."

Messed it up. I messed it up. Like everything.

"I keep trying all these things to help her try harder. To motivate her. But she was so motivated for that sleepover . . . I can't motivate her away from ADHD. I can't. She needs a kind of help I don't understand. And the doctor is good. Careful. Patient."

Mom sighs huge.

"So I'm going to let her try it. The stimulants, I mean. But boy am I going to need your help to get us through this transition. Thank you."

I freeze on that bench and turn those words over in my head a few times.

*I'm going to let her try it.*

They spin and spin until they paint a smile on my tired face.

Something is finally going to work. I'm going to horse camp.

I'm going to be a good kid.

# 15

## SIMILAR GENETIC MAKEUP

The next day I copy Step Four into my Top Secret Notebook. Then I stare at it.

Step Four: I made a searching and fearless moral inventory of myself.

I'm under my lofted bed again with Mr. Jojo's feet padding across my shoulders. My eyes go back and forth between my notebook and my iPad, which is open to the Twelve Steps site.

Step Four has a lot of big words, but I know them all.

*Searching.* As an adjective it means examined carefully.

*Fearless.* It means holding nothing back on account of being afraid.

*Moral.* It means the good stuff or admitting to the bad stuff.

*Inventory.* It means a list of everything.

I read and read what the website says about how to do this

step. I keep coming to the same conclusion.

A "Searching and fearless moral inventory" is a list of things that are bad about me. Like a bunch of terrible things that describe me all numbered on a piece of paper.

Like fifty-four of them.

I already did this step.

I scroll to the next step and copy it.

Step 5: I admitted to ~~God~~, Confidence, myself, and another human being the exact nature of my wrongs.

I don't have to admit the fifty-four things to Confidence because he lives inside my brain. Same with myself. There's only one thing left to do.

I go to bed terrified.

The next day, Monday, my list is in my shoe as always. After lunch I run out to outdoor break. I wave to Hettie and Thaís and Marty where they're standing by the basketball court but don't stop running until I almost crash right into Tyler at the bottom of our tree.

"Braids?" he asks.

"Yes," I say. "Thank you."

I plop down on the grass in front of him and take a deep breath. Carefully I build the glass wall around us and block out all the sounds and movements of our classmates. I have to do this right. I have to do it carefully.

I'm going to show Tyler my list.

"Do you know why my mom's nervous about me riding horses this summer?" I ask, looking for a way to start.

"No," Tyler says. "You already know how to ride them."

"Yeah. It's not about riding. It's about . . . I get angry sometimes."

"Me too," Tyler says. "I'm still going to horse camp."

"Yeah," I say. I shift around on my butt. The ground is still hard and frozen beneath me. We're back in a cold spell. "But I mean really, really angry."

"I used to get angrier," Tyler says.

"I do things without thinking. It's called impul—"

"Impulse control," Tyler says. "I have that too. Or I mean, I don't have it. Because that's one of those things you're supposed to have, right? Not like immaturity, which we have too much of." He finished off my braids.

"Um, right," I say. This isn't what I thought Step Five would feel like. I'm supposed to be more embarrassed. Ashamed. I stand and shift to one foot to take off my shoe. While I'm pulling out my list, I start naming things on it. "I'm also disorganized and forgetful and overly emotional and I talk too loudly and—"

"My meds help with all of that," Tyler says.

"All of it?"

"Yeah," Tyler says. "They . . . even me out. Make me take my time before acting. And . . . well, yeah. All of it."

I stare for a moment, trying to imagine what that's like. What it would be like for me.

I wiggle my foot back into my shoe and hold my list out to Tyler. "Here."

"You're supposed to have impulse control, though," Tyler says. He stands but doesn't take the list. "And you aren't supposed to get so angry."

"Huh?"

"Because you don't have ADHD," he says.

Anger jumps up, awake.

"You don't need to have ADHD to get angry!" I shout. But then Anger closes his googly eyes because I remember. "And, actually, it turns out I do have ADHD."

"I thought so," Tyler says. Then he glances at his feet. "I'm sorry. ADHD stinks."

I shrug.

Tyler reaches for the list, then stops. "Wait. Maybe it's a good thing."

"It is," I say. Maybe it stinks to have ADHD, but it stinks even more to have ADHD and not know you have ADHD, and I'd have it whether or not Dr. Nessa said I did.

"Right! Maybe Adderall will help you with all that stuff, too. And then you can go to horse camp."

"Oh!" I say. I'm shocked. He's right.

Everything on my fearless and moral inventory is about to change.

While I'm being 24. Spacey, Tyler grabs the list from me.

"Give it back!" I say.

I don't want him to see it anymore. He doesn't have to see

it. No one ever has to see it.

"What is this?" he asks.

"Give it back!" I say again, jumping at him.

He twists away from me and unfolds the papers. "Fifty-Four Things Wrong with..." he reads, but then I leap on top of him and pull it out of his hands. It rips a little at the corner.

"Look what you did!" I scream.

"I didn't do that," he says.

"You snatched it."

"You were trying to give it to me," he says.

"Well, I changed my mind!" I'm way way way 23. too loud.

"Whatever. I change my mind too," Tyler says.

"That doesn't even make sense," I spit back.

Tyler's hand comes up and, for a second, I think he's going to hit me, but instead he yanks out my rubber band and my left braid comes loose.

He laughs his crazy laugh.

"Stop it!" I yell.

"Don't cry and be all overly emotional, now. Don't be bad impulse control," he taunts.

"It's *impulsive*!" I say. And then, being 13. Impulsive, I run away. I break through the glass wall and run all the way to Hettie.

"Gwendolyn?" Hettie says when I show up at the picnic table where she's been talking to Thaís and Marty.

"Will you do my braid?" I ask. "Tyler's being a butt."

Hettie and Thaís and Marty all giggle, which surprises me.

"What's so funny?" I ask. I sit.

"Let me do the braids," Thaís says. Her fingers on my scalp are suddenly familiar. I forgot how she used to braid my hair a lot back in third grade.

My friends are still laughing.

"Why is that funny? Because I called him a butt?"

"Yes," Marty says. "That's a funny nickname for your brother."

"I'm going to call Nolan a butt today," Hettie squeals.

"No, don't," I say. "It's mean . . . right?"

"Yeah, but he's my brother," Hettie says. "It's kind of normal to be mean to your brother."

"It is?" I ask.

Thaís is really good at braids. She's halfway done already and it's even tighter than the one Tyler did.

"Yeah," Marty says. "Like, I can't call Tyler a butt. But you can because he's your brother."

"But you're never mean to Nolan," I tell Hettie.

She laughs again. My heart is enjoying making her laugh. My brain is annoyed at it. I'm so confused.

"Um, yes, I am," Hettie says.

"But you never punch him," I say.

"Actually," Hettie says, giggling, "he's the only person I've ever punched."

"Sibling rivalry," Thaís says as she secures my hair elastic. "It's real. Sometimes just the sound of my sister's voice makes me want to scream."

"My brother is so annoying," Marty says. "Yesterday he just took my iPad while I was in the middle of a video. He claimed he had to do 'homework.' I kicked him in the shins." She pauses. "What a butt."

They giggle. I join in. Thaís starts redoing the braid Tyler had just finished without even asking me, and it feels good.

"Why did he need *your* iPad to do *his* homework?" Hettie asks.

"Well, we share an iPad," Marty says. "But still." For some reason everyone laughs again. I do too.

I don't tell them that me calling Tyler names is different than them calling their siblings names.

I don't tell them how my mom says that Tyler and I can't have sibling rivalry. How she says that sibling rivalry is a thing that happens to real siblings who grow up together and share all their parents and have to fight for resources.

How the fact that Tyler and I don't share a mom or a house means we can't share problems either.

I let their laughter calm down the lightning bolts in my brain and double-check for my pencil before Mr. Olsen's afternoon class.

Before lunch on Tuesday, Mom picks me up and takes me to a different doctor's office in downtown Madison. I think it's weird but Dr. Nessa doesn't prescribe ADHD medicine, or any medicine. Mom explains that this doctor is one of the only ones in the city who takes our insurance. So we'll go to him for the meds, and if it's simple that will be that. She said that if things get complicated, Dr. Nessa will recommend a different doctor and we'll have to figure out a way to get insurance to pay for it. "That's confusing, Cupcake, and you definitely don't have to understand it all. But I want to be honest with you that we chose Dr. Nessa because she's the best. We're choosing this doctor differently. I want you to understand I'm working within the limits of the real world. But don't worry. I got you."

I'm not worried at all. I know it will work. All I need is exactly what Tyler already has.

The office doesn't look like Dr. Nessa's. The only things in the waiting room are rows of metal chairs and lots and lots of people. We have to stand in a line to check in with some nurses behind a glass window. Then we sit in two of the metal chairs. They're cold, even though it's finally not freezing outside anymore.

I look around. Most of the people in this room are adults. There's even a TV on the wall playing some sort of grown-up talk show. It seems like the doctors here see people for all sorts of different reasons. I guess I was expecting it to be sort of like my pediatrician's office: one waiting room full of toys and only a handful of doctors who all do the same thing.

My braids are loose because Tyler didn't get a chance to redo them yet. I rub my head on the back of the chair and wait. After a few minutes we're taken down a long hallway to an office with no windows. It's not like a regular doctor's office with one of those plastic half-bed things. It's also not like Dr. Nessa's office. There's a big brown desk in the middle and there are boxes and files everywhere. It looks like the office version of the mess in Tyler's room.

The man behind the desk stands to shake Mom's hand. He doesn't reach for mine.

He has gray hair and a full white beard, almost like Santa. But his cheeks are completely pale—no sign of cherries. And his nose is long and lean, not like a button. And he's wearing a boring white shirt and tan pants. Definitely not Santa.

I feel nervous when I sit in the chair next to Mom. I'm not used to this. Every doctor I've ever seen has been a woman.

"You can call me Dr. Mark," he says, finally looking at me. He looks quickly back to Mom. "So I read her file. It's good. Thorough. Very clear she has ADHD. We'll still start slowly though in order to be sure we don't increase any aggression."

"Increase aggression?" Mom asks.

"If the root source of most of a patient's anxiety is in fact ADHD, then it is more likely the stimulant will calm the anxiety and lead to an increase in executive function, which will further keep the anxiety in check. But it's also the case that an increase in stimulation can multiply anxiety if its root cause is something different, and that can make patients act more aggressively, especially juveniles. There are other side effects to watch out for: depression, hallucinations, etc."

"What?" Mom says. She sounds scared. I'm a little worried that I'm not going to get the meds after all.

"These side effects tend to happen because the prescription is wrong. In other words, because it seems so clear that she has ADHD, those sort of side effects are unlikely. But look out for digestive issues, headaches. Be sure she eats before taking it and drinks plenty of water all day."

My brain is racing through all these long words trying to spell them.

A-N-X-I-E-T-Y

E-X-E-C-U-T-I-V-E

J-U-V-E-N-I-L-E-S

D-E-P-R-E-S-S-I-O-N

D-I-G-E-S-T-I-V-E

I miss most of what he's saying.

"I think it's best to start with Concerta."

"Oh," Mom says, surprised. "I thought you'd say Adderall."

"The good thing about Concerta is that it's long-lasting. Twelve hours. We don't need to worry too badly about the crash."

"The what?" Mom asks.

"But my brother takes Adderall," I say.

Dr. Mark looks at me, then looks down at the papers in his hands. Then back up at Mom. Mom is still asking what he means by "the crash." He interrupts her.

"It doesn't say anything about a brother in this file," he says.

Tyler isn't in my file. I wonder if I'm in Tyler's. I wonder if the next time Tyler sits down with a doctor like this the doctor will say, "I see he has a sister who is also diagnosed with ADHD." I wonder if Ms. Christakos sees how Tyler and I are an *us*, even if it doesn't include our moms. I think that may be true. I think that may be why she helped us. I think maybe it's really only my mom who has been worried about Tyler and me being close.

"He's her half brother. Paternal. He doesn't live with—"

Dr. Mark interrupts Mom again. "Regardless of where he lives, they share similar genetic makeup. That's important information."

Mom frowns but I try not to look at her.

"We'll start with Adderall. If it works for a relative, it's the best bet to work for the patient."

"What about this crash?" Mom asks.

"We'll watch out for it. I'll worry about the meds. All you need to do is pay attention to her, OK? If the medicine is fine, nothing will happen for the first few days and we'll increase the dose. And if it's good, then you'll see an obvious improvement."

Those words—*obvious improvement*—echo in my head as Dr. Mark gets my height and weight and blood pressure.

Mom keeps sighing on the way back to the car. Her bangs

are going crazy.

"That's not exactly what I expected," Mom says.

"What did you expect?"

"I'm not sure," she says, but I think it maybe is one of those things she doesn't want to tell me until I'm older. "OK, Cupcake, let's go back to school."

We get in the car and she starts to drive.

I swallow big. "Mom?"

"Yes?"

"Will you please redo my braids?" I spit the words out as fast as I can, trying to get the question over with before Mom gives me that disappointed look. "It's just Tyler redoes them at outdoor break usually but I wasn't there today and now they are all loose and I—"

"Tyler redoes your braids?" Mom asks, surprised. "Every day?"

"Yes. Well, usually. Well, sometimes Hettie does them."

Mom pulls up to the school and parks in the parking lot.

"But . . . someone redoes them? Every day?" Mom asks. Like that first question wasn't really about Tyler. Maybe it wasn't.

"Yes," I say. "Tight braids help me concentrate. And they don't stay tight all day. I need them redone."

"Every single day?" Mom says again.

"Yes!" I say.

Mom clears her throat like she wants to ask more questions

but she parks and says, "OK, hop on out and stand still."

I study her face as she walks around to my side of the car. I look really closely. But there's not a hint. Not a smidge. Not a note of disappointment.

Maybe Mom is starting to believe in the medicine too.

# 16

## EXTREME SIDE EFFECTS

That night, the night before I get my own little blue pill, the night before my life changes, I sit in my bed with my light on but I don't pull out my list. Instead, I open my Top Secret Notebook.

Mr. Jojo scurries around beneath me in his cage. I hear his little feet tapping across the wood chips and his little mouth slurping at his water bottle. I love hearing him scurry at night just like he's supposed to. I love that someone keeps watch while I sleep. I let his little noises relax me and start to write.

Step Five: Check! Well sort of. I think it counts even if I didn't exactly show Tyler my list.

(I'm never, ever, ever going to let anyone see my list.)

I turn the page and copy from my iPad.

Step Six: I was entirely ready to have him remove my defects of character.

I freeze with my pen still poised on the paper. I don't know what this step means by "him," but I also don't care. The timing is so perfect, I can't believe it. "Him" will be my pill. It will remove all my defects of character. Just like Tyler said.

In the morning there's half a blue pill next to my milk and oatmeal. Mom is standing at the kitchen counter, her back to the table.

"Eat first," Mom says. "You need to take it on a full stomach."

I take a bite of oatmeal. Mom leans against the counter behind me, sipping her coffee and scrolling through her phone. When I'm finished with my food, I pick up the blue half-circle. I start on a mini-dose. I won't feel the meds for a few days. I know that because Dr. Mark told us. Still, I whisper to it, "Remove all my defects of character. Please." Then I swallow.

"What did you say?" Mom asks.

I jump about a foot in the chair. I forgot she was behind me.

24. Spacey

"Nothing," I answer, trying to sound light. I hope she didn't hear me. I know she'd recognize the words as part of the Twelve Steps if she did.

Mom stares for too long.

"You aren't going to feel any different today, Gwennie," she says, eventually. "I don't want you to be disappointed."

"I know," I say.

And it's true that I'm the same fifty-four things today. I'm a little late to school because I forgot to pack my backpack until the last minute (4. Lazy, 31. Poor sense of time). Then as I'm rushing toward the front door at school I crash into one of the seventh graders (26. Clumsy).

Then, of course, in math class when Mr. Olsen tells us to get to work, I don't have a pencil. Thaís is absent so she doesn't sneak a pencil over my shoulder like she did yesterday. I have no choice except to ask Mr. Olsen.

He hands me one and says, "That'll be five percent."

I know the pill isn't working yet, but, in that moment, I feel different, just a little bit.

Usually, when Mr. Olsen says *five percent* I feel like crying or screaming, depending on whether Sadness or Anger is bigger at that moment.

Today, I shrug.

Slowly over that week and the next, the little blue circles by my breakfast plate multiply. For the first few days there's half. Then a whole. Then one-and-a-half. Then two. No matter how many there are, I ask them to remove my defects of character, then swallow.

None of the Fifty-Four Wrong Things is any different because I'm not up to what Dr. Nessa calls a "therapeutic dose." But still, I go two entire weeks without yelling at Mr. Olsen or Ms. Hayley or my mom. I'm forgetful and lazy and picky and impulsive and bad at transitions, but all the mistakes aren't piling up inside me the same way. Instead, each one hits and then *ping* rolls away. I imagine one day the entire list will *ping* away one by one. Number 11 will roll up on itself and somersault off my page, and I'll never be overly emotional again. Number 2 will lace up its sneakers and jump off the loose leaf and *wham*, I'm no longer a picky eater.

Then, one day, I open my backpack in math class and find a pencil.

This is the day. Therapeutic dose day.

Adderall is working.

Thaís is already trying to sneak a pencil over my shoulder, but I turn to her with wide eyes. "I have my own today," I whisper. "Thanks."

I half-expect her to cheer for me. I half-expect Mr. Olsen to give me a high five. I half-expect a song, a party, a parade. *I remembered my pencil.*

But no one notices. A pencil in my backpack is a normal thing that doesn't require celebrating, even though a pencil *not* in my backpack is a huge thing that requires a punishment.

I'm surprised at how big Sadness is, even with my own pencil in my hand and factoring 1,568. Sadness stretches through my shoulders like he agrees with Mr. Olsen that this is no big deal.

Confidence wakes up though. He marches in quick circles inside my skull, then takes off running. *We did it! We did it!* he yelps.

It's weird to have Confidence awake when Sadness is stretching. But that's what keeps happening.

Confidence celebrates again the next day when it's time for

us to hand in homework, and it only takes one second for me to find my complete packet in my backpack.

He celebrates again that night when Mom calls me to dinner, and I start setting the table before she even asks.

*Listen to me,* Confidence yells in my ears. *Don't pay attention to that other guy.*

So I try not to notice how Sadness reaches into my arms and legs and squeezes tight on my brain and heart. I'm trying not to notice how finding my pencil in my bag feels boring. How being able to concentrate on my homework turns Mr. Jojo's scampering from comforting to annoying. How when Hettie asked yesterday, "What should we do during free time?" yesterday—for the first time either of us could ever remember—I had no answer.

Somehow Adderall has made Sadness so big, I even forget how to miss Dandelion.

Friday, in science class, Mr. Olsen organizes a review game, sort of like *Jeopardy!* Adderall performs another miracle and I don't let my team down. Instead, I, Gwendolyn Rogers, get the winning answer.

Confidence is ricocheting around my skull like a bouncy ball, and I try to focus on him and not on how winning should feel better than this. Mr. Olsen congratulates our team and gives us each the grand prize—a mini Rubik's Cube.

The Rubik's Cube steals my brain.

For the rest of class, I keep twisting it under my desk.

When Mr. Olsen dismisses us to the schoolyard I walk with my head down and bump into the doorway on the way out of the room. Some kids laugh but I don't care, and I barely hear them because I have the whole green side completed, and I think I can get the yellow one in like two moves.

Hettie comes up to me in the hallway. She's talking but I don't hear her. She says something about horses. I say "yeah" without listening.

I twist the top row of squares to the right and *yes!* I have yellow done. But now green is ruined.

Suddenly we're in the schoolyard. I don't remember walking down the hall.

"Gwendolyn," Tyler calls. I don't look up. He runs up to me and Hettie. "Did you hear?"

"Hear what?" I ask on autopilot. Red and white are almost lined up, even if that does ruin yellow.

"They announced it!" he yelps.

Two twists to the right and I'll have white all done.

"Announced what?" Hettie asks.

"The dates. Horse camp is the first two weeks of summer. It's two weeks this year!"

"Two weeks?" Hettie yells, jumping up and down.

I just need to get this white side done, and then I can jump up and down with them. But when I make the next move, it ruins all my progress on the white side, but lines up the red side so it's only missing two squares.

"Gwen? Did you hear me?" Tyler asks.

"Yeah," I say.

"What's wrong?"

All that's wrong is that I have one blue square on the red side, and every time I try to twist it, I ruin my white side. And now yellow is all messed up. "Nothing," I say. "I just need to finish."

"Finish?" Tyler says, laughing. "That's a Rubik's Cube. No one finishes those."

Finally, I look at him. My voice is louder and angrier than anyone expects. Even me. "Well, I am going to finish it, OK? So leave me alone."

"Whoa," Tyler says.

"Gwen?" Hettie whispers.

"Sorry," I mumble, my eyes back on the colored squares. "I just need to do this."

Tyler shrugs. "I want to celebrate," he says. He looks at Hettie. "Want to race to the swings and back?"

"Sure," she says.

They run.

A teeny Gwendolyn deep in my gut tries to take off after them. She squeaks like a mouse, "Don't leave without me! Don't leave me out! I'm excited for horse camp too!"

But everyone ignores her. Especially me.

Even as I twist the Rubik's Cube all through PowerKids and on the ride home from school, I realize it: If I take more

Adderall, there will be no more teeny Gwendolyn. There will be no more real Gwendolyn at all.

Adderall is killing her.

An hour later I'm at home, and my Rubik's Cube is in my backpack and I didn't solve it and I don't care. My head is on the kitchen table because I'm so tired, I can't lift it.

My mom puts a plate of roast chicken, green beans, and mashed potatoes next to me.

"Gross," I whine. "You know I hate mashed potatoes."

49. Reactive

17. Rude/Impolite

2. Picky eater

Mom is calm. She's always calm these days. Even though I'm extra rude in the evenings because, when the meds are out of my system, I get hungry and exhausted. "I know you haven't preferred them in the past. Feel free to eat around them," she says.

She sits down next to me. I manage to pick my head up for a second to slice into my chicken. The pile of white mush next to it gurgles at me. It's so gross I want to puke just looking at it.

It's weird. Mom knows how I feel about mushy food. She hasn't tried to get me to eat mashed potatoes in a long time.

"Can you please take them off my plate?" I ask her.

Mom sighs long and slow. She's disappointed but still calm.

"You know I hate them," I say, again. 23. Too loud.

"A lot has been changing," Mom says, standing to scrape

the offensive corner of my plate. "I thought maybe you'd give them another chance."

"I'll never give anything that mushy a chance," I declare.

"Fine, Gwendolyn," Mom says. She sits next to me and takes a bite of her own mashed potatoes. I pick my head up and eat, too.

We're silent, and I don't want to talk to her. Words keep popping into my head anyway, though, and some of them almost make it out of my mouth and into her ears. I want her to be the next to say something, but that never, ever happens. Why can't I eat in silence?

"Mom?"

"Yes, G?" Mom says, like we didn't have that almost-fight at all.

"What did you mean? What's changing?" I feel a little better with some food inside me.

Mom smiles. "You know you were right about meds, don't you? It's been weeks without a phone call home. You've been remembering your books. Your backpack is more organized. You come home from PowerKids with a lot of your homework already done."

"Oh," I say. Sadness shifts into a new pose inside me, tightening his hold on my face and reaching all the way into my legs.

"I thought you'd be happier," Mom says. "I'm telling you that you can stay on Adderall."

"No, I can't."

10. No filter

I didn't even realize I wanted to say it until I do. I didn't even feel the words coming until they're on the table next to my chicken bones.

"What?" Mom asks. She sounds shocked.

"Remembering my pencil isn't making me happy. And today I ignored Hettie and Tyler in after school, even though they were running races together. I kept working on my Rubik's cube instead of having fun," I say. "I know it seems like I'm doing better, but I'm so . . . bored. All the time. It's like nothing matters. Is that how it's supposed to feel?"

"I . . . what? I didn't notice, Gwen."

When I look up, my mom looks heartbroken.

"I know Adderall is making your life better. I can keep taking it if you want."

"No Cup—"

"I thought they were working. I thought they were removing . . ." I stop myself before I say *my defects of character.* "Do I have to choose between being angry a lot and being happy never?" I ask.

"No," Mom says firmly. "That's absolutely not right." She thinks for a minute. Then she says, "I met with Dr. Nessa a few times by myself before we started this medication. I wanted to be sure it was the right decision."

"I didn't know that."

"She told me the key to knowing if a medicine for something like ADHD is working is that it will make you more like yourself," Mom says.

"So . . . It'll make me *enjoy* myself more?" I ask.

"Not exactly. It will make you *be* yourself more."

"Huh? How can I be more like my own self?" I ask.

"That's a good question. But it sounds like on Adderall, you didn't feel like yourself at all. On the right stimulant, you would feel more like yourself, not less. In other words, you should be able to remember your pencil and be happy about it."

"Really?" I say.

Mom nods. "So no more Adderall, OK? I'll talk to Dr. Mark and Dr. Nessa tomorrow. You should be feeling totally you before the morning."

Sadness shrinks away from my face. I smile. "I already do," I say.

I'm thinking about what it would be like to take a pill that makes me remember stuff and still be me. That seems magic and impossible.

"And you know your friends should forgive you for ignoring them today," Mom adds. "They should understand that the real Gwendolyn would never choose a Rubik's Cube over fun."

"Friend," I say.

"Huh?" Mom says.

"It was only one friend. I ignored Hettie and Tyler. Hettie is my friend. Tyler is my brother."

Mom sighs, and it feels like she suddenly loves me a little less. "You know what I mean."

Of course I know what she means, but I don't want her to

mean it. She means Hettie and Tyler are the same. She means Tyler doesn't really count as a brother.

"Anyway, thank you for being honest with me, G. That was brave."

I get up and give Mom a big hug. I go to bed feeling a lot better.

But the next day, when Mr. Olsen is walking around the room collecting our research paper part of our science fair project, I put page one and page three on my desk but I can't find page two. Page one was a bunch of fill-in-the-blank questions, page two was the graphic organizer, and page three was the essay outline, which you had to use the graphic organizer to fill out. I know I did all three pages. But when Mr. Olsen gets to my desk, I only hand him two.

"You're missing something," he says. He says it loud enough that everyone looks.

"I'm sorry," I say. Which is weird because I'm the one who's going to fail and Mr. Olsen looks like he's enjoying it.

"You didn't think the second page was important?" he asks.

"I did the whole thing," I say. "But I can't find it."

He lowers his eyebrows, and I know the sarcastic voice is coming. "You mean to tell me that you somehow kept track of page one and page three but lost page two?"

Everyone laughs. I ignore them.

"Yes," I say.

Mr. Olsen stares at me like he doesn't want to believe me,

then shrugs. "Well the consequence is the same whether you lost it or didn't do it so I suppose your honesty is irrelevant."

"I'm not lying!" I shout. I miss Adderall now. I miss how it meant I didn't lose pieces of paper from the middle of my homework. I miss how it made me so I didn't even care if Mr. Olsen was sarcastic.

"Lower your voice. This is not a gym," he says, and my face burns.

He walks away. I feel a tap on my shoulder behind me. It's a pencil.

"Here," Thaís says. "Just in case."

I whisper "thanks" and take it from her because, of course, I don't have a pencil today either.

I'm upset the whole day until PowerKids when I start playing basketball with Hettie and some boys from our class. It's a tough game, and I'm running and sweaty and out of breath, and all this moving has finally made Anger go back to sleep.

The boys are beating us, but only by one point. I'm about to take a three-point shot. If I make it, we'll win.

The whistle blows before I can try.

We have to go inside now. But I don't move. I don't drop the ball.

I really want to throw it. I want to take this one shot. It'll go in, and then we'll win, and then I'll go inside.

My knees are bent. My elbows are bent. The ball is cradled softly in my fingers. I'm ready to take the shot, but I don't. I know it's not worth horse camp.

"Don't even think about throwing that ball, young lady!"

Ms. Hayley is beside me. How did that happen?

She's yelling even though I haven't done anything wrong. I just wanted to take one three-point shot, which would take three seconds. And I was trying stop myself from doing even that.

I hesitate.

"Put it down!" she screams.

Anger wakes up, sudden and ferocious.

I turn and throw the ball as far as I can away from the basket, into the school parking lot.

"Gwendolyn." Ms. Hayley says my name like it's a curse word.

I hate that sound.

I run after the ball to fetch it but Ms. Hayley screams, "Get back here right now!" like she thinks I'm going to run for the fence again when I'm not. I swear.

I go right back to her, but it doesn't matter. When we get inside, she calls my mom anyway.

When my mom arrives, she's mad at me. She yells at me the whole way home.

What happens to my brain because of Adderall might not be my fault, but what happens because of ADHD definitely is.

I'm bad all over again.

# 17

## SUPERGWENDOLYN

One morning about a week later, there's a different pill next to my oatmeal.

"What's this?" I ask my mom. She's behind me again, pouring herself coffee.

"Hmm?" she says.

I hold up the pill. "What's this?"

"Oh." Mom sits next to me. "Remember how I said different pills will hit you differently?"

I nod.

"This is Concerta. It's different than Adderall in that it lasts all day. It also affects your brain a little differently. I'm hoping it won't have the same antisocial effect you described before. Dr. Mark says there's reason to hope that was actually part of your crash."

"My crash?" I ask.

"You know," Mom says. "The feeling of the medicine leaving your system."

"Oh, you mean eating dinner with my head on the table."

Mom laughs. "I'm sure that was a part of it, too," she says. She kisses my forehead.

I pick up the Concerta. I look at the orange oval rolling in my palm. I'm a little nervous to take it but I'm also sick of everything—forgotten pencils and blank spaces on my homework and Ms. Hayley's phone calls—being all my fault.

"We're starting with a half dose," Mom says. "Just like last time. So you probably won't notice anything today. But remember, if you do, it should feel good. Not perfect. But things should get easier without making you less happy."

"More my own self?" I say. "I still don't really get it."

"Like . . ." Mom shakes her bangs in concentration. "Like a superhero version of you."

I smile at her. "SuperGwendolyn?" I say.

And oops. I'm hoping again.

At first Concerta doesn't feel any different than normal Gwendolyn. Then, the third day, I sit in math class and Mr. Olsen says, "Please take out your pencils and copy the problems on the board." I open the front pocket of my backpack and stare. Ten perfect yellow pencils stare back at me. I did it. I followed all the steps from asking for pencils, to finding where Mom had put them, to putting them into my backpack, to opening the right pocket and now here they are.

I want to sing. I'm buzzing. I could jump off my desk and fly. I have pencils *and* I'm happy.

Concerta is working.

"I suppose you need a pencil, Gwendolyn," Mr. Olsen says. I hadn't realized it, but the rest of my classmates are already copying the problems. "That'll be five percent."

I hate his voice. I hate the up-and-down notes of sarcasm. I hate everything about him. Anger swells inside his shell. I'll make that stupid voice be quiet.

"Not today!" I say, triumphantly. I pull a pencil from my backpack like Arthur pulling the sword from the stone. I hold it over my head like it's a trophy.

Mr. Olsen raises one sarcastic eyebrow at me.

Kids laugh. I don't know if they're laughing at the way I pulled the pencil out or if they're laughing at his sarcastic eyebrow wiggle. Either way each laugh is like a needle scratching my skin. Anger grows larger.

"What?" I demand.

"I'm not sure that'll work out for you," Mr. Olsen says, nodding at the pencil over my head.

More laughing.

I bring the pencil down to my face and look at it.

"Well I only need the pencil *sharpener*," I say.

Giggles. Snickers.

I stand to sharpen my pencil. I'm glad to have a reason to move. I need to let all that laughing soar past my ears. I need to shrink Anger back to his regular size.

Why is he so big? Laughter isn't something that would usually make him grow.

"Sit until you have permission to use the pencil sharpener," Mr. Olsen demands. "And that will still be five percent."

"What?" I say, not sitting.

"I asked you to sit," he says.

"How can that be five percent?" I ask. "I have the pencil."

"Unprepared is unprepared," Mr. Olsen says. "And I said to sit."

"I'm not unprepared!" I shout, still not sitting. I can't believe I'm shouting at a teacher. But the words keep bursting out of me. "I'm prepared. Look!" I shove a pencil toward his face. I bend and grab three more pencils and shove each toward him. "Prepared! Prepared! Prepared!"

"I have asked you to sit," he says.

But I don't sit. I walk toward him so fast he flinches.

The way I notice the flinch is weird. He's standing right in front of me, but that's not how I see him. Instead, I'm looking at the classroom from above. Concerta is controlling my body and my voice, and it was afraid I would sit down and be quiet like he asked. So it banished me to the ceiling.

I watch ConcertaGwen as she walks past the teacher to his desk at the front of the room. She deliberately takes her time lining up the pencil sharpener and inserting her first pencil. It whirrs to life. Her eyes dare anyone to say anything. She beams like she's won.

What was there to win?

Above myself, I'm terrified. But I can't seem to get back into my body.

Eventually Mr. Olsen shrugs. He moves on and starts explaining one of the math problems. I sharpen all four pencils, then go back and copy the work from the board. I'm in my body again, but I'm not sure how that happened.

Later that day, on the ride home, Mom asks, "How does the Concerta feel? Any of the depressive symptoms you mentioned before?"

The first thing I think of is flying out of my body in Mr. Olsen's class today. But then I remember the moment before that. How happy I was to see all the pencils. That whole thing was weird but it wasn't *depressive.* Sadness didn't even register.

Plus, I spent all of outdoor break laughing at stupid jokes with Tyler. I spent free time this afternoon racing Hettie and playing basketball, and I didn't even get upset when we lost.

So what if I got angry in Mr. Olsen's class? I'm always angry. I'm a girl with Anger inside of her. That wasn't Concerta. That's just me.

"Nope," I answer my mom. I'm not 100 percent sure that's true, but more than anything I want my mom to be happy. So I add, "I think it's the SuperGwendolyn medicine."

She smiles at me in the rearview mirror. "I love you, kid," she says.

* * *

Concerta is working. My brain is better. There's usually a Tyler's-room style mess inside my skull, but when my Concerta kicks in, it tidies itself right up and every thought and memory and fact is ready for me on the right shelf.

The only problem is that, when my brain isn't messy, there's more room for Anger inside it. He keeps waking up at random times when he never would have before. He stalks around inside my nice, clean brain like he's looking for a reason to grow. Like he wants me to yell at someone or punch someone or run away, even when I'm feeling fine.

Over the next few days, I spend a lot less time looking for things that are lost and doing the same homework assignments more than once. But I seem to be spending more time yelling at my friends and muttering to myself under my breath.

At PowerKids on Thursday, Hettie and some other girls and I are playing a game of ballet HORSE. It's like regular HORSE except whenever you take a basket you have to stand in a ballet position. Hettie nails a free throw from fourth position. I'm up next.

I walk to the free throw line and imagine the ball going in the hoop. I'm focusing on my mental game when I hear Tyler and his friend, James, approaching.

"Hey, what are you guys playing?" James asks.

"Ballet HORSE," Hettie answers.

I line up my feet. The back one is right on the free throw line. The front one is exactly twelve inches in front. Both sets of toes point out. It is a weird position to shoot a basketball from.

"Can we play?" Tyler asks.

"Sure," Hettie says. "You're up next."

I try to focus.

"Good luck, Gwen," Tyler says. But there's a little laugh in his voice like he's saying it in the sibling rivalry way, not the nice way. There's been a lot more sibling rivalry in Tyler's voice since I started taking Concerta.

I take a deep breath. I tell myself it's OK if the ball doesn't go in the net. It's OK if I get an H. It's OK not to win. I take the time to prepare so that, if I miss, Anger will stay in his shell and not crack my brain.

Then I bounce the ball once and throw it. It's a perfect arc. It goes in!

"Wow!" Hettie says. "You're up, Tyler."

I run after the ball and rebound it to him. He stands on the free throw line and shoots. It goes in but—

"H," I say.

"What are you talking about?" Tyler says. He's louder than he usually is. Like maybe he's a little mad at me. "It went in." Like maybe he came over here just to beat me.

"It doesn't matter. Your feet weren't in fourth position," I say.

"What the freak is fourth position?" Tyler yells.

I step closer to him. "Your feet have to be like this." I demonstrate. "You get an H."

"Let him try again," Hettie says.

"No, he gets an H," I insist. "He took the wrong shot."

"It doesn't matter what position your feet are in," Tyler says. Anger is growing and growing. Soon his shell will burst. "This is HORSE."

"Actually this is *ballet* HORSE. And it's *my* game. And it *does* matter."

"Your game?" Tyler yells. "You think everything is yours." By now every other kid is frozen around us, watching.

"I do not," I say. "But this *game* is mine. I made it up. If you want to play with us, you get an H."

"I don't think so, Bossypants," Tyler says. "You can't say HORSE is your game. Everyone plays HORSE."

"Did you even hear me?" I scream. Concerta takes over again and throws me out of my body. There's no ceiling outside so I'm even farther away when I hear ConcertaGwen shout, "We aren't playing HORSE!" I watch her step toward Tyler. She's right in his face. "We're. Playing. Ballet. HORSE." She pokes him hard in the shoulder with the last two words.

"There's no. Such. Thing," he says, poking her twice right back. I'm so far away from myself I can't even feel it.

"I just told you!" she shouts, her face only an inch from Tyler's, her words spraying all over him. "I made it up!"

"Well it sounds like the stupidest game in the world."

I haven't been in my body so I didn't feel Anger break his shell. I didn't feel him bouncing around my insides trying to reach my brain. But he's there now. He's climbing into my skull. I can see him from where I watch among the clouds.

"I didn't realize my own sister was so stupid."

I'm on Concerta so it's not supposed to happen. It does anyway.

*Crack.*

Then I'm not watching myself. I'm not in my body. I'm not anywhere. My brain cracked so hard, it turned me off.

The next thing I know, Ms. Hayley is screaming "Gwendolyn!"

I'm on top of Tyler. He's lying on the asphalt.

"Gwendolyn!"

My name as a curse word.

I look around and see my brother's lip bleeding, my classmates staring, the teachers yelling.

"Gwendolyn!"

Maybe my name should be a curse word.

I leap off of Tyler's body and run to the cafeteria. I put my own self in the chair where I always wait when they call my mom.

I'm 90 percent Anger and only 10 percent Gwendolyn while I listen to Ms. Hayley on the phone. I'm so much Anger that when I hear Ms. Hayley tell her that I'm officially out of PowerKids forever, I almost explode all over again.

On the ride home, I'm 75 percent Anger and only 25 percent Gwendolyn, so I don't say a word to my mom as she talks about how disappointed she is in me.

At home I'm getting close to 50/50 and then, suddenly, I'm famished and exhausted and my head is on the table next to my plate of pizza. Mom didn't say she ordered pizza because I made her too worn out to cook. But I know that's what happened.

After dinner, when the crash is over, and I'm finally 100 percent Gwendolyn, I climb into bed with my Top Secret Notebook.

Step Six: No check. Adderall didn't remove my defects of character. Concerta added a whole lot of new defects. And God or Confidence or whoever didn't do anything at all. But I'm sick of Step Six.

I turn the page of my notebook and copy the next one from my iPad.

Step Seven: I humbly asked him to remove my shortcomings.

What? I'm pretty sure shortcomings are the exact same thing as defects of character.

What's the point of this? What's the point of any of the steps, or any of Mom's plans, or of any pills? What's the point of trying? Nothing makes me better.

I pause because I hear the *doo-dee-doo*.

I climb out of my loft to eavesdrop without even telling myself not to this time.

"I think we're done with stimulants," Mom is saying. "The doctor agrees."

My body floods with relief, and then the relief rushes right back out. No stimulants means no more randomly getting worse, but it also means all the fifty-four things keep hanging on me like deformed Christmas ornaments.

"OK," I hear Marsha say. "So what's next?"

"I wish I knew," Mom answers. Her voice sounds a different kind of broken. Her words do too. Mom always knows what's next.

Mom has stopped hoping.

I climb back into my loft. I pick up my pen again.

When I was little, my mom called me delightful. She delighted in me. I miss that.

I don't think she ever will again.

I don't think she can.

# 18

## Gwendolyn on Pointlessness

The next day I roll out of my loft and pad to breakfast in my socks. My mom has made the usual scrambled eggs and cheese. There's a jar of salsa on the table because I used to add ketchup to my eggs, but then it wasn't on the food plan so I started using salsa, and salsa on eggs is delicious, so I kept using it.

I sit and stare at the glass of milk next to the plate. It's alone. There's no pill for after I'm done eating.

My stomach growls like it has every morning over and over for the past month. When I'm on the stimulants, I never feel like eating. Which means at night and in the morning, I'm starving. I wonder how my stomach will be the rest of the day today.

Mom comes behind me and kisses my cheek. "Good morning, Cupcake," she says. "Let's get you some nice, tight braids."

I smile because that's a nice thing to say, but the smile is sort of forced.

"Can I use your phone to text Tyler?" I ask.

Sadness is big in me now. Big and furry and stretched around every one of my muscles. He's all there is now. There's no making me better. There's no horse camp. There's not even PowerKids, which means I don't get to hang out with Hettie every day anymore, unless I give up outdoor break with Tyler.

The battle is over.

ADHD won.

"Sure," Mom says, grabbing her phone from her purse and handing it to me. I text.

**Me: Hi. It's G. I'm sorry. I'm really sorry.**

**Tyler: I know.**

**Me: I didn't want to hit you. Not really.**

**Tyler: I know. I have ADHD too.**

**Me: The meds messed with my head.**

**Tyler: Oh**

**Me: I'm not taking them anymore.**

**Tyler: Good**

**Me: But I can't go to horse camp.** But then I delete that one before I send it.

It's weird but Tyler will be more mad about me missing horse camp than he was about me hurting him. Somehow missing me is worse than being hit by me. I don't want to have to tell him I can't go to horse camp. I can't even hope for it anymore because I'm kicked out of PowerKids.

Sadness is huge, but he's mixed with this weird sort of relaxed feeling.

I lean into it as Mom pulls a chunk of hair good and tight so that it almost hurts. I take a bite. Even though I'm hungry eating seems pointless because for a month I've been filling my stomach every morning so I could swallow a pill and it would work the right way.

"What's happening after school?" I ask.

"We're going to see Dr. Nessa. She was able to squeeze in an emergency appointment."

"What?" I say. I want to turn and look at my mom but she's holding three strands of my hair, so I can't. "What about work?"

Mom sighs. "I had to call in sick, Gwennie."

"No, no!" I say. "You can't lose your job. I'll . . . I'll walk home. I know the way."

Mom almost-laughs. "It's ten miles, Cupcake. Anyway, I won't lose my job over one sick day," she says. "It's Friday. That gives us three days to figure out a solution, OK? We'll figure something out by Monday."

"What?" I say.

"What do you mean?" Mom asks.

"What will we figure out by Monday? If I can't go to PowerKids and I can't walk ten miles, what will I do after school?"

"Today I'll pick you up and we'll go see Dr. Nessa. And then I don't know, but by Monday we'll come up with something, OK?"

Tears dance on the outside of my eyes, threatening to touch my eyelashes. But Anger is asleep. Even though everything is unfair, Anger is asleep. It's probably because Mom isn't angry either. It's probably because I'm with Mom, and I can see how the unfairness is surrounding both of us, clutching us, freezing us. She can see how hard I tried to make everything better. She can see how failing isn't the same thing as wanting to be bad.

And I can see how hard she tried too.

"I forgot my pencil," I tell Mr. Olsen that morning. I don't tell him that I took all of the pencils out of my backpack to sharpen them so we wouldn't have to repeat the King Arthur scene. I don't tell him I almost remembered to put them back in my backpack, and now I'm surprised they aren't there.

He sighs and rubs his beard like I've been forgetting a pencil every day for weeks. He should have fresh patience for my pencil-forgetting.

For some reason his disappointed sigh isn't as upsetting as usual though.

*Remove my shortcomings.*

Almost by accident, I'm doing Step Seven. I don't know who I'm asking. God? Confidence? The mess in my brain?

Mr. Olsen walks to his desk and returns with a newly sharpened yellow #2.

"Keep it, Gwendolyn," he says as he hands it to me. "I'll take five percent in exchange." He walks back toward the front of the classroom.

"Actually," I say. He turns. "Can you keep it here for me? That way I won't forget every day. And I have a lot of pencils at home. So I don't need to keep taking yours and then losing them every day. I can use my at-home pencils for homework and the pencil in your classroom at school. You could keep the same pencil here for me, and I'll pick it up on the way into the classroom, and you can take it on the way out, and then it'll always be here, and that will be easier."

It's a perfect solution. I can't believe I've never thought of it before. But, for some reason, Mr. Olsen rolls his eyes.

"You're in middle school now, Ms. Rogers," he says. "You should be able to keep track of a pencil."

I take a second before I answer. I check my rib cage. Anger is still sleeping. Sadness is big and stretched everywhere, and everything, including this conversation, seems to have no point.

And that very pointlessness means I don't have to try so hard. I don't have to pretend I can do things when I can't.

"I maybe *should* be able to keep track of my pencils," I say. "But I can't."

With that one truth something purple and slippery shows up. He's smooth and shiny and shaped like a ribbon and he slides around my body, quickly filling me up. Sadness is still there but this new thing mixes with it.

Relief.

*It's OK that there are things you can't do,* he whispers.

*It doesn't matter that you can't do them anymore.*

*Horse camp is gone.*

"Actually," Mr. Olsen says, "you'll bring this pencil—this exact pencil—back this afternoon."

But I know I probably won't. Anger stays asleep because I don't care.

After lunch, I trudge across the schoolyard toward our tree. It stinks because I don't know when I'm ever going to see Hettie if I keep hanging out with Tyler at outdoor break. But I need to see Tyler.

Even though there are no meds inside me, I'm walking slowly. Things—normal outside things like balls and chalk and screams and the limbs of my classmates—are rushing outside my head, but they don't have the same distracting qualities as usual. The mix of Sadness and Relief has slowed every bit of me down, even my muscles, my brain.

Then I see my tree. I jolt into my own body again. I run. I sprint.

"What are you all doing here?" I ask.

It's not just Tyler inside the imaginary glass wall. It's Hettie and Marty and Thaís *and* Tyler. They're all together, which means I can see them all at once.

"We were talking about what happened yesterday," Hettie says. "It's not fair. It makes no sense."

Tyler clicks his tongue.

Hettie shoots him an annoyed look but I don't think he sees it.

I plop down between Hettie and Marty. I'm sitting in a circle with my brother and my friends. Sadness retreats a little.

"What's unfair?" I ask.

"That you're not in PowerKids," Hettie says.

Suddenly I'm itchy. I turn to Tyler. "Will you redo my braids?"

"Sure," he says. He stands and walks behind me.

"You braid hair?" Marty asks.

"He's great at it," I say, happy for the subject change.

Because Hettie is wrong. It *does* make sense that I'm not in PowerKids. It *is* fair . . . or at least it's fair to me. Because I'm the one who hit Tyler.

But it isn't fair to Hettie. I didn't think about that before. About how Hettie will be alone at PowerKids today when she didn't do anything wrong.

"That's so cool," Marty says, watching Tyler twist and pull my hair.

"I mean, they kicked you out?" Hettie is saying. "They can't do that!"

"I don't want to talk about it," I say.

"But you have to," Hettie insists.

I shift around in the grass. It's poking my ankles where my socks don't quite reach to the bottom of my pants. I keep shifting so that it will keep poking.

"We have to fix it," Hettie says.

"I don't think we can," I say. From the way Thaís and Marty are quiet and Tyler's tongue is clicking, I can tell no one agrees with Hettie. They all know that what I did was super messed-up, even if they forgive me.

I make my voice as quiet as I can. "I want to go to PowerKids, too. I actually need to go to PowerKids. I don't know what I'm going to do after today because my mom had to take the day off just so that I didn't have to walk ten whole miles to get home. But Mom can't just stop working forever."

"See?" Hettie says. "We need to fix this. They can't kick you out for what you did."

"But, Hettie . . . I hit Tyler," I say.

Hettie looks at Tyler, exasperated. He clicks his tongue.

"You were on drugs!" Hettie's voice explodes so loud we all jump. "It's not like you just randomly decided to scream and hit people. It's not like you ever used to hit Tyler before you started taking those stupid pills."

It's quiet when she's finished. Too quiet. I know how she feels because I always lose control of my voice and my volume and stuff, but Hettie never does.

Finally, I say, "That's not how it works. I mean, my mom's in

Alcoholic—" I slap my hands on my mouth when I remember the next word. *Anonymous.*

I did it again.

But then I look around the circle. At people who care about me. Who want to spend a whole Friday outdoor break talking about what I'm going to do without PowerKids. Mom tells her AA people about me. Maybe I'm sometimes allowed to tell some people about her.

"Anyway, she says that she's responsible for all of her behavior. Even the stuff she did when she was drinking. She doesn't drink anymore, and now she's like the most responsible person ever, but she says she's still accountable for everything that happened when she was drunk."

"My mom says that too," Tyler says. "Exactly like that."

Hettie leaps to her feet. She's angry. For some reason my Anger doesn't eat hers. He stays in his shell, peeking out a little like he's curious at what could get Hettie so worked up.

"But you weren't drinking," Hettie says.

"Drugs are the same thing," I say. "I'm responsible."

"No they aren't," Hettie says.

Thaís's and Marty's heads ping back and forth.

"I'm still the one who hit Tyler."

Hettie rushes across our little circle and kneels in front of me. Tyler's still pulling on my hair, and thank goodness. That's probably why Anger isn't awake yelling back at Hettie. Tyler's tongue is clicking like crazy, but he's not saying anything.

"A doctor gave you that pill," Hettie says, almost pleading.

"You followed the instructions. And then it didn't work. It's like if you suddenly puked all over everywhere because you took some medicine that had the wrong side effect. You wouldn't get kicked out of PowerKids for puking."

"But I didn't puke," I say.

"Whatever you did, if you did it because of something a doctor gave to you . . . it wasn't your fault."

"But—"

"Actually," Thaís interrupts me. "I kind of think Hettie's right." She sounds so calm compared to Hettie and me. "When I got my tonsils out, I was super weird waking up. I told my sister she looked like a frog. Usually I'd get in trouble for that, but since I didn't actually mean to say it, and I only said it because the sleeping gas made me weird, my parents laughed instead of punishing me. This is kind of the same thing, right?"

"I'm not . . . I don't think so," I say quietly. Tyler snaps the last rubber band in place and sits beside me, his tongue clicking.

"Wait . . ." Marty says quietly. "At first I thought Hettie was talking crazy but now . . . Yeah. I think she's right. It's not like you chose to take that pill. You had a side effect. It doesn't make any sense to kick you out of PowerKids for that."

"No," I say again. "No."

"Yes," my friends try to insist.

I see their point. But I can't think that way. I can't let them be correct. If I start to believe I'm not getting horse camp even though I deserve it . . . I don't know what Anger will do.

Finally, Tyler speaks up. "Hettie might be right, but it doesn't matter. Gwen and I, people like us . . . we do things we shouldn't all the time. Yeah, it was Concerta this time. But whenever we do bad things, almost every single time, we don't mean to. Right, Gwen? It's Concerta or it's something else. Sometimes adults decide it's our fault. Sometimes they don't. We don't understand one way or the other. We almost never know why we do anything anyway."

"What do you mean?" Marty asks. "People like you and Gwendolyn?"

"People with ADHD," Tyler says.

He looks at me and I nod.

At least I still have ADHD. Even without the meds, I'm not alone anymore.

"It's time to go in," Hettie says. "I'm sorry, Gwen. I still think you shouldn't be expelled."

We stand and start to jog back to the school. Marty comes up next to me. "I don't have any plans Monday," she says. "Want to come over? My mom can pick us up, and your mom can come get you when she's done with work."

I'm so stunned, I stop running. My brain spins searching for any reason this won't work. It seems so simple. It seems so possible.

Mom always comes up with the plans.

What will she think when I tell her I have a plan this time?

It takes too long but then I finally say, "Yes!" I'm too loud. Too fidgety. Jumping as I say it.

Marty doesn't seem to mind.

That afternoon I manage to bring Mr. Olsen's pencil back to class but now a pencil doesn't matter.

Mr. Olsen is walking around the room collecting final drafts. I should say, collecting their final drafts.

The written part of our science fair project. It was due today.

He stands in front of my desk.

"I don't have it," I say.

Usually when I say that it means I lost it somewhere, whatever it is. My pencil or my page two of my homework or my lunch. Usually *it* is in the trunk of Mom's car or on my mess of a desk at home or buried in my backpack, and I find it hours later. This time it doesn't even exist. I didn't do it.

I know Mr. Olsen is not going to understand.

"You don't have it?" he asks. He sounds like the forgetful one. Like we didn't just have a talk this morning about how I can't remember things.

"No," I say.

The whole class is staring. I don't want to say anything else. Maybe if I don't give any explanations or excuses, he'll move on.

My braids are good, but my stomach is jumpy anyway. I tap my feet against the linoleum floor.

"Where is it?" Mr. Olsen asks.

"Nowhere," I say because 52. Remarkably honest for someone who is sneaky.

Kids around me start snickering.

"Gwendolyn, we've been working on these essays for weeks," he says. As if that means anything at all. It's harder for me to remember something for weeks than for just a day.

"So?" I say. "I forgot anyway."

More laughter.

"So . . . You should have written it down," Mr. Olsen says.

Anger is awake now, using my heart as a trampoline, trying to launch into my brain. My brain feels soft, though. Not as fragile and breakable. Relief has done that. Hoping for horse camp was keeping my brain tight like a piece of masking tape pulled taut between two fists. Now it's fluffy. It's cotton. There's room for Anger to climb inside without it cracking.

"I *did* write it down," I say.

I wrote *science fair written report* down in my assignment notebook every day for all the weeks he's talking about. Writing it down didn't help me remember to do it, though, because it was written in there for so many days it became a part of the notebook. I didn't even really see it anymore, like I never see the date or the month at the top of the page. And anyway, I've lost my assignment notebook at least twice since we started working on the essay.

"Writing things down doesn't help me," I tell him.

"Tell me, Gwendolyn," he says. Sarcasm laces his words.

"What does help you then? What helps you remember things like pencils and homework?"

Anger is shaking me now. My whole body is practically vibrating.

"If I knew how to remember things, don't you think I'd remember them?" I say.

"That's enough sarcasm," Mr. Olsen says.

I stand before I realize I'm standing. Anger hasn't cracked my brain but he's in charge of my legs and arms and all my muscles.

"Are you kidding me?" I say. To a teacher.

"Sit down," Mr. Olsen says.

"No!" I shout. "You can't tell me not to be sarcastic. You're sarcastic all the time. You even admit it. It's like you're proud of it."

"Ms. Rogers—"

"OK, here it is without sarcasm," I say. My classmates have stopped giggling, but they've also disappeared. The entire room is Mr. Olsen, me, and Anger. Everything else is gone, and the three of us are crystal clear. "I'm telling you what I can't do and all you are saying is what I *should* be able to do. How does that help me?"

"How does it help *me* to give you pencil after pencil every single day?" he says.

"You're the teacher!" I scream. "Aren't *you* supposed to be helping *me*?"

"Ms. Rogers, you may sit now. Here. Or you may go sit in

Principal Dickens's office," Mr. Olsen says.

If I were still trying for horse camp, I'd sit back down and tap my feet and bite my lips and tug my braids while Anger got bigger and hotter and angrier. I'd force myself to be in that chair until my brain cracked. But I don't have to do that now. There's nothing more to lose.

"Fine," I say. I storm out of the classroom and run down the hallway until I collapse into the chair outside of the principal's office.

"Gwendolyn," Principal Dickens says, coming out her door. "What's going on?"

I shrug.

"You aren't going to answer?"

I shrug again.

"OK, I guess I'll call your mom."

"Fine," I say.

It's not like Mom is at work today anyway.

# 19

## DIAGNOSIS RE-INCONCLUSIVE

A few hours later, Mom bursts into Dr. Nessa's office, angry. She's been angry since she came to pick me up. Or she's been angry since the meds didn't work but now she's done hiding it.

She starts yelling when Dr. Nessa comes into the lobby, before we're even in her office. There are other kids here and my cheeks burn when I think about them hearing her. The words are so loud I can't even understand them. They're like little balls of fire. I know if I tell her she's embarrassing me in front of these kids, she'll say that's ridiculous because I wasn't embarrassed when I threw a fit in front of my whole after-school program, but of course I'm embarrassed that I did that now that my brain is connected, but when my brain is cracked, embarrassment goes away and I can't feel it at all, and right now my brain isn't cracked so I feel mortified.

Thankfully Dr. Nessa holds her office door open and Mom storms in.

"You said she had ADHD! You said the medicine would help her!" Mom is saying.

"I do have ADHD," I say.

Mom doesn't hear me.

"How is it that *you* made things worse?" Mom is saying. "I trusted you. Gwendolyn trusted you. We worked so hard to find someone we could trust. You were supposed to be different."

My eyes go wide at the way Mom uses *we.* I wish she would frame it this way all the time. Like Mom and I are on one team with my ADHD on the other. Like Mom isn't fighting me along with my ADHD.

She didn't used to ever use that *we.* The *we* popped up with the diagnosis.

Dr. Nessa walks around her long table and sits. She gestures for us to sit too, but Mom doesn't. I walk toward a chair then freeze, not sure what to do. Not sure which side I'm on.

"Nina, I—"

"My daughter is doing worse. She didn't even make it through the school day!"

"I can't imagine what—"

"You filled us up with all these promises and I . . . We . . . I . . ."

Mom can't finish.

"I'm so sorry. To both of you. I believed Gwendolyn was exhibiting ADHD. I thought it was a textbook case. I spoke too confidently. I'm genuinely sorry."

My heart stops.

*Believed?*

*Was exhibiting?*

Why past tense?

Mom sputters then freezes with her mouth open. "In all the therapists and psychiatrists and counselors we've seen, I'm not sure any has ever apologized," Mom says. "And believe me some of them really screwed up." She sits.

I'm still standing.

"I don't have ADHD anymore?" I ask, my voice small.

Dr. Nessa sighs. "Well, that's irrelevant now."

Irrelevant?

I-R-R-E-L-E-V-A-N-T.

Unimportant? Not of use?

*Irrelevant?*

It's the most relevant thing ever. It's why Tyler and Hettie and everyone forgave me so quickly. It's why Mr. Olsen should keep a stupid pencil for me. It's what makes me make sense.

"It's not irrelevant!" I scream.

"Oh!" Dr. Nessa looks surprised at my volume but she doesn't correct me. "You're right. Of course. What I mean is . . . We talked about trial and—"

"How can my ADHD not matter?" I yell.

Dr. Nessa and Mom both look at me.

"The thing about a diagnosis," Dr. Nessa says, slowly, like she's making room for me to interrupt her again if I need to, "is that it only matters insofar as it helps you. We don't know if you have ADHD, but we do know the treatment doesn't help you."

"I need to know if I have it," I say. "I need to know what my letters are."

"Letters?"

"Marty and me. We're the letter friends." The words are pouring out of me because I don't have a filter, and I don't have any impulse control, and now nothing can help me with that or with any of the fifty-four things. "You can take away the meds but I still need my letters."

"I'm not sure what you—"

"And the meds did help with some things. They made it so . . . I don't know . . . I need to have ADHD because . . . because . . . my brain needs a name."

"Are you saying life was easier with the stimulants?" Dr. Nessa asks.

"No," I say, exasperated.

Mom is staring at me, openmouthed. Like she somehow didn't realize that losing the letters would be the worst part of this. Like the only thing that matters is my behavior and not why I am the way I am.

"What are you saying, Cupcake?" she asks.

"ADHD is something," I say. "Something people understand. Something people make space for in places like PowerKids and school. If I go back to just having"—I stop myself before I say fifty-four things wrong with me—"you know, general problems, then no one ever helps me. No one ever understands."

"But not having a dis—" Mom starts. Dr. Nessa interrupts.

"That sounds frustrating, Gwendolyn," she says.

"It is. And it's lonely."

Dr. Nessa gives me a small, sad smile. "It must be so lonely," she says. "And I'm not saying you're neurotypical. I believe you have some neurological particularities that make it harder for you to function in the environments that you just listed because of how they're dominated by neurotypical culture and neurotypical people."

That's a weird way to say it. It's almost like she's saying that's hard for me because people don't understand me instead of me being the one who's . . . wrong. Bad.

"I can see how a diagnosis would make it easier for you to ask for what you need in a way that people can understand."

I nod.

"The truth is tricky, and it's not what you want to hear, but I always tell you the truth, OK?"

"Yeah," I say. I inch closer to Mom but she doesn't notice. I wish she'd put her arm around me.

"So here it is: the typical treatment for someone with

ADHD didn't work. It's going to be more complicated to diagnose you and to treat you, and that may make it more difficult for you to access the kind of modifications you deserve in the world. And that . . . stinks."

I giggle. Relief slips around my bones. I want to have ADHD, but the second best thing is talking to someone who understands me.

"And I know you've already been dealing with it. You've already had so many professionals fail you because your case is complicated." She turns to Mom. "But just because helping Gwen will be difficult, perhaps even more difficult than it is with other neurodivergent children, that doesn't mean she deserves the help less. You deserve help. Real help. You both do. And my job is not finished. That is, if you'll let me try again. I'd like to fix the mistake I made."

I expect Mom to answer, but she doesn't. She's staring at me. After what feels like a long silence Dr. Nessa says, "It's OK if you need some time to think about it, Gwendolyn."

She's talking to me.

"No," I say. "I don't need time. I need help!"

Dr. Nessa and Mom both chuckle.

"Let's talk about what happened in school today," Dr. Nessa says. "Why did you get sent to the principal's office?"

"Um," I say. "I sort of sent myself there."

"You what?" Mom asks. She's mad at me again. There's no magic *we* anymore.

"Why?" Dr. Nessa asks.

"Mr. Olsen said I could stop being sarcastic or I could go to Principal Dickens."

"Why did he say that?" Mom asks.

"Because I was being sarcastic," I say.

Mom lowers her eyebrows. "I don't think we're getting the whole story."

"I usually try to be as good and as still as I can, and hold it all in, and then I end up bursting at PowerKids. Today I went to the principal."

"Because you're not on meds?" Mom asks.

"No, because there's no horse camp," I say.

"What?" Mom says. I don't understand how she can be so confused.

"What's this about horse camp?" Dr. Nessa asks.

"I can't go to horse camp so there's no reason to try to sit there and be quiet while Mr. Olsen yells at me anymore," I say.

Mom's eyes go big and she starts to speak, but Dr. Nessa shushes her again.

"Let's rewind back to the beginning. Were you actually being sarcastic with Mr. Olsen?"

"I guess," I say.

"Why?" Dr. Nessa asks.

"Because he was sarcastic with me," I say. "He's sarcastic all the time. He thinks it's funny."

"What?" Mom says. "Why didn't you ever tell me that?"

"You never asked," I say.

"Asked?" Mom says. "How would I even—"

"Hold on, Nina," Dr. Nessa says. "When she's talking, let's try to keep her talking, OK?"

That's the weirdest thing anyone has ever said about me because I'm always talking.

"What was he saying that was sarcastic?" Dr. Nessa asks.

"He wouldn't listen to me. I forgot my science report—" I look at Mom. "Sorry. I just . . . I forgot to do it. And I forgot a pencil. And he wouldn't keep the pencil for me, and he wouldn't listen when I told him that writing things down doesn't help me. And then he started speaking in this voice that made me feel so small and stupid . . ."

Mom's face gets redder and redder. I don't want my words to keep coming. I don't want to make her upset. But they pour out of me before I can stop them.

"I tried to make myself feel better by speaking the way he was speaking. So I got in trouble."

Dr. Nessa nods. "It sounds like you were trying to explain your needs," she says. "And your teacher responded in a way that made you feel insecure and defensive."

"Yes," I say. Relief rushes around inside me even faster.

"That's a way I may be able to support you. I'll be contacting Mr. Olsen tomorrow."

"You will?" I ask, shocked.

"You will?" Mom says at the same time.

"With your permission, yes," Dr. Nessa says. "Sarcasm isn't ever great to use with middle schoolers, but it's especially bad to use with someone like Gwendolyn. Gwen, I can see even more clearly what having a diagnosis means to you. I can see how much easier it would be to explain your needs to someone like Mr. Olsen if you could say you have ADHD."

"Yeah," I say. I guess I can't ever say that again.

"So that means it's up to me to help you communicate those needs, OK? If you don't have a diagnosis to lend you credibility when advocating for yourself, maybe a doctor is the next best thing?"

"Oh," I say. "Um, OK." I'm stunned.

"Also, bear with me, Nina, but I'm wondering if Gwendolyn actually did the right thing by going to the principal's office? She was able to calm down. She didn't end up hurting anyone."

"Anger didn't crack my brain," I say, before I realize that they both won't know what I mean. I'm not sure they hear me anyway.

"It looks like being freed from the pressure of trying to earn a reward allowed Gwendolyn to make a decision that ended up being good for her."

"But what if I was at work?" Mom asks.

"Yes," Dr. Nessa says. "Have you been operating under the idea that the only way to stop school and the after-school program from constantly interrupting your life is to change Gwendolyn's behavior?"

"Well . . . yeah," Mom says.

"That's got to stop," Dr. Nessa says.

"What?" Mom asks. "How?"

"I'm not sure. I'm going to talk to both places about how and when they call you. I'm going to explain Gwen's needs and yours. I don't think we can say they should never call you. Sometimes there are true safety concerns with Gwendolyn but sometimes . . ."

"Sometimes they call me for something so minor my head wants to explode," Mom says.

I had no idea Mom felt that way.

"Exactly," Dr. Nessa says. "So I'll advocate for you until we have a less disruptive plan."

Mom looks even more stunned than I feel.

"I'm here to help you, too," Dr. Nessa says. "Your mental health is critical to Gwendolyn's functioning, and you seem a little . . . overwhelmed."

Mom has tears in her eyes. "You could say that," she says.

Dr. Nessa glances at her watch.

"We're going to be out of time. But, quickly, let's explore this idea that Gwendolyn was able to think more clearly when she was freed from the pressure of trying to earn horse camp. Do you think that's true?"

"Yes," I say. "I wanted to go to horse camp so badly it was all I thought about. And when it seemed like someone would take it away, I got so angry. But now that it's gone . . ."

Dr. Nessa nods. "This happens a lot with kids like Gwendolyn. The things we do that we think will help—specifically structuring consequences and rewards to influence behavior—often backfire. They're behaving poorly because they *can't* do whatever we're asking of them, no matter what we threaten or offer. Rewards and consequences just don't work."

"So I never should have even hoped for horse camp," I conclude.

Dr. Nessa shakes her head. "I'm saying the opposite. You should go to horse camp."

"Wait. So she just does whatever she wants?" Mom asks.

"No," Dr. Nessa says. "That's impossible. I'm not saying Gwen should get everything she wants. But I do think she should be allowed to go to horse camp."

"Why?" Mom lowers her eyebrows.

"Because when I read her original IEP, I was struck by how much success Gwendolyn found with horses. I know equine therapy was frustrating, but that seemed to have little to do with horses and more to do with yet another inflexible therapist that didn't understand Gwendolyn. When it comes to horseback riding, it seems to me that Gwendolyn was thriving."

Mom and I both nod.

"We need to get her used to thriving. She's going to learn the skills she's missing the same way she learns anything: easy problems first, then harder ones. From what I know about her relationship with her favorite horse—"

"Dandelion," I say.

"Right. Dandelion. It seems like when you were with her you were able to demonstrate a lot of frustration tolerance. She was a frustrating horse, and yet in her presence, Gwendolyn remained patient."

"That's true," Mom says. "I never understood that. It drove me crazy."

Dr. Nessa smiles. "That's an understandable reaction. But what I'm saying is that instead of looking at Gwendolyn as mysteriously inconsistent, we can try to use that experience of frustration tolerance and help her apply it to other environments where she's less successful."

"I never thought about it like that," Mom whispers.

"Of course you didn't," Dr. Nessa says. "You've been trying to fix everything for everyone. You've been trying to do the impossible."

"Yeah," Mom says.

"A simpler way to look at this: you know how the meds didn't help, so we stopped them?"

"Yes?" Mom says.

"Well, when you took away horses . . . did that help her?"

"No, it didn't," Mom says.

"Did it help you?" Dr. Nessa asks. She's talking faster and looking at her watch. I like this conversation but I don't think I'm ready for it to be over. I don't like the watch-glances.

"No," Mom says with a chuckle. "I missed Gwendolyn chatting happily about horses. And I missed having another place she could go and be happy so I could—"

"Exactly," Dr Nessa says. She cuts Mom off. My mom looks

at me. Her eyes are clear, finally. "Gwendolyn, I think you're going to horse camp."

She looks so happy, it shatters my heart.

"I can't," I say. "Remember? I'm not even in PowerKids anymore."

Mom's eyes go wide and she smacks her forehead in frustration.

"Oh," Dr. Nessa says. "Right. I'm sorry, I'm so rushed. I can't believe I didn't lead with this: I already spoke with Ms. Hayley. We tried to come to a compromise. She asked that Gwendolyn apologize to Tyler and—"

"I already did that!" I proclaim.

Dr. Nessa smiles. "I'm not surprised."

My face feels warm, in a good way.

"That means you can go back to PowerKids on Wednesday."

"What?" I ask, shocked. "They changed their minds? Why?"

"Because you shouldn't be punished as if you were acting on your own, Gwen. What happened was due, at least in large part, to a side effect of a medication you were taking correctly, as prescribed."

My eyes go wide. *Hettie was right.*

Mom is stuttering. "I can't tell you . . . wow . . . what a relief . . ."

"I actually think even a three-day suspension is inappropriate considering there has already been a medication change," Dr.

Nessa is saying. "But, practically speaking, you were already coming here for appointments today and Tuesday. So I'm hoping that you'll be able to come up with something on Monday, and then this problem will be over."

"We'll take it," Mom says. She almost sounds like she's singing. She doesn't even know that Marty and I already solved Monday for her, too.

"Good," Dr. Nessa says. "Now I have to go. You two have a nice weekend."

"But—wait," Mom says, no longer singing. "What's the plan?"

"We have an appointment for Tuesday, right?" Dr. Nessa says. "You can speak with reception if—"

"No, I mean . . . what do we do this weekend?" Mom says.

Dr. Nessa is half out of her seat. She freezes like that, lowering her eyebrows at Mom like she doesn't understand.

"I understand what you were saying, I think," Mom says. "No rewards, no punishments. But then . . . what do I do? What's the plan?"

"Ah," Dr. Nessa says with a small chuckle. "No plans this weekend."

"What?" Mom asks.

Dr. Nessa starts to walk toward the door. "I think you both need a break from plans," she says over her shoulder.

Mom follows Dr. Nessa, so I follow Mom, but I can see on her face that she's still confused. And maybe a little worried.

"So I just . . . do nothing?" Mom asks as we reach the lobby.

"Rest," Dr. Nessa says. "Nina, you rest."

I can tell we aren't finished but I guess we need to be.

We walk out of Dr. Nessa's building. I'm stunned and I think Mom is too. There are no words between us, which is weird.

I always thought the worst possible thing would be if Mom stopped hoping. I thought I'd know she had stopped hoping if she gave up all the plans. But it seems like Dr. Nessa is saying that's what should happen.

When we get in the car, I ask Mom if I can borrow her phone to text Hettie.

"If you do all your homework focusing and without complaining," Mom says.

But a second later she tosses her phone into the back seat.

"Never mind. Text Hettie. I'm going to have to get used to this."

I open Mom's phone and text **U WERE RITE! I'll be at camp!** Then a bunch of horse emojis.

She texts back immediately. **I ♥ you.**

# 20

## THE NO PLAN PLAN

The weekend is weird. I sleep all the way through Mom's Saturday meeting. When she comes back, she doesn't tell me to turn off YouTube and do my homework. She spends Saturday at the kitchen table surrounded by paperwork while I spend the day in my room with Mr. Jojo and Zombie and Marshmallow. I watch videos of horseback riding lessons. I try to remember the way I bounced up and down when I'd get Dandelion into a trot and how amazing it felt to soar over an obstacle. Soon, I'll be on a horse again. Even if it's not Dandelion.

I'm a little afraid that without a plan, all fifty-four things will get worse. But Anger sleeps all day.

Then again, why would Anger wake up when Mom doesn't ask me to do anything? No chores. No homework.

By Sunday, I'm bored of YouTube and horses, and I do some of my homework at the kitchen table without being reminded. Mom doesn't even glance up from her own work. Usually, when I do homework, Mom sits with me and helps me stay on track and organized, and I keep getting off track and disorganized anyway, and we end up fighting. Today there's no fighting, but there aren't any words either.

She's paying such little attention that I pull out my Top Secret Notebook and start writing right in front of her.

Step Seven: Another no check. But I have to do something. I need a plan for myself now more than ever because Mom doesn't have one. Without a plan, I know I'll mess up. I'm skipping to the next step. Hopefully it makes sense.

I open my iPad and read the next step. Then I breathe a sigh of relief. This one I can do.

Step Eight: I made a list of persons I had harmed and became willing to make amends to them all.

I pull out a fresh sheet of paper and start writing.

People I Have Harmed.

1. Mom

2. Tyler

3. Hettie

4. Thaís and Marty

5. Nolan

6. Dandelion (not a person but it still counts)

7. Mom (I've hurt her so much she deserves two spots.)

I miss having a plan.

I may even miss fighting.

Maybe I just miss my mom.

* * *

On Monday, Mr. Olsen is collecting the science homework. Even without my mom's help, I finished it this weekend. Eight comprehension questions. After a pretty short search, I find the wrinkled loose leaf in my backpack, and it's ready when he gets to my desk.

He glances at me over his glasses. His green eyes are pale, and they make me want to hide.

"The written part of your science fair project?" he says.

My eyes go wide and my heart starts beating like crazy and Anger rattles around. I take a deep breath to keep him inside his shell. I shouldn't be angry. It's not Mr. Olsen's fault I don't have my essay.

I bend toward my backpack and then rummage through it like an essay on the life cycle of the dolphin will suddenly appear on freshly typed, not-even-wrinkled white paper. Of course it won't. It can't. It doesn't exist.

"Well?" Mr. Olsen says.

I don't want to see his eyes again. They will definitely wake up Anger.

"Earth to Gwendolyn?" he says. My head is practically inside my backpack now.

I guess Mr. Olsen didn't listen when Dr. Nessa told him not to use that voice with me anymore. Or maybe she didn't talk to him yet. I don't know because Mom didn't tell me because there was no plan.

"I don't have it," I say to the bottom of my bag.

"You lost it?" he asks.

"No," I say, my head still in my backpack. "I forgot to do it."

My mom's plans make it so that I usually don't make mistakes like forgetting huge assignments. And if I do make that kind of mistake, Mom finds out. Then we fight. But after that, she helps me clean up my mess. I guess she's done cleaning my messes.

And right now I'm a mess.

"If you didn't do it, why do you appear to be looking for it?" Mr. Olsen asks.

Kids laugh. Anger starts peeking out of his shell. Relief is nowhere. Confidence is sleeping.

I hear myself say, "Because your eyes are scary."

10. No filter

17. Rude/Impolite

There's a chorus of "oooh!" around me like I just said something really, really bad instead of something really, really honest.

"My eyes are not the problem, Ms. Rogers," he says. "Your irresponsibility is the problem."

The word appears before my eyes in my handwriting.

44. Irresponsible

I think of all the other things on the list that fit right now.

38. Disorganized

4. Lazy

24. Spacey

45. Forgetful

"Being irresponsible is only one of my problems," I shout. Anger has climbed into my voice.

23. Talks too loud

"And you're implying that *I'm* the other problem?" he asks.

"No," I say. "I have lots of problems." But he's still talking so he probably can't hear me.

"I'm your problem, because, what? I believe that at eleven years old you should be able to keep track of a pencil and an assignment notebook?"

My face is hot.

"No!" I shout. "I have tons of problems but my only problem with you is that you don't help me with any of them."

"Sit down, Gwendolyn," he says. I didn't even realize I was standing.

"Fine."

I sit.

"You lose ten percent on your report. Have it tomorrow or your grade will be a zero."

"Fine," I say again.

Mr. Olsen stares at me. His eyebrows jump like they do when he's saying something sarcastic. He opens his mouth, and I cringe and shrink thinking about how everyone is going to laugh at me when he speaks again.

Then Thaís calls out, "Mr. Olsen, I had a question about the homework."

When he turns his back, Thaís sneaks me a pencil without

even asking if I need one.

She helps in the way Mr. Olsen won't.

Somehow I make it through the school day without cracking. But every time I'm one of the fifty-four things, it reminds me that I have no idea what Mom would say about anything anymore. And that makes me feel like I'm crumbling.

After school that day I climb into the back of Marty's mom's minivan. The way she smiles at us makes me ache for my own mom. It's like I lost my compass.

"It's so good to see you, Gwendolyn!" Ms. Smith says. She has on pink glasses and a sparkly pink top. Her hair is perfectly curled. She's basically the opposite of Marty. All the way at the Female End of the spectrum. I wonder if that means they fight like we do sometimes. Or maybe it means they fit together like puzzle pieces.

Right now it doesn't look like it.

Marty leans into the front seat and gives her mom a kiss on the cheek. "Hey, kiddo," her mom says. "I missed you."

My mom never says that to me. *I love you*, yes. But not *I missed you*. It's too hard to miss someone who causes so many problems in your life, I bet.

It makes me realize that even if we were letter friends, Marty and I wouldn't be the same. NB is just who you are. It's the same as girl or boy. Nonbinary is a long word so Marty uses an abbreviation. But it isn't really a letter thing.

In ADHD, the last letter stands for *disorder*. It's something actually wrong with your brain. And now I lost the *A* and the first *D* and the *H* but I still have the *Disorder* part.

No wonder Marty's mom misses her. It's easier to miss a kid who doesn't have a disorder.

When we get to their house, Marty's mom sends us up to her room with a plate of cookies and two glasses of milk. Marty's room looks like a rainbow exploded inside it. There's a rainbow bedspread and pillows and a big rainbow flag that says PRIDE hanging on the wall.

"I know it's a lot," Marty says. Her cheeks turn a little pink like she's embarrassed. "When I first figured out I was nonbinary, Mom sort of didn't believe me. She thought I was too young to know. Or she thought it was a phase or something. Then we started seeing a family therapist and Mom completely flipped her approach and now she's, like, determined to prove that she accepts my gender identity." Marty shrugs. "It's still weird but better than when she thought there was something wrong with me, so I'm not complaining."

I sit next to her on the rainbow bedspread.

"Your mom thought there was something wrong with being nonbinary?" I ask.

"Her and everyone else I know."

"Why?" I say.

"People are stupid," Marty says. She pauses and looks out her window. "That's sort of why I haven't changed my pronouns yet. I want to. I don't like being called *she*. But I also don't want to explain a million times a day that people need to call me *they*. I don't want to hear people mess up. Especially Mr. Olsen. He'd probably be all gross and sarcastic about it."

"Why would he be sarcastic about a pronoun?" I ask.

"I don't know. He's sarcastic about everything."

"Oh, believe me, I know," I say scooting backward so I can cross my feet on the bed. "I'm an expert on the Sarcasm Voice. He's sarcastic whenever I forget a pencil. Or lose my homework. Or wiggle in my desk. But you're different."

"What?" Marty says. "Why?"

"Because there's nothing wrong with you," I say.

Marty nods, still looking out the window. "I know."

"Why should he care about a stupid pronoun? That would be a dumb thing for even Mr. Olsen to be sarcastic about."

"I know," Marty says. "I know that . . . now. I'm in therapy."

"You are?" I ask.

Marty nods. "But don't tell anyone, OK?"

"I'm in therapy too," I say. I take a bite of cookie. "I didn't know that I knew anyone else who's in therapy."

"Right here!" Marty says, like it's a joke.

"But . . ." I trail off.

Marty rolls her eyes in a way that makes my face burn. "I'm guessing you *just have some questions*." She sounds like Mr. Olsen. Sarcastic.

I should probably stop talking. But 10. No filter.

"No, I just don't get why you would need therapy. I mean, it's not like there's something wrong with you."

"Oh," Marty says. The sarcasm is gone as suddenly as it came. "Um . . . I guess I'm in therapy because . . . other people think there's something wrong with me?" Marty shrugs. "My therapist says some people get mad when they don't understand something. Or someone."

"That's a stupid reason to get mad." Anger shakes my rib cage, just a little. Where did he come from?

"Yeah," Marty looks down. "People get mad at me for just being me. A lot."

"That's not OK!"

Anger is awake *for* Marty. That's new.

"I know," Marty says. "My therapist says there's a whole lot of people who think that gender is just about what's in your pants. And they think, for some reason, that I should live my whole life the way they want me to, even though they aren't me."

"Then *they're* the ones who should be in therapy!"

Marty's face scrunches up.

"Right?" I ask, confused.

"Um, I don't know. This is weird."

My heart thumps. "I'm sorry."

"No," Marty says. "You're being . . . fine. It's . . . usually, I don't have to explain why other people get upset. Because everyone gets upset. My mom. My dad. My sisters. My teachers. Even Thaís and Hettie didn't get it at first. That's why, when we weren't talking, I figured you had a problem with me. Now it turns out you get it best of all, you just didn't know. Go figure . . . And I'm mad because I really could have used you last year."

I understand best? That's impossible. I'm never the best.

And I don't get it.

"But . . . there's nothing wrong with you."

"You keep saying that." Marty says. "I know there's nothing wrong with me, but that doesn't mean everyone does, OK?" She looks annoyed even though she keeps saying such nice things about me.

No.

*They* look annoyed even though *they* keep saying such nice things about me.

I'm going to practice talking about Marty the right way in my head so that I don't mess up when they're ready to ask everyone to use the they/them pronouns.

"Nonbinary isn't, like, a problem," I say, trying to explain myself to them. "It's not a disorder. It's just . . . a description. It's not like ADHD after all."

"Oh," Marty says. "Oh. That's what you mean. That's . . . true."

"See? I don't get it," I say.

"No," they say. "You do."

"But I'm in therapy because the problem is in my own self.

Not because other people are stupid. I'm not saying that's worse, just that . . . *I'm* worse."

"No, Letter Friend," Marty says. "There's nothing wrong with you either."

I shake my head. I'm too sad to speak. Too sad to explain I don't even have letters anymore.

"I don't think there's anything wrong with having ADHD," Marty says. "It's like . . . a different way to have a brain. But not a bad way to have a brain. Even if the stupid people do call it a disorder."

"I don't even have ADHD anymore," I tell them.

"You don't?"

"I'm undiagnosable. *All* I have is a disorder. I can't even be a letter friend."

"Oh." Marty thinks for a moment, then throws their arm around me. "OMG! You know what? I can't actually be a letter friend anymore either!"

"What?" I ask. "Why?"

"It's sort of complicated, but it's cool that we figured it out at the same time, right?"

"What did you figure out?" I ask.

"OK. In my support group this weekend, I was using the letters. You know, NB?"

I nod.

"It turns out we aren't supposed to use those letters. In, like, internet words or whatever, NB also means Not Black, so my support group was talking about how we shouldn't also use those letters. Especially because a lot of the kids in my support group are Black, so they're nonbinary but not NB." Marty laughs like she's remembering something funny. I'm looking at her and trying to understand, but I'm just confused.

"So, it turns out nonbinary people are supposed to spell out the letters when we text. Like text them the way they sound. E-N-B-Y. Get it? Enby."

"Oh," I say. I understand the spelling, but I don't really get her point. No matter what letters you use, there's nothing wrong with being enby or NB, or enby but not NB.

"So that's a word. You write it like a word. Not letters. Get it?"

Marty sounds all excited. I shake my head slowly.

"Now we can be the ex-Letter Friends!" Marty proclaims. "We both figured out we can't use those letters at the same time." They laugh.

After a second, I giggle with them. "It is kind of cool that we lost the letters at the same time," I say. "Even if it's really different."

And it is really different. Marty lost the letters, and they don't seem to care. I lost part of my identity. A part I've been looking for forever.

Marty stops giggling as soon as I do. Almost like they read my mind.

"And . . . we're the same in the main way, still, too. Right?"

I shrug. I stuff another cookie into my mouth so more words don't burst out. I wish this hangout were happier.

"We are," Marty insists. "Because they don't get us. The rest of the world. The world wants everyone to act the same and think the same and be the same and, you and me, we challenge them. That's why you get me, Gwendolyn. And I get you too."

Then, I smile.

# 21

## THE WORST POSSIBLE THING

The next day after school, I'm sitting in Dr. Nessa's waiting room with my Top Secret Notebook on my lap. Mom is behind the glass door talking to Dr. Nessa. Their heads are bent together and I know they're talking about me. I'm trying not to pay attention. Not to be 16. Sneaky. For ex. eavesdrops or 13. Impulsive or 19. Doesn't respect others' space or 39. Immature or anything else.

I lean over and write.

Step Eight: ??? I don't understand how writing a list of names was supposed to help me. I already knew I had hurt all these people. What I don't know is how to stop. What if I can't? What if Dr. Nessa took away all the plans because she knows nothing will ever really help me? What if I'll always be bad? I was so convinced meds would help, and then they didn't. I've been sure these Twelve Steps would help too but

I pull the two lists out of my notebook. Fifty-Four Wrong Things that have hurt at least seven people (counting me). I scooch to the middle of the couch so I have space on both sides. On my left I lay out the list of people I've harmed. On my right, I place each page of the list of fifty-four things.

This is me: the filling in a disaster sandwich.

if these steps were helping, wouldn't these lists be getting shorter? At least the meds helped me remember my pencils. But the Twelve Steps aren't helping me do anything.

Suddenly I'm writing furiously. I can't look up. My pencil keeps moving faster and faster across the paper.

I love a lot of the people on this list. I love my mom and Tyler and Hettie and Thaís and Marty and even Nolan. Why do I keep hurting the people I love? Why can't anyone help me be . . . something. Something different than a problem.

I don't want to

"Gwendolyn?" It's my mom. I drop my pencil. It rolls across the tiled floor of the waiting room. A pencil rolling isn't supposed to be loud but it sounds that way to me.

"You didn't hear us calling you?"

"No," I say.

15. Hard to redirect

24. Spacey

My heart is beating like crazy. I lean forward to cover my writing with my chest. I can't let her see it. She can't know what I'm doing.

"What is this?" Mom asks, reaching for my lap, my Top Secret Notebook.

"No!" I say. I pull it tight to my body.

"Oh!" Mom steps back and her hands are far enough away that I know she's not going to snatch it. "I didn't know you kept a diary."

"I don't." I say.

Why did I say that?

10. No filter

"Oh," Mom says. She takes a step toward me again but sort of to the side, like she's going to sit down. I lunge away, taking my notebook with me so there's no way she can see it. And then I hear the pages crunch under my butt.

My list. It's everywhere. I somehow forgot that I had spread it all around me and now my mom is here and . . .

"Well Dr. Nessa is ready for you," she says.

But to my ears it sounds all deep and wobbly because the world is moving in slow motion. Mom keeps walking closer. Then her hand is reaching for the list of fifty-four things like it's nothing. Like she just wants to move it out of the way to sit next to me.

But it's not nothing. It's everything. It's the worst thing Mom could see.

I drop the notebook. I dive for the paper, but I'm too late. She's not sitting. She picks one of them up. It's the first page and it's in her hands. I see her eyes scan the title.

"Gwendolyn?" she says. She sounds shocked. Scared. I stare at her for what feels like hours as she glances down at numbers 1 through 23. I see her fingers shake as they hold the loose leaf. "Gwendolyn," she whispers. "What is this?"

I open my mouth to answer, but no words come. She turns to look at me. Her eyes are broken. They look like two precious marbles that someone dropped on a concrete floor. There are black fissures spiderwebbing through the green and white parts of her eyes.

I stand.

I run.

# 22
## THE FIRST CRACK

There was a time before plans. There was a time when I was so small, I didn't have to worry about wiggling my brain until it fit with someone else's because sitting in my mom's lap felt like fitting inside a puzzle.

I had a dollhouse back then. It was huge. Three floors with a dining room and a dark brown dining room table. Five bedrooms with pink and yellow and purple and white bedspreads and little dust ruffles around the bottom of each bed. Tiny things like chandeliers made of sparkly toothpicks and teacups the size of my pinkie nail. Little details that made it seem like the fanciest people ever lived there.

It didn't matter that the things were tiny and precious. It didn't matter that it's the exact kind of thing that would terrify me now. Because I was small enough that I never had to clean the dollhouse or remember where things were. I played with it, and then Mom cleaned it up. I know I can't be in the world that way forever, but back when that was OK, it felt like life worked. Like I worked. Like my brain made me delightful instead of broken.

At night after Mom gave me a bath and pulled my nightgown over my head and combed my hair and brushed my teeth, she would bring me over to the dollhouse. We'd say good night to each doll and tuck them into their beds before climbing into mine together with a pile of books.

This is all I can think about as my feet pound out of Dr. Nessa's office and down the hallway. The dollhouse is huge in my brain as I run through the front doors and into the spring air of downtown Madison. My legs pump and my breath gets steady as I run down the sidewalk and turn the corner.

I can hear Mom behind me. "Gwendolyn!" she's yelling. "Gwendolyn!"

She thinks I'm running away from her but I'm not. I'm just running. I can't be still in a world where Mom knows about my list. I'm going to run forever.

I won't cross the street though. I run all the way around the block, and I hear Mom pause behind me when I get back to the door to Dr. Nessa's building. But then I run right past it.

I'll run around this one block for the rest of my life.

"Gwendolyn!" Mom screams.

I hear my name again but in a different voice. "Gwendolyn!" Dr. Nessa is chasing me too.

My feet pound. My breath in-and-out, in-and-out. Sweat creeps under my armpits and across my hairline.

The dollhouse bounces in my brain.

*Good night, boy doll. Kiss. Into a bunk bed.*

*Good night, girl doll. Kiss. Into a bunk bed.*

*Good night, baby doll. Kiss. Into the crib.*

*Good night, Mom doll. Kiss. Into the big bed.*

"Gwendolyn!" Mom yells. But her voice and footsteps are getting farther away.

This time I hear Dr. Nessa yell, "Nina!"

My feet keep pounding. The dolls in my brain start to move on their own. Into and out of their bedrooms. Into the bathroom with a toilet that sounded like it really flushed. Around the dining room table with those tiny teacups. Back into their bedrooms.

Mom's voice behind me has disappeared, and that's good because the voice in my brain is better. It's Mom laughing with me. Enjoying me. Delighting in me.

But my brain keeps moving through the memory. I can't force it to stop at the good part. I got a little bigger. Anger was supposed to shrink after the terrible twos. After the threenage years. After preschool. After kindergarten.

But Anger kept growing with me.

I didn't fit in my mom's lap the same way. I didn't fit anywhere the same way. The dolls saw it all happen. They saw me turn from baby to bad.

One night I didn't want to go to bed. The dolls didn't want me to go to bed either. We all wanted to stay up late and play together, but Mom said we had to go to bed over and over until she was shouting and I was screaming.

And then—

*Crack.*

*Crash.*

I collide right into my mom. She must have gone around the block the other way to find me. My head hits her collarbone and my body falls backward so that I'm a heap on the sidewalk. Dr. Nessa is behind Mom and they crash together, too. Then Mom kneels beside me and gathers me into a hug.

"Baby," she says. "Cupcake. Gwendolyn. Baby."

Somehow I fit.

"I'm sorry. I'm sorry I broke the dollhouse," I say.

Mom's eyes go wide.

"I'm sorry I'm . . . this way. I'm . . . I'm sorry."

"Oh honey," Mom says. She scoops me into her lap and I'm too big for this, too old for this.

I fit anyway.

"Gwendolyn. You aren't some way. You're . . . you're wonderful."

Her tears mix with mine and she holds on to me like if she lets go I may fall apart, which is true. I might.

Dr. Nessa watches. She doesn't correct Mom. She doesn't say I can't be wonderful because I'm fifty-four other things. I don't say it either.

I don't say I can't be wonderful because I'm bad.

Right now, in my mom's lap, for once I can be both.

# 23

## CROSS-OUTS

When we get back to Dr. Nessa's office, she says this is now an emergency session and I'm her last patient of the day, so we can stay as long as we need to. We'll stay until we feel safe leaving.

I don't know what that means. I don't feel safe leaving or staying. I'll never feel safe again.

I wiggle my chair closer to Mom's. The feeling is only half there now. The feeling that I can be bad and wonderful at the same time.

Dr. Nessa has my Top Secret Notebook and the list of fifty-four things sitting in front of her. She's across the table from us. The notebook is closed and the papers are underneath.

"Gwendolyn," she says. "I think it's really important that we look at these. But I don't want to betray your trust. I want to tell you that no matter what I find in here, I will still think of you as the funny, brilliant, creative, and striving girl I know, OK? May I look?"

"Yes," I say. As usual, I speak without thinking.

But Mom has already seen the list. Nothing matters anymore.

Dr. Nessa starts with the notebook.

"What is this . . ." she says slowly. "Twelve steps? Like AA?"

"What?" Mom says. "Gwendolyn is a lot of things . . . and I know I'm not perfect . . . and *I* started drinking very young but Gwendolyn: she hasn't been drinking," Mom finishes.

"What?" I say. "*Drinking*?" Without a plan it's like my mom doesn't know me at all anymore.

Dr. Nessa hands the notebook to Mom. I don't try to stop her. "She replaced the word *alcohol* with *anger*."

Mom's eyes move fast as she scans the pages. "Gwendolyn," she says, so quietly I can barely hear it. "Cupcake. This isn't how it works."

"How what works?" I ask.

"This isn't how the Twelve Steps work."

"Yes it is," I say. "I followed the directions super carefully."

"But, G . . . you aren't an alcoholic," Mom says.

"I can still follow steps," I say. "I read a website and I did everything it said. I have a higher power. I prayed. I did it perfectly, just like I took the medicine perfectly, but it still didn't work. Just like every other plan."

"That isn't . . . I don't know where to start. I'm so confused," Mom says. "You aren't an alcoholic, so the Twelve Steps aren't for you. And they're only one part of AA. There's also the community aspect. The sponsor. The Twelve Steps work for alcoholics because we do them with people who understand us. You were trying to do this all alone."

I stand up so fast the chair tips over. Anger is jumping around in me, pinging off every bone. "Because *no one* is like me!" I yell.

"Shh, Gwen—" Mom says.

But Dr. Nessa says, "No. Don't pay attention to the volume. Just listen."

So I get louder. "*No one* else has fifty-four things wrong with them. *No one* can be my sponsor because my problem doesn't even have a *name*."

I fix my chair and sit. I feel better without those words inside me.

"Wow, Gwendolyn," Dr. Nessa says. Her voice is sad. "Thank you for sharing that."

I don't say anything.

"What fifty-four things?" Mom says. "Where did that even come from?"

Now I'm the one who reaches across the table. I hand her the list. I tell myself it's OK because she already saw it. I tell myself it's OK because she already knows all of this about me. But I still hold my breath as I give it to her. Shame starts sliding, slimy, around my insides.

Mom reads the list from the top to the bottom. Then she starts again. She reads it slowly and carefully, over and over again, like she's me in my loft going to sleep at night.

Mom keeps trying to talk but her words are shattering in her mouth. Finally she says, "Socially inept? Do you even know what that means?"

"Yes," I say.

"I . . . there's so much to say. I don't know where to start. But . . . socially inept?"

"You told the IEP people that I only have one friend and that I don't know how to make more. Even though I actually have three friends. And a brother."

"No," Mom says. "No, no, no."

"I read it," I say. "I know what you said."

I expect Mom to be surprised that I read it. Or maybe not surprised because she should know I'm 16. Sneaky. But I expect her to be mad that I read it.

Different words burst out of her so desperate I know they're true. "I never said that!"

"What?" I ask.

"I was shocked when I read that in the report. You were always well-liked and social. I never, ever said you had trouble making friends. That's part of why I was so disgusted with that report. That was clearly a mistake, like they had copied and pasted old reports and just replaced your name here and there."

"No," I say. "No."

"Yes," Mom says.

"But the rest of it was true," I say.

"Well, let's look," Dr. Nessa says, pulling the list closer to her. "Hmm." She reads. It looks like she's reading a regular book or the news or something. It feels like we're all working on a school assignment or a project together instead of talking about everything that's wrong with me. My feelings are too big for the curious and calm look on Dr. Nessa's face. She says, "Number twenty-five. Is it true that you're picky about your appearance?"

"I need my braids super tight," I say. "Otherwise I can't think."

Dr. Nessa's eyes go bright like she just had an idea. She doesn't say what it is though. "I remember. But is that about how you look?" she asks.

"No," I say. "It's about how it feels."

"Right," Dr. Nessa says. "But you know what appearance means, don't you?"

"Yes," I say. Anger is still too big for me to spell it and define it like usual. It's like Anger is huge but something else is blocking his power so my body is still doing what it's supposed to. What's blocking Anger?

Then I see him.

He's kelly green and shaped like a many-pointed star. He's sticky like those toys you throw against a wall. He's wiggling to get his tentacles between all the folds in my brain so that Anger can't crack it.

Curiosity.

"Why?" I ask.

"Because it sounds like your need for tight braids has nothing to do with your appearance."

"Yeah. You're actually not picky about your appearance at all," Mom says. "And you aren't a picky eater either."

"I hate mushy food," I say.

"Right," Mom says. "And you have trouble concentrating on eating at school, I think. But at home you'll eat almost anything except mashed potatoes and applesauce. Not liking mushy foods doesn't make you a picky eater. A truly picky eater could have never followed that diet, and you did that like a champ."

"Mashed potatoes are just too mushy," I say.

Because I can't say what I'm really thinking. Which is that we're down to fifty-one. That's still a lot of things, but it's not as many as fifty-four. Does a girl with fifty-one things wrong with her have an easier time at school? At horse camp?

I grab the list from Mom and a pen from Dr. Nessa, and neither of them says anything about snatching. They watch as I cross out number 2, number 6, number 25.

"Let's talk about four," Dr. Nessa says. Then she taps the Top Secret Notebook. "You aren't lazy. A lazy person would never do this much work on herself."

"The report said I'm lazy. I know it used that exact word."

I interrupt Dr. Nessa when she tries to answer.

"Also, Mr. Olsen thinks I'm lazy. And Mom does too, sometimes."

"I never said that," Mom says. But that's not the same thing as *you aren't lazy.*

"You have a lot more to work on than your average eleven-year-old," Dr. Nessa says. "You're working really hard on a lot of things, and maybe sometimes that means you don't work as hard on your schoolwork because the other work you're doing is exhausting. But the bottom line is you're doing more work than almost anyone I know."

"But Mr. Olsen—"

"Also, when you do a homework assignment, lose it, do it again, and lose it again, that's not laziness. Even if the assignment ultimately never makes it to the teacher," Dr. Nessa says.

"So I'm *not* lazy," I say in wonder. I cross it off.

"Let's keep looking," Dr. Nessa says. "I want to also point out that there are a lot of things on this list that almost always appear in school reports about *girls* who are having a hard time and almost never on reports about *boys.* Like, *talks too much, talks too loud, overly emotional.*"

"Only girls are that way?" I ask.

"No," Dr. Nessa says. "They were in your report because girls are too often expected to be quiet and docile and hide their emotions. There's nothing wrong with talking a lot and showing the world who you are. Those things didn't belong in the report because, even if they're true, they aren't problems.

We should be encouraging you to use your voice. Not criticizing it."

"Cross them out!" I say. She does.

"And Gwendolyn is not demanding or attention-seeking," Mom says. "All kids deserve attention, and Gwendolyn usually gets in trouble because the attention gets turned onto her. Not because she's looking for it."

That's so true. I think of Mr. Olsen's class and all the missing pencils. I never wanted anyone to pay any attention to that. I was avoiding attention.

I look at Mom. "I want *you* to cross those out," I say.

I watch her hands as a black line appears through numbers 1 and 3.

I'm down to forty-five.

Dr. Nessa and my mom keep talking.

They say I'm not obsessive. And I'm not that hard to redirect if you get my attention. And there's nothing wrong with being a little clumsy. That doesn't make me a bad person. And immature is a stupid thing to say about a kid who doesn't need to be mature yet anyway.

They say it's silly to say that I'll only do what I want to because I do a lot of things I don't want to do, like my math homework and the dishes and even making this awful list. Dr. Nessa says that I'll only do what I'm *able* to do, but that's true for everyone.

I'm not actually sneaky because the goal of my sneaking is

always to understand my own self better.

Interrupting is a part of impulsivity.

Having a poor sense of time is a part of being disorganized.

By the time we're almost done, there are cross-out marks and arrows and notes about what's universal or not a problem or biased because I'm a girl or even a good thing.

Only a few things are left unmarked:

Hyperactive

Impulsive

Disorganized

Aggressive/Explosive/Reactive

(These all have the same meaning and never should have been three separate things anyway.)

So that's four. I lost fifty.

There are only four things wrong with Gwendolyn Rogers.

Dr. Nessa shoves the paper away.

"Gwen, why did you continue this notebook after we agreed to no more rewards and consequences? Did you realize you were breaking our agreement?"

I lower my eyebrows. "I was?"

Dr. Nessa nods. "This feels like another way to reward or consequence yourself. I thought we agreed to rest for a while."

"Resting wasn't working either. I didn't want to rest."

"What did you want to do?" Mom asks.

"Get better. I tried every plan Mom came up with and nothing worked. I thought maybe I needed the same plan

Mom used to get better a long time ago when she was out of control and a mess." I look at Mom. "I mean, that's how you describe it."

She smiles. "Yes, I do. Keep going, Gwennie."

"Then, last week, Mom and I didn't have anything to talk about," I say. "I kept making mistakes but Mom wasn't there to help. She couldn't even lecture me because that would be a consequence. So it was almost like she wasn't on my team anymore. I needed some sort of direction . . . I can't get better if there's no plan."

"Ah," Dr. Nessa says.

"I see. I'm sorry. I had to rush us out of the last session and I didn't realize it, but I left you both flailing. The point of cutting rewards and consequences isn't to cut communication," she says. "I should have made that more clear. You're right, you do need a plan. A practical one. Rest was only supposed to be the first step. So let's get practical. First—"

"You mean practical like medicine?" I ask.

"No," Dr. Nessa says, screwing up her face like she doesn't understand me.

"But you do mean something like that, right? A solution?"

"Gwen," Dr. Nessa says. "There isn't really ever going to be a solution. That's not how neurodiversity works. In order for there to be a solution there has to be a problem. And there isn't a problem."

"Yes, there's . . ." I almost say there's fifty-four problems but then I trail off.

"Your brain isn't a problem," Dr. Nessa says. "And it's the only brain you're ever going to get. You need to learn to love it."

"I love it," Mom says, sturdy and solid. She says it without thinking.

My mom loves my brain.

"When I say practical I do mean something that you can check off a checklist. Something that you know you've done. Something much more concrete than these Twelve Steps."

I breathe in. "OK," I say.

"Here's the first step: whenever you and your mom find yourself in a moment where you'd usually be discussing behavior or homework or plans or consequences, don't. But don't stop talking. Instead, talk about horses."

"Horses?" I say.

Dr. Nessa nods. "Or Mr. Jojo, or your fish, or Hettie. Something like that. Something fun. We're going to focus on connection instead of behavior for a while." She turns to Mom. "You've had the weight of the world on your shoulders," she says. "Everyone in Gwendolyn's life expects you to be able to control her even though no one can ever control another person. So, I'm going to take that responsibility away from you. Do the one thing in your control: love Gwendolyn."

"That's it?" Mom asks.

"Pretty much. Keep everyone physically safe. Take care of your own self. And love Gwendolyn. That's it."

"Wow," Mom whispers. "I can do that." She's trying not to cry. But also . . . she's smiling.

"Eventually, we'll work on problem-solving some of the tough moments and helping Gwendolyn learn the skills she needs to control her anger. But for now, we need a solid foundation to build from. And that foundation is you.

"Secondly," Dr. Nessa says. "I'm interested in the braids and the mushy food."

"What?" I say. It feels like we were driving in one direction and Dr. Nessa took a sharp turn.

"I think you may be sensory-seeking," she says. "It's a kind of Sensory Processing Disorder. What your body is feeling and what your senses are perceiving have a profound impact on your behavior and your other skills. But that's only one of many things going on with you so I don't want you to latch onto that the way you did ADHD, OK?"

I nod.

"Regardless, I'm going to give you a prescription to start some sessions of occupational therapy. It should happen at school and be covered by insurance. Like everything else it's not magic, but it should help."

My eyes are wide. I didn't know there could be a way to help me that's not medicine and not talking and not getting in trouble.

"What would I do?"

"It's mostly playing. Running and jumping. Pressing things into you. Also, do you have a weighted blanket?"

"No," I say.

"Gwendolyn's really picky about her blankets," Mom says.

"I just need them tight," I say. Because it's like the braids. I don't care what they look like.

Dr. Nessa smiles at Mom. "This gives me further suspicion that we may have some sensory processing stuff going on. A lot of kids who are sensory-seeking love to sleep in a sleeping bag with a weighted blanket on top."

"Wow," I say. "That would work. I could even adjust it myself in the night."

"Wow," Mom echoes. "That's so simple."

"This is what I mean. Let's start with ideas that don't seem difficult to either of you. Here's another one. Nina, I'm going to help you start the documentation that will get your insurance to cover visits with my colleague who is a psychiatrist. We're done with stimulants, but I think Gwendolyn would benefit from some gentle medication. There are some great non-stimulant ADHD meds that I believe would really help her whether or not what we're seeing is ADHD or SPD or something we won't be able to diagnose for a while." Dr. Nessa looks right at Mom. "And they aren't habit-forming."

"OK," Mom says. "OK."

My jaw is dropped. My arms and legs feel like warm jelly. I'm the most relaxed I've been in ages. A new kind of therapy. A different medicine. A weighted blanket that will never be loose at night. Talking about horses. Dr. Nessa already did four things to help me, and I only have four things wrong with me.

"The only other step I can think of right now is the one we discussed last week. Let's get Gwen back on a horse."

Mom laughs. "Horse camp starts in two weeks. She's all signed up."

"I'm all signed up?" I ask.

A jolt of excitement runs through me, but when it burns out I'm a little sad. When Dr. Nessa said *back on a horse,* of course, I pictured Dandelion. And I still can't go back to Millington Stables.

But Mom and Dr. Nessa are smiling, and missing Dandelion is going to be every day. This is the only day where I'll ever lose my list. So I smile back.

"I want to make sure we're clear about one more thing," Dr. Nessa says. "No one did anything wrong here. Gwendolyn, you may feel guilty for keeping this list from your mom. But it's OK for you to process things on paper. If you're putting words on a computer or the internet or something, your mom needs to know. But anyone is allowed to have a secret with a piece of paper. So if you want to write things down, do. Even things that seem ugly like this. Writing them down is an adaptive behavior."

A-D-A-P-T-I-V-E. It means something that helps someone progress in their current situation.

It means I did something more than not-wrong when I wrote stuff down.

I did something *right.*

"And, Nina, you may feel like you betrayed Gwendolyn by

reading these private thoughts, but when a human being who can read encounters a piece of writing that is of great interest, it's impossible not to read it. The same way it's impossible to drive past a car accident and not to look. Do you understand what I'm saying?" Dr. Nessa is looking at me.

"No," I say.

"It's fine for you to keep your feelings on paper. But if you leave that paper out somewhere and your mom reads it, that's not *her* fault. Your mom won't go snooping for notebooks. She'll respect your privacy. But if paper is lying around, the rule has to be that she's allowed to read it because, just like we aren't asking you to do things you can't, we won't ask Mom to do the impossible either."

I nod. "OK."

"So, how are you feeling?" Dr. Nessa asks.

I take a minute and close my eyes. I check on them all. Anger is asleep. Sadness is small. Confidence is awake but in a lounge chair wearing a pair of neon pink sunglasses instead of marching around in my skull. Relief is everywhere, making my muscles loose and heavy. Curiosity is sticky all through my brain.

"I think I feel happy," I say.

Dr. Nessa smiles. "That's usually what follows when we're brave enough to share something as big and scary as this." She taps the crossed-out list. "Happiness."

# 24

## HETTIE'S LIST

Mom doesn't say it but I think she's feeling happy too. We get in the car and buckle our seat belts. Someone should say something. Someone should say how this plan feels different. There are no ifs in this plan. There's no messing up. We know we can do it.

But before either of us says anything, the phone rings. Mom answers it through the Bluetooth on the stereo.

"Nina?" Hettie's mom's voice fills the car. "Can I ask you a favor? My mom is not well and . . . I have to get to her and . . . well, could Hettie sleep at your place tonight?"

My eyes go wide. I've never had a sleepover at my house. I've never even asked for one. It always seemed like if I did I'd be faced with an everlasting list of things I had to get good at before Mom would let me.

But there aren't any *ifs* anymore, so Mom doesn't even hesitate before she says yes.

"Gwendolyn and I are in the car right now. We can swing by and pick up Hettie."

"Thank you, thank you!" Hettie's mom says.

A few hours later, Hettie and I are clearing out the furniture in the living room so that there's space for us to sleep. Mom ate pizza with us and then even brought out the cinnamon rolls from the pizza shop for dessert. I'm so not used to dessert, I can actually feel the sugar buzzing in my blood as Hettie and I spread out our sleeping bags on the carpet. Mom says good night and goes into her room.

"It's weird to sleep here," Hettie says. She stands on her sleeping bag and stretches her arms toward the ceiling. Her pajamas are pink with tiny avocados printed all over them.

"Are you OK?" I ask. I know Hettie loves her grandmother. I wonder if she's scared. Mom didn't tell me more of what's going on, but that's only because she doesn't know much herself.

"Yeah," Hettie says. "I don't want to think about Nana."

"OK," I say. "But you said it's weird to sleep here."

"Oh." Hettie drops onto her sleeping bag. "I just mean it's weird I'm sleeping here because even though you're my best friend, I'm barely ever here."

"That's because my mom is embarrassed by our house," I say. The words fly out of me. I don't think I've ever realized that before, let alone said it out loud. "Hardly anyone ever comes here," I say.

"Really?" Hettie spreads onto her stomach and scoots

closer to me. "But it's so cute."

"Well, *I* love it," I say. "I love our living room and how the kitchen's right there and how my mom is never too far away from me because where could she go?"

My face flushes. I'm eleven. I'm not supposed to talk about how much I like to be near my mom anymore.

My brain almost says 39. Immature. But I stop it. Immature is crossed out now.

"I love your house too," Hettie says.

"Do you want to watch a movie?" I ask. "Or play a game or . . . well . . . I sort of want to show you something. Is that OK?"

Hettie nods. "Whatever you want to do," she says, like always. She sits up and crosses her legs on her sleeping bag.

I reach into mine and pull out my papers. Even though most of the words are crossed out, my heart is beating like crazy. I can't believe I'm about to show yet another person. Before I can stop myself, I shove the papers into her lap. I can't look at her. I keep my eyes on my toes.

"Fifty-Four Things Wrong with Gwendolyn Rogers," Hettie reads out loud. I guess I forgot to cross out the title.

"It's only four now," I say.

Hettie squints. "What is this?" she asks.

So I tell her the story. The whole thing.

"That's what you meant when you said your brain is weird!" Hettie says. "I was wondering."

"You were? Why didn't you ask?"

"I don't know." Hettie sighs. "I'm not good with, like, feelings-questions. That could go on my list. Some Number of Things Wrong with Hettie McFee."

I shake my head. "You don't need a list," I say. "There's nothing wrong with you."

Hettie laughs. Or snorts. It's a Mr. Olsen laugh. Sarcastic. "A lot is wrong with me. Believe me," she says.

I shake my head again. Hettie is basically a perfect kid. She never gets in trouble at school. She never gets put in time-out at PowerKids. Teachers never call her parents or send her home early. And she still manages to be friends with someone like me.

"I could write a list right now," Hettie says. "Number one, doesn't ask about other people's feelings. Number two, jealous. Number three, boring. Numb—"

"Stop it!" I shout.

23. Talks too loud

No, not too loud.

"Don't write a list. I don't want you to have a list like this. And anyway, you aren't boring. You're fun."

"Not as fun as Tyler," Hettie says. She looks sad. I thought she was sad about her grandmother, and I understood that, but now she looks sad about Tyler. "See?" she says. "Number two, jealous."

"No," I say. "Did you have this list already? Or are you making it up right now?"

"I already knew these things but I've never numbered them."

I shake my head. "Don't do it," I say. "I did that and for a long time all I could think about was all the things that other people said were wrong with me. Did you know I stopped being friends with Thaís and Marty because someone wrote down that I only have one friend? And then I, like, *made* it so that I only had one friend, which was you, of course, because you're my best friend—"

"I *was* your best friend," Hettie says.

I stop mid-story. The rest of the words want to tumble out—about how I don't want Hettie to write a Some Number of Things Wrong with Hettie McFee list because it will make more things be wrong with Hettie McFee, and it will make Hettie McFee miserable, and I love Hettie McFee.

But I hear what Hettie said and I make my words stop.

"No, you *are* my best friend," I say. "Now. Always."

"What about Tyler?"

"He's my brother," I say.

Hettie shakes her head. She leans away from me a little bit.

"He is!" I insist because if one other person tries to deny that I have a brother, I think I may explode.

"I know," Hettie says. "I didn't mean he's not your brother. But he's also your best friend. You want to be with him all the time. It's not like Nolan."

"But you love Nolan sometimes," I say.

"I love him all the time. But it's different than how I feel with you. Nolan and I fight. There are times I can't stand him. I get so jealous whenever things go his way. Everything seems so unfair when I get in trouble and he doesn't."

"But that *is* how I feel about Tyler. That's half of why I get so mad at PowerKids. He does the same bad things as me but they never call his mom."

"Yeah, I've noticed," Hettie says. "They never call boys' moms. That's not fair."

"Really?" I say. "It's all boys? Not just Tyler?"

Hettie nods. "Yeah, you know Jack and George are always in trouble too. They never call their moms."

"I never noticed . . ." I say. "Actually that's the point. Tyler and I, we aren't the only two kids who do bad things, you know? I don't even know if they call anyone else's moms. It only feels unfair because Tyler is my brother. It's sibling rivalry. We have to shove all that rivalry into school hours because that's the only time we get to see each other."

Hettie stares at me, or sort of past me, like she's trying to piece a puzzle together in her brain.

I keep talking. "But you . . . I just love you, Hettie. You're easy. You'll always-always be my best friend no matter how many brothers we find out about or how many terrible lists we write. If you got in trouble during PowerKids, I would want them to *not* call your mom."

"Really?" Hettie says. Her eyes look brighter. I can tell she believes me. I can also tell she needed to hear me say that.

I nod, firmly. "TBH: you're the only easy thing about my life," I say.

She laughs.

"If Tyler and I got to grow up like you and Nolan, I probably wouldn't even want to see him at outdoor break or after school. But we don't live together and we just met and . . . I needed to find out all about him. I can't explain it. It's something I needed like food or water. But he's my brother. You're my friend. My best friend. Always."

Hettie jumps to her feet. "I have an idea!" she squeals. "I . . . I have an idea. *Me*. Is that OK?"

"Of course," I say.

Hettie runs to the fridge and pulls down the magnetic notepad and pen my mom keeps up there. She collapses next to me.

Across the top of the paper she writes:

**Things That Are Awesome About Gwendolyn Rogers**

I giggle, but I'm nervous. How many things can go on this list? There's no way she'll reach fifty-four.

But four, I remember. There are only four things wrong with me now. Maybe Hettie could come up with four.

It'll only count if they're true. She better not write stupid stuff that's supposed to make me feel better.

Hettie writes.

**1. Comes up with the best games**

I smile because that is true. I do come up with the best games.

Hettie keeps writing.

**2. Really, really nice**

"No," I say.

Hettie looks up. "What?" she asks.

"I'm not nice," I say.

"Yes you are," she says, like it's obvious.

"I threw a computer at Ms. Hayley. I talked back to Mr. Olsen. I punched Tyler. I yelled at Nolan when he was only six. Six!" I shake my head. "I'm not really, really nice."

Sadness has been so small all night, but now he grows a little, stretching into my ribs and wrapping around my heart. Hettie is going to say that actually I am nice when I know that nice girls don't do any of that stuff. Hettie is going to say the thing people always say about how I'm good even if I don't act like it. But I know that's not true, so it's not what I want to hear.

Hettie chews on the end of the pen and looks up to the corner of the living room. Then she writes again.

**2. Really, really nice (to Hettie)**

And that . . . is true. I'm so relieved that I start to laugh. Then Hettie laughs.

We dissolve into giggles. We laugh so hard that we end up crying. We laugh so hard that we're tumbling around together. And it feels good to hug and cry and laugh and be with my best friend. We laugh so hard that I hear Mom's door open, and I'm sure she's going to come out and tell us to be quiet, but when I look up, she's only standing in the doorway smiling. We laugh so hard that we fall asleep and that's the end of the Things That Are Awesome About Gwendolyn Rogers list.

It turns out I only needed two things on it.

In the night, I wake up spread across both sleeping bags. My teeth are sticky because I never brushed them after all that cinnamon and icing. My skin is all goose-bumped because it's chilly on the living room floor. I roll over onto my sleeping bag and my hand hits the magnetic notepad. I tear off the paper and zip it into my sleeping bag with me. I'll sleep with this list now.

Unlike me, Anger is sound asleep. But there's something new awake inside me. She's hot pink and shaped like a stick bug with six leg-arms and a long body and antennas. She jumps and buzzes in my abdomen, tickling until I smile. She picks up the little blue marble that's rolling around her many feet and tucks Sadness into her shirt pocket. Then she burrows deep into my gut, so I feel warm and cozy and content.

She's a hot pink many-legged stick bug with a front pocket that can hide Sadness.

Happiness.

Hettie's list gave birth to Happiness.

# 25

## AWESOME THINGS

I wake up early because I hear a quiet *doo-dee-doo* through Mom's door.

I shouldn't listen. I know. But her door is cracked open and she knows I'm in the living room. This feels a little like what Dr. Nessa was saying. It's impossible not to listen the same way it's impossible for Mom not to read my lists if I leave them lying around.

Especially when the first thing Mom says is, "I had a breakthrough when it comes to understanding Gwendolyn."

I don't crawl over to her door. I don't strain to hear. I don't even sit up. But still Mom's words find me.

"She's been trying. Like really trying. All this time I thought I had to try for her. I thought she was being insolent. I thought if I could just find a way to make her want to behave, she would. But you know what? She wants to behave. She went so far as to try to cure herself using the Twelve Steps."

"The Twelve Steps?" Marsha's voice says. The cartoon librarian in my imagination is laughing.

"She replaced the word *alcohol* with *anger*." Mom chuckles.

I know they're laughing at me, but there's so much love in Mom's voice, it's OK.

"You sound happy," Marsha says.

Mom's quiet for a moment. Then she says, "You know . . . she's a good kid. If she's trying to be good . . . well that's enough for me. That alone makes her a good kid."

Happiness was sleeping as I slept but now she opens her eyes and yawns.

"Teaching her some executive-functioning skills. Doing things with her. Loving her . . . all of that seems so much more doable . . . I was trying to do the impossible."

"And—"

Mom cuts Marsha off. "You were right. I know, I know. You were right."

"And—"

Mom cuts her off again. "And I have amends to make," Mom says. "I . . . I don't know. I've been through the steps so many times. I accepted her amends years ago. I . . . well, it's going to be tough, but I think I'm finally ready."

Could she be talking about the same *her*?

"I'm proud of you," Marsha says.

"My kid's trying so hard to be good. I better put in a little effort, right?"

"Gwen's a great kid, Nina."

"She really is."

I roll over in my sleeping bag and close my eyes again.

I'm good.

A few hours later, we drop Hettie off at the hospital so she can visit her grandmother. Hettie's mom called earlier and said that her nana is going to be OK. Before Hettie gets out of the car, I tuck a little piece of paper into her hand. It has seven things on it, Seven Awesome Things About Hettie McFee.

"It's just a start," I whisper to her.

Afterward, we go to Mom's meeting. I sit outside and watch YouTube videos. Mom decides to skip brunch with her friends even though I offer to sit outside and watch YouTube for that too.

When we get home, Mom asks, "How was the sleepover?" She's folding my sleeping bag and putting the living room furniture back to where we usually keep it. I stand next to her to help, but I don't move. The new list is in my sock. I can feel it starting to paper-cut my heel.

Then I remember what Dr. Nessa said about how happiness often follows sharing things that are scary to share.

"Can I show you something?" I ask her.

"Of course," Mom says.

I take off my shoe and pull out the little square of paper. Mom looks nervous as I unfold it and put it on the coffee table, straightening it out.

Mom squints. I see a little smile playing on her lips.

"Is this Hettie's handwriting?" Mom asks.

I nod.

"Is it OK if I add a few more things?"

My eyes go wide and I nod again. I can't imagine what she'll write. I just hope it's true. She goes to her desk and takes a pen out of the drawer.

Mom writes.

3. Compassionate with all animals, especially horses

Well, that's true. Dandelion. The ornery-est horse. I smile even though that one makes me miss her.

4. Compassionate with her friends

That's true too. Like with Hettie last night.

5. Incredibly accepting of everyone who is different

Yeah, that's like when Tyler clicks. Or even Marty, who some people think has a problem, but I know that's stupid, and it's not really a problem.

6. Creative

That's sort of the same as number one, right? Being good at games? But maybe it's different. Maybe I'm also creative in other ways. And the fifty-four things had a lot of repeating.

7. The best person to talk to

"You have to sign that one," I say.

"Huh?" Mom says.

"You have to sign that one. Like Hettie did for number two."

Mom adds (for Mom) and Happiness buzzes and buzzes

and buzzes. "You really love to talk to me?"

Mom nods. "More than anything, Gwen. I've been so overwhelmed. You're right here with me and I think about you every minute of every day, and yet I realized last night that I miss you. I've been doing life backward. I've been thinking only about the stress and not at all about the wonderful stuff. The delight. Of being your mom."

Mom sits on the couch, like cleaning the living room can wait. I sit next to her.

"Should we talk now?" I ask.

Mom smiles. "Tell me about horse camp."

I didn't know Happiness could buzz any louder but her little pink wings take off with a flurry and they spray pink and silver glitter all over my insides.

I open my mouth to talk about horse camp, but I end up talking about Dandelion. How much I loved her. How much I understood her. How much it hurts to know Tyler gets to see her when I can't.

Mom listens.

The next Friday, it's the last day of school, which means it's the last day of PowerKids. Hettie and Tyler and I race around the schoolyard one, two, three, four times before going into the cafeteria. Hettie has been much nicer to Tyler since our sleepover. She doesn't even roll her eyes when he clicks his tongue anymore.

Inside, Hettie and I walk over to the fifth-grade table, but

Tyler is still running like he forgot to turn off his motor.

*Crash.* He knocks right into Ms. Hayley. She was carrying a computer and a phone and a bunch of papers and a metal coffee cup. It all goes flying. The cup rolls and brown liquid spills across the green linoleum close to my table.

"Sorry! Sorry!" he says.

He bends to help her pick things up and, when he does, their heads bang together.

"OW, Tyler!" she says. "That's enough."

*It was an accident.* I stop myself from shouting. I don't want both Tyler and me in trouble on the last day of school.

He looks up, rubbing his own forehead. "I said *sorry*," Tyler says.

"Let's just get through this last day, OK?" Ms. Hayley says. "I don't want any more trouble out of you."

"I was trying to help you." Tyler says, but louder this time.

He bends to pick up more papers, muttering to himself under his breath.

"After the year we've had it's hard to know what's an accident and what's . . . why are you laughing?," Ms. Hayley says.

"You don't know what an accident is?" He squeals. It's not a normal laugh. It's the kind of laugh I have when my heart wants to cry but my body is all confused about it.

This isn't supposed to happen to Tyler. Tyler takes meds.

"Can I help him clean up?" I ask Ms. Madeline.

"Sure," she says.

I scurry over to him. Even though I'm moving fast, things around me go in slow motion. Everything is clicking into place.

Tyler's blue pills are good because they are a real plan and not an *if* plan. But they're not perfect. I understand it for the first time as I watch Ms. Hayley tell him to stop laughing over and over again.

Tyler can't stop laughing.

By the time I get to him, he's uncontrollable.

"Stop it," Ms. Hayley says pointlessly.

"You don't know the difference between on purpose and an accident?" Tyler giggles. "What are you, stupid?"

Kids laugh.

"Stop!" Ms. Hayley yells.

I bend down to help. I pick up the coffee cup and shove some of the papers away from the spill.

Tyler picks up a paper near his feet and immediately drops it again. "Oops," he says.

"That was purposeful," Ms. Hayley says.

"Very good!" Tyler says in a fake-teacher voice. "Try again."

He picks up a paper and drops it again.

"That's enough, Tyler. Thank the good lord this is the last day of this year. I can't take you anymore."

How can Ms. Hayley not realize by now that being mean to Tyler will make him worse? He could go from laughing to screaming in a second.

"Tyler," I whisper. He has to get away. Ms. Hayley is never going to help. "I can clean up for you. Do you want to go to the bathroom or something?"

He doesn't look at me. He's gone. I'm worried his brain has already cracked.

He drops a pencil. "Any guesses, Ms. Hayley?"

"You're delaying the end-of-year celebration for everyone in the room," she announces.

Now everyone stops laughing. They start to whine.

I hand some papers to Ms. Hayley and tug on my brother's arm. "Leave," I say. "Go cool down."

"Thank you, Gwendolyn, but Tyler will stay right here and clean up this mess," Ms. Hayley says.

"Sure," Tyler laughs. He kicks a paper that's on the floor. "Oops," he says again.

"Enough!" Ms. Hayley screams.

She doesn't remember that this really did start as an accident. She doesn't see that if she hadn't yelled at Tyler for running into her when he didn't even mean to, he'd be nowhere near this upset.

"The end-of-year celebration is canceled," she sing-songs to the room. "Don't blame me. Blame Tyler."

I'm right next to him so I swear I hear it. His brain cracks.

"What?" he screams. "It was an accident, you—"

Then he curses. At a grown-up.

My jaw drops and my hands shake a little where I'm lapping

up Ms. Hayley's coffee with some napkins. I've never heard a kid curse at an adult. And I've never heard Tyler curse at all.

But also . . . cursing is better than hitting. Right?

"Sit at my table in the back!" Ms. Hayley screams. Tyler goes. Finally.

He's there for the rest of the day. Ms. Hayley un-cancels the celebration. I keep looking over at my brother while the rest of us play games and eat ice cream.

Eventually he's crying. I know how this feels. He isn't supposed to be in trouble anymore. The pills are supposed to make him less crazy. But there's no magic cure for ADHD, just like there's no magic cure for whatever I have. Tyler still needs more help even though he has the blue pills.

During free time, Hettie and I sit at the side of the school with a pad of paper.

Awesome Things About Tyler Rogers I write at the top.

1. Does the best, tightest braids

Hettie adds,

**2. Treats boys and girls the same**

Then I write,

3. Fun to play with

4. I never knew how much I needed a brother until I met him

Hettie adds,

**5. Great at basketball**

At pickup time I pass it to him all folded up. I don't even watch him unfold it and read it before I get in Mom's car. I want him to be able to keep it for himself, private, if that's how he wants it. And I don't need to see him read it anyway. Tyler is like me, so I know how much he needs a list like that.

"See you this weekend, Gwen," Ms. Christakos calls from her car as they pull away.

"This weekend?" I ask Mom. I figure she's going to be all weird about it like she was the last time I went to Tyler's house. Like she's always all weird about everything when it comes to Tyler and Ms. Christakos.

"Yes, Ida and I had lunch today," Mom says.

"Ida?" I ask.

"Ms. Christakos," Mom clarifies.

"You had lunch with her? Wait, you called her Ida?" I'm not sure which one is more shocking.

Mom laughs. "Yes, she told me to. She actually told me to a long time ago. You know, Gwen, if I had a list of Things Wrong with Mom, one of the things on it would be that I'm too bitter. I hold grudges. I've been mad at Ida for too long because of how differently our lives turned out after your father left town."

There's so much to say to that but my mouth is talking before my brain can form questions. "Maybe," I say. "But on your Awesome List would be that you're a really good mom, and that you still let me hang out with Tyler, and you're a great cook, and you—"

"Gwen!" Mom says. "It's OK, honey. It's not your responsibility to make me feel better. I'm apologizing."

"You are?" I ask, surprised. I will always and forever be surprised when adults take the time to apologize to kids.

"Yes," Mom says. "When you met Tyler at school I didn't . . . I resisted. I was worried about you guys being close. I was worried you'd compare all the things they have to what I'm able to give you. I was worried you'd be mad that you ended up with me."

"What?" I say. "But I love you!"

"I know," Mom says. "I know. I'm sorry. It wasn't fair. I didn't want Tyler to be like a real brother to you. I didn't want you to have this whole family that has nothing to do with me. But you do have it. You have a brother. You have a dad out there somewhere. And one day, you'll probably find aunts and cousins and stuff. The only thing that makes sense is to make myself a part of it. I'm so sorry it took me so long to realize."

"Oh," I say. I chew my lip. Then I take out my science notebook and write in the back of it because I have a lot of questions, but I'm not ready to ask them all right now. And writing them down is adaptive.

1. What aunts and cousins?
2. When did Ms. Christakos say we could call her Ida?
3. Who else does Mom have a grudge against?
4. What's happening this weekend?

Wait, I'm ready for that question. "What did she mean when she said she'd see me this weekend?"

"That's what we concluded over lunch. You guys are

brother and sister. It's a fact. The more you get to know each other the more you're acting like it. You aren't hanging out like friends. You're growing up together."

"Right," I say. Mom can finally see it.

"So we decided to help you. And both Ida and I are always a little overwhelmed, to be honest, so we decided to help each other too."

"How?" I ask.

"I think we need to work on making you more like siblings and less like friends. So every Sunday, we're going to get together. Either you'll spend the whole day at Tyler's or he'll spend the whole day with us. Not for some special event but just for a regular day. You'll do homework. We'll do chores. We'll run errands. We'll be a family, together. One day a week, you get to be part of each other's families. I want you to be able to focus on school stuff at school and family stuff at home. So that means you and Tyler have to be home for each other. But it's only going to work if you both like this plan."

I like that plan. I love that plan.

Those aren't the words I say.

"But Tyler goes to Millington Stables for horse riding on Sunday mornings."

Mom nods. "That's right," she says. "This Sunday we'll pick him up from there, and then he'll spend the rest of the day with us until dinner."

"Oh," I say.

"So what do you think?" Mom asks.

I blink. I guess that's really what makes Tyler my brother instead of my friend. If it were Hettie riding Dandelion, I'd be jealous, but it wouldn't feel this cosmically unfair. I don't know how I'm going to handle seeing Tyler right after he sees Dandelion every single weekend. But I'm learning that's part of having a brother. Dealing with it being unfair.

"Thanks, Mom," I say. "It's a good plan."

Sunday morning we pull into the gravel parking lot in front of Millington Stables. My heart is mashed into a tiny sliver because Sadness is wrapped so tightly around it. He's also shoved himself into my throat so I can barely breathe or talk. Tears gather at the edges of my eyes, even though I keep telling myself I won't cry.

I expect Tyler to hop in the car, but instead Mom pops the trunk. I don't know why.

"You coming?" she asks me.

I shake my head. "I don't want to smell it. Or hear it. It's hard enough to see it."

Mom doesn't say anything else. She gets out of the car and shuts her door so I'm all alone. I guess she has to go in to get Tyler.

I close my eyes.

In a few minutes, I'll be with Mom and Tyler. Three of us together for a whole day. A day of normal stuff. Like real brother and sister. And the first of many days like that.

And tomorrow, I get to go to horse camp. I won't get to ride

Dandelion, but at least I get to ride horses. And spend two weeks with my brother and all of my friends.

There's more good stuff than there's ever been . . . but I still miss Dandelion.

A minute later someone knocks super loudly on my window. I jump and turn to look, expecting Tyler. But Mom's standing there. She's holding two riding helmets.

"Come on!" she yells.

I open the door. "What?" I say.

"Get out of the car," she says. Her smile is so big, it's goofy. She's holding out a helmet to me.

"But . . . but . . . I can't ride here anymore," I remind her.

Mom smiles. "That's why there are two helmets."

"Huh?" I say.

"I'm going to ride with you," Mom says.

Mom doesn't ride horses. She never has.

"Dr. Nessa and I had a talk with Ms. Kate. We discussed some of your needs, and I explained how much riding means to you. I explained why the equine therapy session was such a frustration for you and how that led to disaster. Then I told her that keeping you away from riding has hurt you."

"And she said I can ride Dandelion again?" I ask.

Mom's smile is a little smaller. "She really wants you to be able to, but she's still hesitant, to be honest, Gwen. Because horses are living beings and you really scared her when you were here last. But then Dr. Nessa suggested that I ride with you to start, that we do some parent-kid lessons until Ms.

Kate feels you can be trusted around horses by yourself again. And she agreed. So on Sundays, we'll come ride. How does that sound? OK?"

OK? *OK?* This is the best Mom-plan ever.

"But you don't ride horses," I say.

Mom shrugs. "I'm going to learn."

"But you never wanted to before," I say. Now I'm climbing out of the car, though.

"I want to learn," Mom says. "I want to learn about everything you're into."

"You do?" I ask.

Mom nods. "I've been too busy to do a lot of what I wanted. But this new plan with Ida and Tyler frees up some time for me too. So, let's go! Dandelion is waiting."

Sadness shrinks so suddenly there's a gap inside me as we walk toward the stables. But then there's that hot pink buzzing and a pile of glitter filling in all the empty space. Happiness is there. She's big but quiet, almost like she knows we have to be calm and steady to be near horses.

And she does know that. Because she's me.

Then we're inside. I freeze when I see her. The chestnut brown fur. The white spot on her back leg. She's stomping and whinnying for the man who is tacking her up, but she freezes when she sees me too.

My Dandelion.

We stand, stunned, in each other's gaze for a long, long time.

Happiness buzzes so hard, I think Dandelion could probably see the glitter flying through my eyes.

A few minutes later, her nose is in my palm digging the remnants of a sugar cube out from between my fingers. I giggle at her warm tongue. She remembers me. Of course she does. Here, with Dandelion's nose in my palm, I'm not a list of Wrong Things or Awesome Things. Standing here with Mom and Dandelion, I'm not a list at all. I'm Gwendolyn. And I'm home.

Ms. Kate is teaching Tyler's lesson so we have an assistant, Mr. Greg, as our teacher.

"Gwendolyn, you stay here with Dandelion while I teach your mom the basics of tacking up Sunflower, OK?"

I nod again, too quiet and calm to talk.

Mr. Greg looks at Dandelion. She's nuzzling my neck.

"Wow," he says. He doesn't need to say the rest. I know he's thinking that Dandelion never looks this un-ornery.

She doesn't have to be ornery when she's with me. She doesn't have to be difficult or willful or an attitude problem.

She's home.

A few minutes later I'm in the saddle and so is my mom.

She smiles at me from below her helmet. I can tell she's nervous but she's also happy. Sunflower sidles up next to Dandelion, who moves over to make space. The uneven stride of her hips bouncing me back and forth is straight out of my best memories.

“We’ll do a trail ride today,” Mr. Greg says.

“Sounds great,” Mom says.

Our horses follow Mr. Greg’s horse toward the trails.

Mom squeezes her reins and winks at me.

Together, we ride.

# AUTHOR LETTER

Dear Reader,

Have you ever failed a test you were ready for because you numbered your paper the wrong way?

Have you ever checked your bag before leaving your house, confirming one million times that you have your math homework, just to realize you forgot your keys?

Have you ever spent an hour crafting the perfect text message for a friend, and then forgotten to send it?

Have you been called *lazy* and *careless* even when you're trying so hard and you care so much that you're crying?

If you have, then you're something like me. Except, I used to think no one was *like me*. When I was six, my parents realized I was having trouble in school, so they brought me to an educational psychologist. She labeled me, but not in the way you'd expect.

She said: *Caela is a conundrum.*

At the time, the 1980s, being a *conundrum* seemed like a better deal than having an official diagnosis. And the educational psychologist recommended a supportive school where I was able to love learning and achieve the skills I needed in reading, writing, and math.

I did all right in school from then on, but still, it felt like I kept messing up. It felt like I should be able to do things that were impossible for me.

I don't remember a school professional ever going through my backpack with me and helping me organize it, but I do remember many who yelled at me or teased me about how messy it was. I couldn't keep my backpack organized any more than I could fly. I've never been ashamed I can't fly . . . but the thought of my grade school backpack still makes my face burn with humiliation.

It took me until I was a full-on grown-up to realize that it wasn't my brain that needed fixing. That I deserved for the world around me to have space for me, even though I was different. And until I realized that, I couldn't see anything about my conundrum-ness except my screwups. I couldn't embrace all the strengths that come with the way my brain is wired.

I'm technically not a conundrum anymore. As an adult, I was officially diagnosed with ADHD and dyslexia. For me, that's been a relief. But, because I spent so much of my life as one, I'll always identify, first and foremost, as a conundrum.

The truth is that, if there were a kid-version of Caela in 2021, she would be much more likely to get the help she needed. And that makes me happy.

But there are a lot of ways to be a conundrum. There are a lot of kids who aren't getting the help they deserve. Who are refused help because it seems too hard . . . or because they seem too unpleasant . . . or because we look at them and mistake the things they *can't* do as things they *won't* do. There are still a lot of kids who face more blame than help.

I don't ever want to be a grown-up who sees a conundrum as a problem. Who encounters a kid I can't help and sees it as the child's failure instead of my own. Who shames kids for being unable to fly.

So, my fellow conundrums: this is for you.

Love,
Caela

# ACKNOWLEDGMENTS

I owe enormous thanks to all of the people who gave me the space to yank this story out of the hidden corners of my heart, and to all of the people who helped me shape it.

Thank you to my agent, Kate McKean, for your wealth of knowledge, enthusiasm, and understanding.

Thank you to my editor, Karen Chaplin: you make me a better writer over and over and over again.

Thank you to everyone at Harper who has helped to mold this book and get it into the hands of readers: Bria Ragin, Celina Sun, everyone on the Sales and Marketing team, and everyone on the School and Library team. Thank you to Maeve Norton for the perfect cover illustrations and to Molly Fehr, Erin Fitzsimmons, and Catherine San Juan for the wonderful cover design!

Thank you to Amy Ewing and Alyson Gerber for all of your critiquing genius.

Thank you to Thaís Rodrigues. This book would not exist without you. Thank you to the many family members, teachers, camp counselors, babysitters, etc., who give my children the village they need to thrive, and the village I need to be able to work.

Thank you to the many parents who talked to me about what school and life is like for neurodivergent kids right now. And thank you to all the kids who have shared your stories with me.

Thank you to my parents, Bill and Beth Carter, for raising me in a house full of books and dreams and creativity. Thank you to my large and growing family for all the support and enthusiasm. Thank you to each of my wonderful, brilliant, and inspiring friends.

To my kids—Elijah and Maebh—I love you more than you can imagine.

To my husband, partner, and teammate-in-all-things, Greg, thanks will never be enough. I love you times pi to the power of a googolplex.

# Also by CAELA CARTER

harpercollinschildrens.com